SUNSET DREAMING

AUSTRALIAN SUPERNATURAL - BOOK FIVE

NICOLE R. TAYLOR

AUTHOR NOTE

The author would like to acknowledge the Traditional Custodians of country throughout Australia and their connections to land, sea and community. She pays her deepest respect to the elders past and present and extends that respect to all Aboriginal and Torres Strait Islander peoples today.

All representations of Indigenous Australians are used fictitiously and neither represent persons who live or have died.

For more information on Reconciliation in Australia, please visit:
https://www.reconciliation.org.au/what-is-reconciliation/

CHAPTER 1

Sunset arrived at the same moment Coen looked upon a land long forgotten.

Light played across the sunburnt outback like a herald, welcoming his footsteps on the unspoilt earth. The ancient heart of Australia bloomed red, orange, and gold, rippling with magic that called out to all who touched it.

It was the first time in a hundred years that Coen had seen behind Andante's veil, and he'd almost forgotten how magnificent the limestone karsts were.

The rock formations were some of the largest of their kind, only comparable to Purnululu in the west. Those were the first Coen had seen—the banded rock alive with colour revealed by erosion over millions of years, just as these were.

The rugged domes reared upwards, their tops reaching for the blazing sky where the first stars were appearing through the dimming light of the sun.

If the place the druidess had claimed for her home had a name given to it by the mob who roamed this land, he didn't know. There were none who lived who remembered. To forget country brought a sadness to his heart, for country held a special place for all who remembered.

"I knew if I opened the door, you'd walk right in."

Coen chuckled, his warm eyes finding the druidess Andante's silhouette on top of the rise ahead. "Of course. It's been a long time since I saw this place."

"I did an injustice locking it away, didn't I?"

The Indigenous man walked along the path and climbed the rock to stand beside the old woman. She came from another world and had seen many that were the same but existed alongside. She'd seen the hurt humans could do to each other and to the land that gave them life.

"Perhaps," he told her. "Perhaps not."

Andante looked over the karsts, her long silver hair ruffling in the warm breeze. "I've known them before. That's why you've come."

Coen nodded.

"I remember what they did to the world I left behind," she murmured. "And they were just as meddlesome as the Old Ones. I see their touch in this place, too."

Coen waited, listening to the lonely sounds of the outback. The magic here kept out more than just humans and supernaturals—it also dulled the song of country.

Andante sighed. "They descend from above, desperate to become part of what they left behind, but they should never have come back." Her brow creased as her irritation rose. "Even if they had the best of intentions, they've destroyed and turned their backs from it. Instead, they leave others to do what they will not."

Her gaze turned to him and he saw the weariness in her heart. She had seen many things...things that could help Eloise Hart. This, he knew.

"But what I still can't see," Andante went on, "is the true nature in *your* heart, wanderer."

Coen smiled. He liked that name, 'wanderer'.

"I lost my name a long time ago," he told her. "I haven't found it yet."

Her eyebrows rose. "Then how did you come to be called Coen?"

"An elder gave it to me." He remembered the man—the same man who'd told him the story of Bunjil the great eagle—and the night they'd met. In a crash of thunder, Coen had arrived. It was a simple story, really. "A great man, a great leader."

"You remind me of them."

Maybe he did, but Coen didn't see it.

"One power sleeps while another wakes." He swept his hand across the sky and a million stars appeared, burning iridescent silver against the fading sunset. "It is a time where all will be tested. No one can hide behind shimmering veils."

Magic thickened in the air and the druidess stirred.

"You've seen her," Coen said. "That's why you helped."

"It's the same story," she murmured. "It's always the same story."

"Perhaps, but that doesn't mean the ending can't be changed. The fate of this reality has not yet been written, and it's not yet set in stone."

Andante sighed, her true age beginning to show. "I fear for her. I fear what they might do."

"And still, she must go to them," Coen said. "It is the only way. She is awake, but she cannot *see*."

The druidess remained silent, for there were no more words to say. There was only one path through the darkness, and only Eloise Hart could walk it.

Coen watched the last of the sunset fade across the horizon and looked through Andante's veil towards Solace. The glow of tainted magic ebbed into the sky, creating a dome over the little outback town.

Yes, there was hope for this world, even as the fabric that held it all together began to fray. The ending had not yet been written...for Eloise Hart held the pen.

All that remained was for her to make the final mark on the page.

Eloise Hart was the key to the destruction of an entire reality.

For years, she'd been plagued by a malevolence that'd tried to corrupt her soul, to twist her magic for its own gain, but her dreams had been undisturbed ever since she'd sealed the Black Mountain.

But...there was always another 'but' in the supernatural world—a loophole, a curse, a threat. A forgotten ancient power disturbed by the unknowing.

The seal that lay underneath the outback opal mining town of Solace was deteriorating. The corrosive magic it'd held at bay for tens of thousands of years was leaking through the cracks, spreading its poison into the earth. And it made itself known a little bit more with every passing day.

One problem after the other kept presenting itself, and the Exiles, who called the remote town home, didn't know where to even start. Fighting back against the struggling Old One seemed like an impossible task.

Wally's mine, where he went to ride out his monthly werewolf transformations, was a festering pit of tar-like sludge. Earth elemental Kyne couldn't get out to his claim to mine more opal after the track was washed out by the magical storm that'd ravaged the area. Without opal, vampire Hardy was idle and had been put to work repairing storm damage that didn't seem to want to stay repaired—metal was rusting at an accelerated rate and nails crumbled to ash in his hands. Business at the *Outpost* was faltering—any fresh produce that entered the store wilted within an hour and was totally rotten by the end of the day, and not even Vera's witch legacy could stop it.

And those were only the problems on the surface.

Eloise stood in the shadow of the large boab tree that grew just to the north of the *Outpost*, her brow furrowed.

Despite the mild weather, the sun felt hotter on her shoulders lately. It was the wet season, otherwise known as late-autumn, but it was feeling a lot like the height of summer. The dry season was fast approaching—Kyne told her it usually spanned May to October-ish, depending on the weather, which, as the years passed, was becoming more unpredictable. The cracked seal underneath Solace wasn't helping matters, but neither were human-made carbon emissions.

She took off her hat—a slate-grey Akubra—and wiped her damp brow. The usually vibrant tree looked a little withered around the edges. Trying to dip into her elemental powers, she sighed when she only came back with the faintest trickle of magic.

Still empty.

It'd been two weeks since Eloise had travelled through time and space with the dingo-shifter Drew to the Black Mountain. There, they'd met up with Finn, the fae's walkabout merging with her own path—and also that of the mysterious supernatural being, Coen.

The Old One—the ancient celestial being who was hellbent on destroying the world—who was trapped under the mountain had drawn them there, desperate to be freed so it could complete its work. Fortunately, Eloise was ready to face the menace and was able to repair the seal, plugging the hole in reality with her unique elemental magic.

But now there was another Old One's decaying prison to contend with...and a mission to banish both entities from this reality forever.

"It's not a pretty sight, is it?"

Eloise glanced up at the sound of Vera's voice. The witch joined her in the shade and looked up at the boab.

The elemental shook her head. There was nothing good to say about the state of it, so it was best to remain tightlipped.

Vera glanced at the highway. "It's quiet."

"It's always a little sleepy around here," Eloise told her. "It's just the weather. Siora's storm did a real number on the roads." It was the corrupted fae's storm that'd cracked the seal in the first place, but Eloise was tired of thinking about it. There was no use dwelling on what had caused the problem; they had to focus on the solution.

"No," Vera said with a shake of her head, "it's different. At this rate, I may as well close the store."

"But Clarke said the highway was flooded, and the road was covered in clay."

"Even so, they never let a road like that stay closed for long. This is the main route to Longreach." The witch's gaze shifted to the horizon. "The road trains have to detour through Lightning Ridge, putting hours onto their routes."

Road trains were enormous trucks that towed three trailers worth of goods along the lonely outback highways of Australia. They roared through Solace at all hours, sometimes stopping at Blue's pub for some grub or at Wally's garage for diesel or repairs. They kept the outback alive in more ways than one, and now that Eloise thought about it, she hadn't seen a single truck since she'd come back from the mountain.

"It was a struggle to get that delivery last week, and I doubt I'll even sell a quarter of it," Vera said. "No one wants to come this way, though they can't seem to explain why."

Eloise sighed. Human minds couldn't comprehend what was happening in Solace. Not even Vera's boyfriend, Police Sergeant Andrew Clarke—who knew the truth about all of it—did the best he could, but it still wasn't enough.

She held up her hand and squinted, focusing on the boab behind, then on the outline of her fingers. She narrowed her left eye, then her right.

Vera leaned forwards, her wild red hair entering

Eloise's field of vision as a blurry blob. "What are you doing?"

"Trying to focus on my magic."

"How's that working out for you?"

She lowered her hand with a groan. "As well as the fruit and veg."

"Don't worry. Your magic will recharge."

"And how long is that going to take?" she asked with a huff. "It's already been two weeks and look at the state of this place!"

Eloise had to get her magic back, then she could search for the elementals. Coen seemed to think they had the answers to their Old One problem—and she could see why—but how much time did they really have?

The mountain may have been leaking poison out onto that forest for forty thousand years, but what she'd seen there paled in comparison to what was happening to Solace in the span of two weeks. That amount of time was a grain of sand on a beach the size of a grain of sand.

"Eloise," Vera said, her voice gentle, "we can only do what we can do."

"I know, I'm just..." She pinched the bridge of her nose.

"Under a lot of pressure?"

"That's an understatement."

The witch placed a hand on her shoulder. "We're here for you. All of us."

"I know. It's just hard watching everyone suffer while my magic is still checked out."

"I wouldn't call it suffering..." her friend replied. "More like, putting up with the neighbour from hell. The neighbour who dumps grey water on your lawn and chucks their rotting rubbish on the nature strip. Oh, and who deliberately leaves their outdoor lights on so it shines through your curtains and keeps you awake at night."

"That's quite the analogy," she drawled.

"Don't be so hard on yourself. We'll work it out together."

Eloise felt the dull spark of her magic and grimaced.

"Where's Kyne?" Vera asked.

"With Hardy in the workshop," she replied with a shrug. "They're planning, I suppose."

"Thick as thieves, those two."

Eloise's frown deepened at the mention of Kyne. She hadn't told him about the elementals yet...and for good reason. He'd been brutally rejected when he'd gone to find them last year, the blow causing him to lose his connection to his magic temporarily.

Grow some balls, Eloise, she thought. *You faced an entity as old as the universe and won. You can tell your boyfriend about this.*

"Eloise?"

She looked up at Vera, who was peering at her with a curious expression.

"I've got this...*thing* to do," Eloise blurted. "I'll see you later."

"*Sure*," Vera muttered as the elemental took off down the path towards the opal shop. "Everyone's always got a *thing* these days."

CHAPTER 2

Vera was still lingering by the boab when the sound of a diesel engine echoed along the lonely highway leading into Solace.

It hadn't been *that* long since someone had ventured through town, but the presence of anyone at all was a revelation. If she was being honest, considering the magical invisible human repellant that lingered in the air these days, it was a downright miracle.

Leaving the shade of the boab, she darted under the cover of the *Outpost's* verandah and spotted the glint of shiny metal on the horizon. A familiar white and blue 4WD came into view, and she smiled as the outline of the vehicle wobbled through the mirage. *He got through.*

She waited in the shade as the 4WD advanced; the tyres crossing the invisible boundary the Old One's magic had cast around the town, then as it did a wide

U-turn across the white line, and finally pulled up outside the *Outpost*.

Sergeant Andrew Clarke slipped out from behind the driver's seat and set his boots on the gravel. He wore plain clothes—lingo for being out of uniform—and it was a strange enough sight that Vera had to do a double-take. Dusty blue jeans, rugged boots, a tight-fitting grey T-shirt, and aviator sunglasses made for a delicious delivery right to her doorstep.

"You're not in your uniform."

"Rostered day off," Clarke replied, rubbing his palms over his jeans. "Something wrong? Should I call the fashion police?"

Vera laughed and shook her head. "Definitely *not*." She leaned down from her advantageous elevation on the verandah and kissed him on the lips. "What brings you all the way out here?"

"Thought I'd come and see how things are going... and to see you."

"It's a wonder you made it."

He raised his eyebrows. "What makes you say that?"

"Well," she nodded towards the road, "the magic leaking out of the seal is making everything go a little sideways."

Clarke took off his sunglasses and glanced over his shoulder. "I thought there was a strange feeling in the air..."

"There's something about the stuff leaking out

that's keeping humans away," Vera told him. "From what I can tell, it's acting like the Old One in the mountain. Drew told me some things, like how the landscape was twisted, how humans steered clear of the whole area, and how the wildlife grew... I reckon it's only a matter of time before it happens here, too."

"And it's already keeping people away," Clarke said with a sigh. "Seems fast, right?"

"A little." She sat on the edge of the verandah, her sandalled feet dipping into the gutter. "It took tens of thousands of years for things to deteriorate at the mountain."

Clarke sat beside her and rested his hand on her knee. "Maybe this one's stronger?"

"If it gets any worse, we might have to do something drastic."

"Like?"

"Make sure people stay away," she murmured.

"A cordon?" Clarke rubbed the back of his neck. "I suppose I could wrangle something with the local government..."

"And with my magic and Hardy's mind control, we can shut down the entire highway."

Clarke spat and swatted his hands at his face as at least a dozen flies circled. "Is it just me or are the blowies out of control?"

"Here." Vera reached into her pocket and took out the small perfume atomiser she kept on hand for emergencies like these.

Clarke took it and eyed the small glass vial. "What is it?"

"Repellant." He shot her a look, and she snatched it back with a chuckle. "It's just a little vanilla, a dusting of cayenne pepper, water, and a drop of Brinewold magic. It won't make you grow a second head, but it will stop you from being eaten alive...and driven insane. Here." She spritzed the pale yellow liquid on the inside of his wrist, then on his neck. "Rub your wrists together."

He did as he was told, then raised his arm for a whiff. "You're right. It smells like vanilla essence. And would you look at that..." A grin broke out on his face. "The flies are gone!"

"Told you." She poked out her tongue.

"Speaking about flies...where's Drew? It's not like him to be absent."

Vera shrugged. "He's always off with Coen these days." Ever since they got back from the mountain, in fact.

"Doing dingo things?"

"I suppose so." She stood abruptly and slipped the atomiser back into her pocket. "Hey, do you want to head over to the pub for a drink?" She nodded at the *Outpost*. "It's a slow day. I've already got the sign up." A bit of laminated printer paper had already become a permanent fixture inside the door—her flowery handwriting stated that she was out, along with her mobile phone number in case anyone wanted to buy anything, but she wasn't holding her breath.

"How's the business holding up?" Clarke asked as they wandered towards the pub. "I can't imagine the lack of customers is doing wonders for the overhead."

"It's not great, but it's out of my control," she replied with a shrug. "I'm losing money every day, what with the loss of income, spoilt produce, and refrigeration costs—which I can't run on solar." She sighed. "And it's not just me, it's everyone. Solace is becoming a ghost town."

"In the span of two weeks?"

"In the span of two weeks," she echoed.

"Well, I can spend a bit of cash at Blue's. Grease the local economy a bit."

"If only I could sue the Old Ones."

"If only I could arrest them," Clarke countered, his shoulders sagging. As a human, there was little he could do to combat all the supernatural threats that'd emerged in Solace over the past year. At least he was trying, and that meant the world to Vera.

"C'mon," she said with a smile, "let's forget about all that for an afternoon, huh? Let's get day-drunk."

Clarke chuckled and opened the pub door. "Ladies first."

As they stepped into the cool, a voice exclaimed from the kitchen, "Customers! My first customers!"

Finn's head appeared through the partition behind the bar, and Vera choked on her own spit.

Seeing Vera and Clarke standing by the bar, the fae's excited smile turned sour, and he self-consciously tugged at the fine black netting around his midnight blue dreadlocks.

"What?" he demanded, his silver eyes flashing.

The witch composed herself before she answered, "You're wearing a hairnet."

His scowl deepened. "Yeah, and it's ruining my credibility."

"If anything, it gives you some," Clarke quipped.

The fae picked up a spatula and brandished it at the sergeant, leaning half out of the opening. "So, it's a hamburger with a side of spit, huh? I'm working my saliva glands as we speak! I've got a reservoir!"

Vera waved a hand at him. "Oh, don't be so dramatic. It's not like anyone will see. That apron is *darling*."

"You're seeing me right now."

"I'm talking about tourists. Truckies. *Humans*."

"Right. *The thing*." The fae eyed Clarke. "Just as I get my first job, too."

"Finn, I know what's going on," Clarke stated.

"*Of course you do*."

The sergeant sighed as Blue set two pots of beer on the bar. "Settled back in all right, I see."

"Don't take it to heart," Blue told him. "He's like that with everyone."

Vera raised her eyebrows. He wasn't like that with Eloise, especially after returning from his walkabout.

Whatever had happened to him out there, it'd been life changing...but not quite enough to take the edge out of his bone-dry Unseelie sense of humour—though he wouldn't be Finn without it.

"You gave him a job?" Vera asked the publican.

"He begged me for it." Blue chuckled. "It had something to do with potatoes."

"Are you ordering or what?" Finn asked, raising his voice.

"Nope." Vera shook her head. "It's too early for lunch."

Finn let out a disgusted snort. "Then I'm going for a ciggie break." The spatula clattered as the fae tossed it over his shoulder.

"But you don't smoke," Vera called.

"It's a figure of speech."

"Smoko," Blue informed the fae. "It's called *smoko*, and there're no cigarettes involved. It's just slang for a break."

Finn curled his lip. "Then why is it called *smoke*-oh?"

"Probably for the same reason I'm a redhead called Blue."

The fae clucked his tongue, strode across the kitchen, and shoved out the back door.

"He's so excited," Blue told them, his eyes sparkling. "He's never really been involved with the human world. I think it'll do him good now that the others have..." he hesitated, "*you know*."

Vera didn't want to bring it up, either. The fae had come to an awful end—corrupted by the Black Mountain, turned into shadow creatures Finn was forced to kill with his secret ancestral magic. Now he was the last fae in Solace, perhaps even the whole of Australia, considering his dependance on the seal's magic for his continued survival.

She glanced through the partition to the backdoor. "Give me a minute?"

"Go for it." Clarke sighed and picked up his beer. "I'll be right here."

Ducking through the kitchen, Vera headed out the back. A wall of heat slammed into her as she left the air-conditioned pub, the dryness sapping her energy.

Finn was sitting on an upturned beer keg in the shade of a low hanging gumtree laden with gum nuts that smelt like pollen and eucalyptus. He looked up, saw her, then looked back down.

She noticed he was wearing the talisman she'd made him—the same one she'd given to Eloise when she'd gone to the mountain looking for him. It was a simple piece of clear quartz wrapped in gold and silver, and while the magic she'd charged it with was long gone, it warmed her heart to see him still holding onto it.

"Finn?"

"I snapped at you..." It was the closest to an apology she was going to get.

"It's understandable." She sat beside him,

perching on a second keg. The metal immediately heated her backside to uncomfortable levels, but she persevered. "You were looking forward to your first customer."

"*Pfft.*" He ripped off his hairnet and shoved it into his apron pocket. "Whatever."

Vera worried her bottom lip. "It's not about the food, is it?"

"The food doesn't matter. It's a wonder it hasn't rotted away yet."

"Finn, whatever it is, you can tell me." She waited, but when he said nothing, she added, "We're in this together. How can we hope to protect Solace, let alone the entire reality, if we don't know all the details? If you know something..."

Finn glanced back at the pub, looking unsettled. It was a new thing for him, and it didn't do anything to ease Vera's wobbly stomach.

"Finn, what is it?"

"I don't think she realises..." the fae began, his eyes downcast.

"Who? Eloise? Realises what?"

"How close she came to setting the Old One free."

Vera's heart almost stopped. "What do you mean?"

"When she was tied up in the vision, the whole mountain began to shake."

"Yes, I know that part. The earthquake."

"It wasn't just an earthquake, Vera," Finn told her. "Fissures opened all over the mountainside, and within...there was a strange green light. An essence I believe was the Old One itself."

Vera hadn't really thought about what an Old One might look like, but as an eternal celestial being, it stood to reason that it'd be more energy than biological.

"That doesn't sound good," she murmured, wondering what it meant for Solace.

"Siora fell into it, and if it wasn't for Drew, I would've, too."

Her heart fluttered. "Oh, Finn—"

"To defeat the Old Ones, she'll have to walk right to the precipice," Finn murmured with a shrug.

"And she'll either fall in or save us all."

He nodded, and they didn't have to say anything else. What they'd all face at the final confrontation was clear, though the path to it was still hidden.

"She has to go to them, doesn't she?" Vera turned to Finn. "The elementals?"

"It's the only logical move."

She shook her head, her mind working overtime. What did they have to do with all of this? Whatever had happened on that mountain, there were still pieces of the story the others hadn't told her yet—her, Hardy, Wally, and Blue. The Exiles were split down the middle, and she didn't like it.

Vera mightn't be needed for the final battle, but she was still a guardian of the seal and of Solace, so that's what she'd do.

"Can you feel it?"

Finn nodded. "It's different than the mountain."

"Andante called it the heart of the ocean."

"Maybe it touches one in another reality…"

"Or the one that used to be here?"

"Why call it a heart, anyway?" He rolled his eyes. "They seem pretty *heartless* to me."

"Yeah," Vera muttered, looking towards the highway, "sure seems that way."

Hardy leaned against the side of the truck and squinted at the sky just above Solace.

He closed his right eye, then his left, alternating between the two. The air shimmered faintly with a smear of colour that reminded him of the multi-coloured surface of a soap bubble. If *he* was seeing the effects of the magic poisoning the land—and during the day, no less—then it was getting worse far quicker than they'd anticipated.

"What are you looking at?" Kyne asked, doing some squinting of his own.

"Just the looming presence of our subterranean friend."

The miner sighed. "It is what it is." He nodded towards the truck backed up between two large gum trees, its front tyres squashing down a rather nasty patch of spiky spinifex grass. "First things first, huh?"

They were out with Wally and Drew on the hunt for a new site to dig a bunker to house Wally's werewolf transformations. The cool-room at the *Outpost* had taken a beating on the last full moon, and there was only so much damage it could withstand; not to mention Vera was fretting over the cost of repairs, so Kyne had rented another Caldwell drill from a bloke over in Lightning Ridge, this one bigger than the rig he'd brought to sink a new shaft at his claim, Black Hole Mine.

It'd been about three weeks since the storm and the outback was still showing signs of the soaking that'd been dumped on it. The large yellow truck had a thick layer of craggy dirt stuck to the mud flaps that crept up the sides, giving the whole thing a two-toned colour. Even his boots were caked with the stuff, his feet feeling like a pair of bricks. He knocked them against the ground as the sound of approaching footsteps reached his ears.

Hardy glanced up at the arrival of a golden dingo, the animal padding towards them with bright, intelligent eyes. Drew.

"*I can't smell any magic,*" he said to the Exiles. "*I reckon this is a good place to try.*"

"Righty-o," Wally declared, turning towards the controls on the side of the rig.

"Guide her down slow," Kyne told the old werewolf. "I'll use my powers, so watch that the drill doesn't get away from you this time."

The machinery ground into life, whirring and rumbling, and the drill began to descend. If the old wolf and his dinted pride had heard Kyne, he didn't let on.

The Caldwell drill burrowed down into the earth, grinding through the topmost layer of rust-coloured dirt and rock. The time, the bit held steady and remained on target.

"Third time's a charm, huh?" Hardy quipped.

Drew looked up at him and bared his teeth. *"Don't jinx it, mate."*

With all the goings-on in Solace lately, it was becoming difficult to find ground that wasn't already tainted by the magic leaking out of the seal. The last two shafts had all filled with the same blackish-tar they'd pumped out of Wally's old mine—the abandoned opal diggings that sat out the back of his garage—and Kyne had quickly filled them in with his earth elemental powers.

"If only there was a way to test for ground contamination," Hardy muttered, watching as Kyne lingered by the drill, watching its progress.

"Can't test for Old One juice," the dingo told him. *"Just have to keep poking holes until we get far enough away."*

And how far did it go? There was no guarantee that if they dug here, that it wouldn't be flooded with contamination by the following full moon, let alone tomorrow.

If they couldn't figure this out, then they'd either have to chain Wally up—which Hardy wasn't sure would work at all—or he'd have to leave Solace until things with the Old Ones were over…if they could find a way to lock them out of this reality for good. But that was another problem with another ambiguous solution.

"Ho!" Kyne shouted, holding up his hand. "Shut it off!"

Wally pounded the red stop button and the drill ground to a halt.

Hardy glanced at Drew, but the dingo was already lowering his nose to the ground. "*I don't like it…*" he muttered.

The vampire joined the others by the drill and added another disappointed sigh to the daily tally. Black tar oozed through the bright reddish-brown earth, the acrid smell burning the inside of his nose.

"*Bugger it,*" Wally cursed, taking off his hat and wringing it in his hands. "This is the third hole!"

None of them said anything for a long moment. The stillness of the outback settled around them in a dull roar in the wake of the noise of the drill, the wind whispering through the storm-weary gums and across the battered scrub.

Hardy looked up. "Eloise is coming."

The elemental appeared around the back of the truck. "I've been walking for ages," she said, coming to meet them.

Drew snorted. "*As you can see, we haven't found the edge of the corruption yet.*"

"Oh…" She looked down at the blackish mess in the shaft and wrinkled her nose. "It's farther out that I realised."

"Yeah." Hardy shrugged. "We'll just have to try again, a little farther out this time."

Eloise leaned towards Kyne. "I've got something I need to talk to you about," she said. "Come for a walk?"

The miner glanced at the others, but Hardy waved him off. "Go on. Between the three of us, I reckon we can drill a hole…even without elemental assistance."

As the two elementals walked off, Hardy wondered what Eloise wanted to talk to Kyne about. She was the key to freeing or defeating the Old Ones after all, and curiosity almost got the better of him. It wouldn't be hard to overhear their conversation, but he shook his head and turned back towards the drill. After all they'd been through together, he trusted Eloise more than he trusted himself.

"All right," he said to Wally. "We better reverse this thing out of there and find a new spot."

"I don't know how much more I can do," the werewolf said, putting his creased hat back on.

"We do it until we find the edge of the corruption." He clapped a reassuring hand on to the old timer's shoulder. "How ever many holes it might be."

CHAPTER 3

As Eloise and Kyne wandered through the scrub, the sound of the truck's engine turning over followed their steps back towards Solace.

Her mind began to mull over the coming conversation about the elementals, formulating the exact words she wanted to say, then reordering and rearranging again until it was all a garbled mess. Bringing the elementals up with Kyne would never be easy, and she didn't realise how nervous it made her.

The moment they were far enough away from the truck, he asked, "What's up?"

"How many holes have you tried?" Eloise blurted, panicking.

"Three so far," Kyne replied, not picking up on her nerves. "All of them were full of that black tar."

"I've never seen anything like it."

"Not even at the mountain?"

"No. No, it wasn't like that there." It was a separate

Old One, and if there were different kinds with different powers, they would probably never know. "At least, not that I saw."

Wally's garage came into view through the scrub, and they made a beeline for it. The sun was hot on their shoulders and the air was dry as a bone, so they sought refuge in the shade cast by the building.

"So...what's up?" Kyne turned and leaned against the brick wall, the brim of his hat dipping low.

"Well... Uh..." Eloise squirmed, wondering if she had time to run to the toilet.

"*Eloise*..." He sighed as his frown deepened. "I know you don't want to talk about everything that happened at the mountain, but—"

"I know. It's just..." She bit her bottom lip. "It kinda... Well, it kinda concerns you this time."

"Me? How?"

"When we were at the mountain, Coen told us a story," she began.

"Coen's stories are always vague at best," he told her. "For as long as I've known him, he's been telling them that way. Why is this time any different?"

"Because when I stood in that mountain, I felt it." She pressed the heel of her palm over her heart. "It was about how the seals were first placed."

He scoffed and pushed off the wall. "We need to close the rifts between realities, not seal them up again."

"That's my point. What I did at the mountain was

temporary, but it was the story Coen told us that holds the answers. Kyne...I think the elementals put them there."

This made him pause. "The elementals...? They made the seals?"

"*Yes.*"

He scratched his chin. "What exactly did this story say?"

"In the beginning, when Australia was formed, a shadow grew—the Old Ones. The spirits, the ancestors, and the Indigenous peoples came together to push the shadow away, but they weren't strong enough. So, the great emu who lives in the sky—what we now see as the arm of the Milky Way—sent down a group of people to help. People who came from the dark places between the stars and were made from light and memory. But somewhere between there and here, they were broken; they lost the ability to defeat the shadow. That's why they placed seals made from meteorites...it was all they could manage."

Kyne had listened to everything she'd said patiently, but he perked up at the mention of the seal. "Meteorites?"

Eloise nodded. "Yes. The one in the mountain was, and the one in Solace has to be, too. I didn't get a good look at it because of all the water, but I'd bet my life on it."

"So, the elementals were broken." He rolled his

eyes. "Well, that'd explain a lot. They aren't exactly...*sane.*"

"They're the only people we haven't spoken to yet," she went on. "My magic fixed the seal in the mountain, so two and two equals elemental. It all lines up."

Kyne said nothing, his expression darkening the longer the story sat with his thoughts.

"Kyne?" It came out as a hesitant squeak.

"You want to find them."

"Yes, I do," she snapped, sensing an argument about to explode. "*I have to.*"

"Eloise..." Kyne sighed and ran his hand over his face. "That path only leads to heartache. They tossed me out like I was rubbish! What makes you think they won't do the same to you?"

"*I won't let them.*"

"They never gave a crap about us, Eloise! They abandoned us as babies to the human world with no idea of who or what we were. Look what it did to you!"

Eloise tensed, her thoughts wrenching to her parents. They *hated* her, all because she didn't understand what she was. She did that to them. *She did*, no one else.

"Yeah, you're right," she murmured. "They did do those things to us, and who knows how many others out there...but they were broken when they came to Earth. Maybe they don't understand what they're doing."

Kyne curled his lip. "You're defending them now?"

"I am!" she shouted.

Her sudden anger slapped Kyne into silence and he stared at her with wide eyes.

"The fact of the matter remains," she went on, her anger simmering. "We are their descendants. I have the magic the Old Ones need to break free—the magic used to seal them away in the first place. The elementals came to lock them out *forever*. No matter your feelings towards them, they are where my path leads...and when I go, I want to take you with me. Not just because you know the way, but because they owe you answers as much as they do me and this world. Kyne...don't make me leave you behind again."

"You'd leave me again?" he asked, his voice low. "For *them?*"

"I don't want to argue about this." She grasped his arm. "I love you and I thought I'd never find anyone I could *touch*, let alone *love*...but this is about the fate of our entire reality. I know it's going to be hard, but it has to be done, and only we can do it."

"We? You're the key."

"Why can't it be us?"

"Because you're the only elemental who can travel the rivers, Eloise. Only you. I may be *like* you, but I can't see them."

He was right. Whatever she did to repair the seal in the mountain was something the true elementals weren't able to do. Maybe that's why she was the 'key'—did she have what they were missing?

No matter how Eloise looked at it, searching for the elementals was their only path, and by the look on Kyne's face, he was beginning to understand it, too—not that he was happy about it.

"The elementals will know why," she murmured. "They were there."

"If they'll speak to us."

Eloise felt her anger rise again. "*They will speak to me.*"

Her words hung between them, the abrasive threat out of character—compared her usual level-headed calm approach to things. A year ago, she would never have been able to say something like that out loud, and definitely not with such impassioned gusto.

Kyne seemed surprised because it took him several minutes to formulate a reply.

"I found them in the Pilbara," he told her. "It's not a place for the faint of heart...or the unprepared. Even a pair of elementals can die out there without the right equipment."

Eloise felt her cheeks flush and she bit her bottom lip. She knew it was going to be a trek, but Kyne was making it sound like a death march. Was it really that perilous?

"Yes," Kyne said, reading her expression. "*Really.*"

Elementals could only manipulate what was there...and if there wasn't water, they would be just as screwed as everyone else.

"I don't like it," Kyne went on. "Actually, if we're being honest, I hate it, but we've got time."

She raised her eyebrows. "Time for me to recharge my magic, or change my mind?"

"Both."

"Well, at least you're being honest."

Kyne snorted and tugged her towards him. "Also, there's time to prepare. We're going to need a lot of gear."

She leaned against his chest and buried her cheek into the crook of his neck, the movement knocking the hat off her head into the dirt. It was way too hot to embrace for long, but she held on tight, her fingers fisting into the back of his shirt.

"Kyne?"

"Hmm?"

"I'm..." She didn't know how to articulate what she was feeling, but she was feeling all the things at once— fear, anger, hope, excitement. Warring emotions had her heart and mind up against a wall where her magic was still a microscopic spark.

"I know," he whispered. "I know."

Finn tugged at his hairnet and scowled at the cutting board in front of him. The carrot seemed to be doing everything in its power not to end up diced as finely as he desired.

His considerable skills in knife combat hadn't translated as well as he'd assumed to the kitchen and the itchy hairnet wasn't helping. There were a few teething problems, but it was his first actual job that didn't involve being a solider or a rebel...on any world.

Slamming the knife onto the carrot, he cursed as the orange vegetable split in half, one half flying off the counter and onto the floor.

Swearing in fae, he bent over to retrieve the carrot, but hesitated as his fingers brushed against a withered stalk that used to be said carrot.

Holding it up, his eyes widened as it continued its devolution, growing green fur and emitting a smell that was so foul, he gagged.

"Uh, Blue?" he rasped, his voice echoing across the kitchen.

The publican came in from the bar, wiping his hands with a tea towel as he went. "What is it now?"

Finn held up the withered mess and made a face. "We've got a problem."

"It's a bad carrot. There's plenty more."

"Uh, I don't think so." Finn lifted a cardboard box that was now full of sludgy, stinky, furry carrots. "It's like *magic*...if you know what I mean."

"Bloody hell." The tea towel slipped from Blue's hand and fluttered to the floor.

Finn set the box down, his nose wrinkling. "I'd check the fridge if I were you."

The publican rushed to the nearest fridge, opened

it, and immediately slammed the door as a potent explosion of organic decomposition wafted out.

Blue shook his head, his mouth hanging open. "It's all spoilt. All of it." He opened the freezer and flipped open the top of a cardboard box. "Bloody hell. Even the frozens are gone."

As the publican turned away from the freezer, Finn poked his head inside and looked around the box. The chips were still icy-cold and solid, but they'd turned the same rancid black colour as the carrots. What'd happened to the meat didn't even bear mentioning.

"I don't get it," Blue murmured. "The cold is supposed to preserve food. Can magic really do that?"

Finn nudged the freezer door closed, the rubber seal making a soft sucking sound as the two sides met. "Magic as old as the universe...?" He shrugged. "I suppose it could do just about anything it wanted if it put its cosmic mind to it."

Blue screwed up his nose and waved his hand in front of his face. "Ugh, I can still smell it." He fled from the kitchen to the bar.

Finn followed, tossing his hairnet over his shoulder as he went.

"I don't know what I'm going to do if I have to shut down," Blue said. "All that food...*gone*."

It wasn't just Blue, but all the businesses in Solace. *The Outpost*, Wally's garage, the pub, and the opal workshop. Hardy was the only one who could set up shop elsewhere by the end of the day, Kyne was loaded from all that black opal he'd mined, and Eloise was taken care of by her relationship status. Vera, Blue, and Wally would lose everything. Kyne wouldn't let them become homeless—he'd do anything to help—but it was more a matter of pride than anything financial.

And what about him? Finn knew he could stay in Solace, but he didn't know for how long. The poison here was different than it was at the mountain, and he'd been able to resist its corruption, but here...? There was no telling what it could do to a creature who relied on the exact same magic to survive.

For once, Finn didn't have anything sarcastic to say; he just rolled up his sleeves and scraped the rotten carrot into the bin.

"There's nothing we can do about that right now," he said, tossing the rest of the withered food. "But we can't leave this stuff sitting out. It's already stinking up the place."

Blue ran his hand over his face, his palm scratching his wiry grey handlebar moustache. "You're right. It's all going to have to go in the bin. The veggies, the meat..." His gaze darted to the bottles of booze lined up behind the bar.

"*The alcohol?*" Finn paced a couple of times, then declared, "Hang on a second!"

The fae snatched up a packet of salt and vinegar chips from the basket behind the bar and tore it open it, the foil crinkling noisily. Thrusting a hand inside, he pulled out a crinkle-cut chip. It was broken, but fresh as a daisy; the smell of vinegar potent as it burned his nostrils.

Why wasn't it rotting like the other food?

Because that stuff had been fresh.

Blue took the packet of chips from him and looked into the bag. "They're fine. There's nothing wrong."

"It's the water," Finn murmured, holding up the chip. "It's the water that's reacting to the Old One's magic."

"The heart of the ocean..." the publican muttered.

Finn clapped his hands together. "Anything with water content is fair game."

"But there's got to be *some* water in potato chips, right?"

"There's always loopholes in magic, and they don't always make sense. This time I reckon it's the preservatives and chemical flavouring..."

"Wait a sec. Water..." Blue's expression fell suddenly, and he reached out and grasped the bar. "The human body is made up of sixty percent water... Does that mean what I think it does?"

"Well, I don't think it's that dire," Finn told him, even though he was thinking the same exact thing. "Carrots don't exactly have a central nervous system, or internal organs or brains. If we were going to rot, it'd take a long time. And that's if it happened at all."

"You're not reassuring me, mate."

"You look like you're going to throw up."

"*Not helping.*"

"Shall I bring you a bucket?"

Blue groaned and slid onto a stool. "Start by dumping those carrots into the bin out back. After that, start on the rest of it. I'll..." he took a deep breath, "I'll be out to help in a minute."

Finn backed towards the kitchen, his frown deepening. There wasn't anything they could do to stop it, only Eloise could do that...but in the meantime? The loss of control over the corruption plaguing Solace frightened him more than that moment a thousand years prior, when he knew what he'd become when he finally ran out of magic. This time, there wasn't a cave on the planet that would save him if the Old One broke free.

What could Finn do about it? Nothing. But what he *could* do was clean out the fridge, so he held his breath, opened the door, and began filling the bin with rotten sludge.

My first job, he lamented. *My financial freedom ruined by a stupid tentacle monster!*

CHAPTER 4

The whirring sound of a vacuum cleaner echoed across the scrub.

Eloise was on her hands and knees in the cab of her motorhome, jamming the little handheld into all the tight corners under the front seats, trying to get the last bit of red dirt out of the crevasses. Bashing her knuckles, she yelped and pulled her hand back.

Sitting on the side step, she sucked her scraped finger. Sweat dripped down her back and she reached for her water bottle with her free hand.

The Pilbara seemed like a thousand miles away—it literally was twice the distance, but it felt like it in a metaphoric way. If they took sealed roads, it was around four thousand kilometres from here to there, depending on where 'there' was. Kyne knew how to find the elementals, but so far, he hadn't spilled the beans.

Despite the reason for their trip, Eloise was excited

to get on the road and travel again. Sitting behind the wheel with an open sky before her, the freedom to go anywhere brought a smile to her face and a spark to her magically-depleted heart.

Raising the bottle to her lips, she swallowed the cool water, ice cubes clinking inside. She curled her nose at the tangy metallic aftertaste, but the additive Vera had cooked up last night was an unfortunate necessity.

Blue and Finn had figured out that the Old One was contaminating anything with a significant water content, which was why all the fresh food was rotting and why every hole Wally, Kyne, Drew, and Hardy drilled kept filling with black goop.

It was probably why the Exiles had been feeling ill since the crack appeared, too. So far, Blue and Clarke were the only ones who hadn't experienced any symptoms. Their humanity was their shield against the contamination, which was the first time their lack of supernatural prowess had worked in their favour.

Still, it was only a matter of time before the Old One's corruption sank deeper and got into the ground water. That meant they couldn't use the bores or catch any rainwater, so bottled stuff with a little witchy cordial was the safest way to go. The moment water became undrinkable was the moment Solace would be lost.

No water in the outback meant certain death, and

not even the supernatural could withstand dehydration.

The rumble of a diesel engine floated up the hill towards the dugout, and Eloise stood. The glint of sun reflecting off metal shone through the scrub as the rumble increased in volume, then a big, blocky, 4WD came into view.

Spotting Kyne behind the wheel, Eloise stowed her water bottle in the van and went to meet him. What was he up to now?

The whole thing looked top heavy—the rear had an extension on the tray, with a pop-top installed on the roof—with monster off-roading tyres and a snorkel on the front. At one point in its life, it'd been painted white, but after what looked like decades traipsing across the outback, the outside had turned into an artful, cream to rust ombré.

The miner parked the beast beside the carport and leapt out of the cab, a huge grin on his face. *Boys and their toys...*

"What is *that?*" Eloise raised her eyebrows, wondering where Kyne was taking her exactly.

"It's a Toyota Landcruiser Troop Carrier," he declared, looking rather pleased with himself. "Otherwise known as a Troopy...and the camel of the outback."

"That thing?"

"It's not much to look at right now, but she's solid, the engine's good, and the drive train is in excellent condition. I got it off a bloke in the Ridge for a steal." He slapped the side, dislodging a shower of dust. "I'm going to hook up some solar on the roof, refresh the interior, get a lithium battery system going..."

Eloise frowned and glanced at her van.

"Your magic will be charged up by the time I'm finished," he went on. "And we can get most of what we need here in town, though I thought we could stop in Lightning Ridge to stock up on food and water. It's well out of the Old One's sphere of influence, so we won't have to worry about any spoilage. There's a forty-litre water tank on this thing."

"Oh, I..." She dusted off one of the Troopy's side windows.

Kyne took a deep breath, the first he'd sucked in since he'd started talking about the car. "What?"

She glanced at her van again. "I thought..."

"Eloise..." He grimaced and pulled her in for a hug. "Your van is only a 2WD. Where we're going, it won't cut it."

"Oh." Her heart sank a little. "Where *are* we going exactly?"

"The Pilbara."

"Yeah, I know. But *where* in the Pilbara?"

Kyne drew back. "There's a billabong at the end of a gorge up near..." His brow began to form a crease. "In the..." The crease deepened. "The billabong was..."

Eloise tightened her grip of Kyne's shirt. "A billabong, where?"

He pulled away, his expression twisting into confusion, and began to pace. "I'd been on the WA coast up near Eighty Mile Beach and Broome..." He ran a hand over his face, almost knocking his hat off. "I'd spoken to an Indigenous guide about heading inland, into wild country. Spiritual lands... Country is important, so I'd wanted permission to travel, especially there."

Eloise nodded, after meeting Coen and listening to all he'd had to tell her, she understood the meaning of country to the Indigenous peoples, and now that she'd discovered her elemental heritage, she felt it, too.

"Where did you go from there?" she prodded.

"Back on the road. Inland... I can't..." he hissed and kicked the rear wheel of the Troopy, dislodging another plume of dirt. "They took my memories! They just *love* taking things, don't they? Insult to injury." He spat out a foul word and kicked the tyre again.

"*Kyne*." Eloise reached for him, but he'd already resumed pacing, more aggressively this time. His boots kicked up enough dust that she was forced to close the sliding door on her van to keep the cloud out of her freshly vacuumed interior. "It sucks, but we already knew they didn't want to be found. Taking the memory of their location seems like a logical thing to do."

"Logical?" he scoffed and ceased pacing, his back to her.

She saw his expression reflected in the Troopy windows and her shoulders sagged. "Kyne..."

"How are we going to find them if I can't remember?"

"You found them once, and you'll find them again."

He faced her, his anger melting into something that looked a lot like despair. "What if they're not there anymore?"

"Then we keep searching."

"You make it sound so easy."

"Kyne... W-we have to." She shrugged and looked at her feet. "*We have to.*"

His arms wrapped around her, and even though she was sticky with sweat, he held her close, their embrace lasting a long time. Long enough for her worries to fall back to a place where they didn't seem so immeasurable.

"We'll figure it out." He ran a comforting hand through her hair. "Four thousand kilometres on a wish and a prayer. Harder mountains have been climbed, right?"

"*Black* mountains," she whispered.

Eloise felt her magic rise and reach for Kyne's, but it spluttered and fell back into the depths of her body. She still wasn't strong enough to leave, but soon.

Soon...

"So," she said, wiping away a stray tear before untangling herself from his arms. "Can I look inside this Troopy of yours?"

"Sure, but it's *ours*." Kyne grinned and nodded towards the back. "It's got more space in there than you realise. There's even a portable dunny tucked in the back corner."

Eloise smiled up at him, her fears forgotten for the moment. "Just so we're clear, I don't think we're far enough along in our relationship for an open-door policy."

Kyne laughed and jangled the keys in his pocket. "Noted."

Drew stood on the ridge overlooking Solace and sniffed the balmy night air with his dingo nose.

The cloud of magic leaking from the damaged seal hung over Solace in a dome, glowing like electric blue bioluminescence in a dark ocean. The sight of it hanging in the night conjured images of black-lit jellyfish and microorganisms floating in the deepest parts of the ocean. In any other circumstance, they were beautiful things, but knowing the cloud of magic was poisoning everything it touched took the shine off it. After all, unnatural colours in nature often signified poison.

The earth lurched underneath his paws and the line where the sky became outer space blurred, and he found himself standing in another time and place. It was as if he stood on the surface of an alien planet where all the atmosphere had been stripped away.

It seemed like he was having a vision of a future

where the Old Ones had won, and they'd begun dismantling the entire reality. Was this how it would happen? They'd hit rewind and evolution would go backwards until the Big Bang sucked in on itself?

It was a terrifying thought, one Drew wasn't too proud to admit having. The seal was a ticking time bomb, and they were just waiting for the fuse to catch the dynamite.

Drew sensed Coen as he appeared out of the rivers, the Indigenous man's bare feet almost silent as he stepped towards the tip of the ridge. He was back in the real world, though he'd never left.

"*The Old One's magic is different than the mountain*," Drew said, watching as the cloud billowed, the plume undulating in slow waves. "*Why is that?*"

"Because it is a different Old One."

Drew resisted the urge to roll his eyes. "*Obviously, but all supernaturals are tied to what they are. Shifters, shift. Vampires, vampire. Werewolves, werewolf. Why aren't they?*"

"They are not bound by the rules of creatures of flesh and blood. The Old Ones shape all that is around them."

"*So they can do anything they want?*"

"I suppose they can."

"*Great. We're screwed.*" This time, Drew did roll his eyes.

"Not yet."

If Coen still thought there was time to fight, let

alone hope they could win, then it was enough to calm his worry for the time being. Besides, there were more pressing matters—the rotting food, Wally's next full moon, protecting the unsuspecting humans who passed through, not to mention their own wellbeing, too.

Drew could seem to shake the serious 'under the sea' vibes the usually invisible poison cloud was throwing off. "*Andante called it the heart of the ocean*," he said, throwing the thought out there.

"An ancient ocean once stretched from the north, rising inland across the outback," Coen said, catching the thread. "This country was once coastline, the shores littered with coral reefs, teeming with life. The Rainbow Serpent swam here, carving the way for all."

"*So when the Old One first broke through here, it was ocean?*"

"Yes."

"*Way to state the obvious, then.*" Drew frowned and looked back down at the town. "*I wonder who had the naming rights?*"

"Sometimes things name themselves; other times, deeds bring names. And sometimes, time itself changes all names."

Drew was seriously beginning to wonder if Coen had a split personality. Sometimes the Indigenous man spoke dreamily, while other times he was direct—it was as if he wasn't sure who he was supposed to be.

"*Coen?*" Drew turned away from the electric blue cloud. "*How long have you been here?*"

The Indigenous man grinned. "Five minutes."

"*That's not what I meant.*" He waited, but an answer wasn't forthcoming, so he added, "*Then how long ago were the seals placed?*"

"Time has become immeasurable," Coen replied with a shrug. "This country has changed so much, and I've travelled so far... It's difficult to remember."

There was archeological evidence that people had lived in Australia for up to, or even longer than, forty thousand years. The story Coen told them about the great animals—the emu, the eagle, the dingo, and the serpent—spoke of things from the oldest stories told by mobs all over. If he was a betting dingo, Drew would say the seals were placed at least that long ago.

And Coen...?

Coen's story was a mystery, and Drew wasn't entirely sure the Indigenous man knew all of it, either.

"*How old are you, Coen?*"

The man's expression took on a strange hollowness, the spark in his eyes dulling. "Time is immeasurable. Remembering... If you leave the Dreaming, you are lost."

Drew flicked his tail, his heart thrumming. "*Coen?*"

He blinked as if he was clearing fog from his mind, then nodded towards Solace. "The cloud is growing, but I can see the warmth within." He pointed towards the hillside. "Look."

Drew followed Coen's finger, his sight drawing him to a point of golden light lying below the dusty red surface. *Eloise.*

"*Her magic is growing,*" the dingo murmured.

"Soon, a new path will be made."

"*A new path?*"

Coen nodded, his expression still fallow. "They must go walkabout where none have walked before. They must walk for us all."

"*They?*"

"Eloise and Kyne."

"*So we can't go with them?*"

Coen stood tall, his gaze moving to the stars above. "They must return to their people."

Drew sat and looked back down at the point of golden light. *A place only elementals could go.*

Was his part in the story over? Or was there more to come?

The only thing Drew could do was wait and see.

CHAPTER 5

Eloise set her fork down as the dulcet tones of Blue's worn *Greatest of Aussie Rock Anthems* CD filled the pub. It was currently playing a classic AC/DC song, *Highway to Hell*, which was an ironic coincidence.

Dinner had been a muted affair ever since the storm, and more so after her return from the Black Mountain. Everyone was under pressure, not just Eloise, and it was beginning to show.

Every facet of life in Solace was touched by the poison leaking from the seal, and it was becoming clearer by the day that the Exiles might have to leave their homes...not that anyone was brave enough to say it out loud.

"Sorry," Blue said, breaking the morose silence. "It's not the greatest food tonight. I scrounged up everything edible from the mess out back."

"The corruption is growing," Finn stated. "It's expanding a little every day."

"And we've figured out the edge is currently halfway across the kitchen," Blue added. "Everything south of the island bench is good, but that means everything in the freezer is toast."

"Except a box of frozen chips jammed up against the south wall," the fae reminded him.

The publican sighed. "Except for the chips."

"Hallelujah," Drew drawled. "At least the chips are saved!"

"At least you have something to eat," Finn fired back. "Go out back and smell the bins, then you can thank me for the chips, dingo."

"Oh, we can smell the bins," Hardy muttered.

Silence fell over the table, and if it wasn't for the CD, there'd be nothing but awkward clacks of cutlery to accompany their side of gloom and doom.

"Has anyone noticed any other changes?" Kyne asked.

"Same old, same old," Wally replied. "I'm still looking for a hole for the next full moon if anyone has any ideas."

"We can put you back in the coolroom," Vera said, waving the old wolf off before he could complain. "Don't worry about the damage. You can't control your transformations, and your safety is more important than a few dents in my walk-in refrigerator." Her brow furrowed. "I've lost more money over stock anyway… can't make a bad situation any worse."

"I've duct taped the kitchen floor," Blue said. "I'll keep testing the border. Get a baseline for the expansion of this thing."

"That's a good idea," Vera said. "If we know how fast it's growing, we might be able to get ahead of it."

"Get ahead, how?" Drew asked with a roll of his eyes. "We can't stop it. There's no dam we can build and there's no magic spell strong enough."

Eloise squirmed and looked down at her plate. Studying the smear of tomato sauce on the off-white china, she frowned as she noticed the edges of the red condiment start to sprout fur. Her stomach squelched.

"We have to keep throwing stuff at it," Vera told the dingo. "Something will work."

"That's not a solution."

"Of course, it's not," the witch snapped. "Everything we do now is about buying time."

Eloise felt the Exiles' eyes turn to her, and her cheeks reddened under the weight of their expectant gaze.

"We're almost ready to go," Kyne said, grabbing her hand underneath the table. "I don't have much work to do on the Troopy, and Eloise's powers are growing every day. Here…" He took out a folded map from his breast pocket and spread it over the dirty plates.

"What is this place?" Finn asked, looking at the map. "Pill-bah-rah."

"No, no, no," Vera said. "If you want to say it like a local, you have to drop at least half of the letters. It's Pil-brah."

Kyne tapped the tabletop. "The Pilbara covers 502,000 square kilometres of the northern part of Western Australia, from the coast all the way to the border with the Northern Territory. That's a thousand kilometres at least, as the crow flies."

"502,000 square kilometres?" Drew asked with a sigh. "That's like finding a needle in a haystack..."

"Yeah, and the haystack's a grain of sand on a beach fifty k's long," Wally grumbled. "I don't know how you ever found anything in all that."

"Three different deserts lie within the boundaries," Kyne continued, ignoring their complaints. "The Great Sandy Desert, the Gibson Desert, and the Little Sandy Desert. The Tropic of Capricorn runs through the southern end. There's also gorges, billabongs, and caves, so it's not all dry outback. There's big iron ore mining operations, as well as small prospectors looking for gold, but a vast majority of the land is unpopulated. The weather is too harsh in the dry season, and the wet brings more dangers the more remote people are. One good storm and communities could be cut off for the entire season with no food, no fuel, no fresh water."

"I can see why people don't want to live there," Finn said. "And why these elementals do."

Hardy nodded. "With how humans have spread

themselves out, it's one of the last places on the planet they can live without being discovered."

"What was the land like forty thousand years ago?" Vera wondered. "It's got to have been at least that long since the seals were placed." She pointed to the map. "Look how the lakes have formed here. A river once cut across this entire region."

Eloise studied the map. There was a path cutting through the swath of desolate ochre that looked a lot like a dried-up river. The whole region was basically desert now, but tens of thousands of years ago, there'd been water—and there was still a little holding on today—and where there was water, there was life...and the hope of elementals.

"And you think we'll find them there?" she wondered.

Vera looked up at Kyne. "You said you found them at a billabong, right? What do you have to search for? You know where they are, don't you?"

The miner coughed, his eyes darting away. "Um..."

Hardy turned. "Um, what?"

"He can't remember how he got there," Eloise said. It was better to rip off the Band-Aid.

"You can't remember?" Finn blinked and leaned towards Eloise. "And you have all this land to search?"

"You were at the mountain," she hissed at him. "You saw what the Old One could do, and you can feel what's happening here. We have to search for the elementals, and this is where they are."

"It could take a lifetime," the fae grumbled. "I don't think we have—"

"It's not like I forgot on purpose," Kyne snapped. "They don't want to be found. At least, not by me."

Eloise met Drew's gaze across the table. The dingo raised his eyebrows, his expression echoing the suspicions she held in her heart. Her magic made her the key, so maybe the elementals wanted her to find them...and *only* her.

"Maybe there's a way to make you remember," Blue offered. "There's lots of different magic sitting around this table."

"I'm out," Hardy said. "I can't use compulsion on another supernatural. I *may* be able to dig into Kyne's mind, but only at superficial levels."

"I didn't know vampires could delve into people's minds," Eloise said.

Hardy shrugged. "Only a few have the skill to delve into the subconscious and view what's there, but it's how mind-control works—planting suggestion into the subconscious."

"I'd have better luck," Vera offered. "This is much more a witch thing, anyway."

Kyne looked at her, worried. "Do you really think you can bypass elemental magic?"

"With what we're up against, I don't think we have any choice."

"*Great*," he grumbled. "Your magic always hurts, you know."

"No pain, no gain," Finn declared, digging underneath the map. Dishes clattered as the paper danced up and down.

"I think it's a good idea," Eloise murmured, taking Kyne's hand again. "Even if we can narrow down the search area, we'd be miles ahead."

His lips thinned as he shrugged. "Yeah. Okay."

"Tomorrow?" Vera asked. "I need to make a few preparations."

Kyne grimaced and glanced at Eloise. "Tomorrow."

"Preparations?" Finn asked, reemerging from underneath the map with a stack of dirty plates. "Do you need to write one of your poems?"

"No, I don't need to write a poem," Vera spat. "And for your information, spells aren't poems, and not all spells require anchors in chants."

"I'll be there," Eloise murmured to Kyne as the Exiles began to debate the mechanics of Vera's magic. "If you want me to be."

"Of course I do..." He glanced at the door, looking a little pale around the edges. "You want to head out? I need some air."

A pang of concern rippled through her heart, but she nodded, comforted by the fact that he wanted her to go with him.

"Vera, I'll come find you tomorrow morning," Kyne said, interrupting the debate across the table.

"Oh?" Vera looked between the two elementals, her head tilting to the side.

"Uh, see you tomorrow," Eloise said as Kyne hurried out the door.

The witch's gaze followed him out, and she frowned.

"He'll be there," she added, glancing around the table. Catching Finn's eye, she smiled. "*E'shrilae.*"

"*Rilae*," the fae said with a grin. "Goodbye is way too final."

<hr>

Kyne was sitting on the table outside the pub when Eloise emerged. Overhead, the stars sparkled like they did every other night. The invisible plume of Old One magic felt like a fairy tale, but she knew it was there—her skin always tingled a little when she was out in the open.

As she approached the table, Kyne ran a hand through his black hair, sweeping his long locks out of his face. Without his hat, it kept falling into his eyes, and she knew it annoyed him. He needed a haircut, but who had time when they were planning a scavenger hunt across the Pilbara?

She came to a stop in front of him and rubbed her palms over his knees. "Are you okay?"

"I'm trying to decide if I want to puke or hold it in."

"Better out than in. Just give me a warning so I can step out of the firing line, okay?"

He managed a weak smile. "Sorry. All this... I

thought I was okay with searching for the elementals, but I don't think..."

"I get it." Eloise knew he didn't believe he was over what had happened to him. He couldn't say the words yet, which only confirmed it for her. She smiled, knowing their journey was just as much about him and his past as it was her and the fate of the world.

"And then everyone was piling on..." he added, "talking about it like it was so easy."

She took his hand and tugged, coaxing him to stand. "We've been through so much together, and I think they forget some things are still private." She wound her fingers through his. "C'mon, let's walk."

Their boots crunched on gravel as they followed the lonely highway north. Solace felt different, and Eloise knew *why* but couldn't quite find the words to describe how.

The windmill looked sadder than ever after the storm. Lightning had blown off quite a few of the rusted metal fins, which had embedded in the ground several feet away. The tank sported new holes, as well as a charred patch where the bolt itself had struck. It was a miracle the whole thing hadn't exploded into millions of jagged bits of shrapnel.

"Glad you didn't paint that mural?" Kyne asked as they passed.

"It would've been a lot of work for nothing," she murmured. "At least Finn might feel some satisfaction about it being blown-up."

When the entity that lived beside Vera's Nightshade legacy had been corrupted by the Black Mountain, the witch had imprisoned Finn inside the tank and used him as a living conduit to access the power inside the seal. So when fae magic had blown it up—albeit by random—it was rather ironic...and fitting.

"I reckon."

They strolled in silence, stopping only when they came to the settler's cemetery. Hardy had been busy clearing the spinifex and scrub from the historical site, exposing old headstones and restoring their carvings. He'd even built a new white picket fence in an attempt to keep the stubborn plants out, though the crisp paint was already tinged 'outback red'.

Amongst the markers was the memorial the vampire had built for his human family. The slab of rock Kyne had dug from his claim at Black Hole Mine was threaded with a river of opal seam. It only carried potch, which was colourless opal, but it was a beautiful piece, nonetheless.

Eloise looked down at the stone and remembered Hardy's sad story—an older brother trying to care for a sick sister in Victorian London, to his journey to Australia as a convict where he ultimately became a vampire, who was unable to return home.

"How did you seal the mountain, exactly?" Kyne asked, breaking through her thoughts.

Remembering the split in the meteor inside the cave, she replied, "The Old One took me into a vision."

"A vision?"

"Yeah…" Her fingers traced the line of milky-black potch in the rock. "It was the day I turned my parents against me. I…" Tears welled in her eyes, the sudden spike of emotions catching the words in her throat. "I had to fix what I broke." She felt Kyne's hand on the small of her back. "If I failed, then I would've set it free."

"It was that close, huh?"

Eloise swallowed hard, her gaze studying Hardy's memorial. She hadn't mentioned it to anyone, but she knew Finn understood how fine that line had been. Maybe Drew had too, considering the fissures that'd opened around the mountain.

Still, none of them had asked her about it, and she hadn't offered.

"When I opened my eyes, the cracks in the meteorite were filled with gold," she added. "I don't really understand how I did it."

"A lot of what we do is tied to our emotions and subconscious," Kyne explained. "On a physical level, I don't really know where the gold came from, but how it got there is an easy one."

If they ever go through this, Eloise would be content with never knowing any more secrets to the universe. She didn't want to understand where, why, or how. The thought of something other than the ancient, unemotional Old Ones pulling the strings was terrifying. It was best no one knew. *Ever.*

"If we beat this thing…" she murmured, her gaze running over the memorial. "If I can perform the miracle everyone's counting on, then I need to go back and fix it for real."

"Your parents?" Kyne's warmth was comforting beside her.

"Yeah. It was my fault and after everything they did for me—the adoption, raising me, putting up with my rebelliousness even before I changed them… It's not right leaving things when I know I can put everything back to how it's supposed to be."

"Then that's what we'll do," Kyne said, taking her in his arms. "I'll drive you all the way to Perth myself."

He kissed her, and Eloise felt the force of his love in his touch. Warmth grew inside her, and the world glowed with golden light as threads of silver spooled around them.

Kyne gasped, his eyes sparkling. "Your powers—"

"Are coming back," Eloise said, winding her arms around him.

"I'll say." His chest rose as he breathed deeply. "When you said your powers awoke, I didn't realise… No wonder you filled that meteor with gold."

Her hands trembled as she grasped the front of Kyne's shirt to steady herself. The light around them faded and night returned, along with the stars and the lingering presence of the Old One underground.

"You want to head home?" she managed to get out. "We've got a big day tomorrow."

"Sure." He cupped her cheek. "You okay?"

"Yeah." She nodded but didn't know how convincing she was. "I think it's low blood sugar. That dinner was *awful*."

"It was far from Blue's best work." Kyne chuckled and grasped her hand, never taking his gaze from hers.

Eloise's unease only grew as they crossed the highway and made their way up the hill.

It was almost time to leave, and when they did, she wasn't sure what was going to happen. But tomorrow…

Tomorrow would reveal where their path truly led.

CHAPTER 6

It was nine a.m. when Vera heard a knock on her front door. Opening it let in a sharp shard of bright morning sunlight and revealed Kyne and Eloise. *Right on time.*

"What is it about elementals and punctuality?" the witch asked, shuffling back down the stairs. She flung aside the beaded curtain, the plastic clacking together, and headed for the kitchen. Yawning loudly, she managed a garbled, "Coffee?"

"I didn't know you drank coffee," Eloise said as they followed her to the rear of the dugout.

"I don't," she called over her shoulder, "but it's polite to offer caffeine this early in the morning."

"People do wake up before ten in the morning, you know," Kyne drawled, looking around the lounge.

"Depends on your body clock." Vera laughed and turned to face the elementals. "Are you ready for this?" He totally wasn't, but she couldn't resist poking.

Kyne took off his hat and flung it onto the couch. "No, but there's never a time I will be."

Vera glanced at Eloise, who shrugged. She knew him well enough to know he was uncomfortable about what they'd might see, more than what he'd face inside his own mind.

Of course it was going to be tough. It wasn't a secret that Kyne had come back from the Pilbara disappointed, angry, and without his powers. They'd tossed him out like a lump of coal—he'd been branded unloved, unwanted, and nothing but a dirty stain on the planet. That had to do a real number on someone's self-esteem.

Besides, Kyne was still half-human, so Vera knew there was a high chance he'd done a little unconscious remodelling himself. There would always be two halves to his psyche, and trauma did strange things to ordinary people, let alone half-supernatural ones.

Long story short, they all understood this was going to hurt. *A lot.* No wonder he was trying to draw things out, despite their world-ending predicament.

"Should you really be doing this?" Kyne added. "I mean, haven't you been feeling sick?"

Vera rolled her eyes and waved a hand at him. "I *was*, but I hardly feel it anymore."

It seemed the more magic that leaked out of the seal, the better she felt, which was curious and slightly alarming, but so far there hadn't been any side effects.

The Nightshade was long gone and along with it, any foothold the Old One might find on the witchy corruption scale.

Kyne raised his eyebrows but didn't push for an answer.

"And what about you?" she asked. "Are you feeling sick? Or is it just nerves that's twisting your stomach? The toilet is through the back. You know where."

"*Vera*," the miner grumbled.

"Either we've all gotten used to it or the nausea is confined to the goop now that it's loose," Eloise said. "Anyway, with the amount of magical bits and pieces down here, I'm sure we'll be fine."

"Yeah," Vera said with a wave. "I've got more crystals down here than a New Age market in Byron Bay."

Eloise chuckled as the tension began to ease.

Kyne's eyes flickered around the room. "So...what do I need to do?"

"All you need to do is sit down and don't fight me," Vera told him. "You'll want to, but you shouldn't."

"Why not?"

"Because you'll make it hurt more than it ought to." She flexed her fingers and rolled her neck. "Want to get started?"

Kyne squirmed. "I thought you said you needed to make preparations?"

"I did."

"Doesn't it involve herbs and crystals and…stuff?"

"Not every spell requires a toolkit," the witch said with a sigh. "A good night's sleep and a can of energy drink is more than enough for a little mind-walking."

"Stop stalling." Eloise placed her hand on the miner's shoulder. "You'll be okay."

"Men are such babies." Vera clicked her fingers and pointed to the chair in the middle of the room. "Here's a chair I prepared earlier. *Plant it.*"

Kyne sank onto the chair, and she positioned herself behind him. He tensed the moment Vera's hands grasped his head, her fingers splayed across his skull.

"Stop being so dramatic," the witch muttered. "I haven't done anything yet." She took a deep breath. "Relax, keep still, and breathe. Forget about me and focus…"

Eloise sat on the couch, her gaze fixed on Kyne.

"I'm going to let go of my magic in a moment," Vera went on. "And when I do, I want you to focus on what you do remember. What the billabong looked like. What you felt when you walked the path towards it. The moment you met the elementals."

"But that's the problem," Kyne grumbled. "I don't remember."

"You remember *some* of it, so humour me." She called on her witch legacy and felt the warmth pool in her blood and rush towards her hands. "Take a deep breath and remember... Remember the path through the outback. Set your feet on the ground and walk..."

Vera's magic flowed into her palms and descended into Kyne's mind, seeping through the barriers of flesh and bone, melting into him like water soaking into parched earth. The miner jerked as she made contact, then was still.

"Follow the Brinewold," she whispered. "Let it guide you."

Kyne didn't resist, not at first. He took the invasion of her inside his mind like a champ, easing his breathing and allowing her to walk beside him. The path was foggy, but she could make out the rusty earth, the smear of sapphire in the sky, the towering cliffs... They stood in a gorge that smelled of wet coolness and carried the electricity that Vera often felt around Kyne and Eloise.

"Vera?" Eloise's voice echoed through the hazy vision, and she opened her eyes.

Below her, Vera frowned as she saw a strange translucency playing across Kyne's forearms. A light shone within him, illuminating his skin and the veins that ran underneath.

The elemental shifted closer, her gaze fixed on Kyne's bare arms. "Are you seeing this?"

Vera glanced at Eloise, then back at the glowing spots racing across the miner's forearms. The light had faded some, but his skin had taken on the lustre of a pearl. Patches of creamy-white rose and fell through his human body, shimmering with shades green, blue, and purple. It crept up his neck and onto his face, but never lingered long enough to take over completely.

His flesh was a shell for what lay underneath. Was this what they truly looked like?

"Vera," Eloise gasped, "*his hair.*"

Vera's breath caught as she saw clumps of Kyne's black locks turn white—not the silver-grey that came with age, but strange, translucent threads that reminded her of the thick, shiny spiderwebs that hung in the forests surrounding her childhood home in Ireland. Clear threads that reflected light...and the glow of her steely blue Brinewold magic.

"What's going on?" Eloise whispered.

"I don't know," she replied. "But I'm not doing it."

"Is it...is it the elementals? Did they...?"

Vera swallowed hard. Did they do something to Kyne—something more than just taking his memories?

She tightened her hold on her magic. She had to keep pushing, it was the only way they'd find answers.

Kyne jerked and clenched his teeth as her legacy drove into his mind.

"*Vera...*" The concern in Eloise's voice grew.

"Don't touch him," she warned. "If the connection is severed now, I don't know what it'll do to his mind."

"I don't like this."

"Trust me," Vera rasped.

"I do, I just—"

"It doesn't matter. I can't stop now. I have to let the wave break on the shore..."

She had to have faith in the Brinewold legacy. The magic of her family and her blood would guide her to where she needed to go. It would burst through the dam placed by the elementals and rush into his mind, showing her the source. Then it would be up to Kyne to piece it all back together.

Vera pushed on, her magic delving deeper into his subconscious.

***

Kyne knew he sat in Vera's lounge room, and he knew he was in Solace, being watched over by Eloise. He knew these things, but when he closed his eyes, he felt himself being swept away.

Then he was in a dark river, being swept into the dark places in his mind—the bits the elementals had taken from him.

Water rushed all around him, the briny taste lingering on his tongue. At first he struggled against the current, pain exploding through his body as he swam towards the smudge of golden light in the distance. Back towards Eloise.

But he remembered what Vera had told him and relaxed. As his body became limp, the water took him, washing him towards the blank spaces...but as he drifted closer, he saw they weren't so empty after all.

Colours and shapes blurred into being, focusing then blurring again, but never quite sharpening to complete clarity.

Then Kyne stood in a fractured landscape, where the sky was stripped away from the Earth and the universe hidden behind the flimsy protection of atmosphere was laid bare. He stood, free of pain and completely dry, his ties with his physical body loose enough that it frightened him. The river was gone just like a cut scene in a movie, but his attention was pulled towards the world above and he forgot all about it.

He knew all those stars burned at impossible distances, making space seem lonely—soundless and empty—but to him, it was full of energy. Frequencies, sounds, light, and *memory*. Full of the things no human could comprehend on their own, not without technology to aid them.

To think such small things like nitrogen and oxygen had kept all this at bay. Without it, life wouldn't stand a chance.

A drip hitting the surface of still water echoed around the emptiness and Kyne turned as it radiated outwards, filling the blank spaces the elementals had left behind.

Remembering his path, he stepped into the gorge in the heart of the Pilbara, sliding his body into the thin opening. His bare arms scraped against smooth rock as he passed, the trickle of water splashing as he dragged his boots through the tight space. He barely fit, but at least thousands of years of erosion had smoothed the way.

He felt their magic all around him and knew their mark on this place ran deep—after all, the same energy ran in his veins. There was no mistaking this was where he'd come from.

A sliver of light broke through the dim light of the narrow gorge, and he pressed towards it, the tang of salt guiding him through the press of tangled memories.

Then the gorge opened before him, revealing an oasis inside the lonely, wild Earth. A billabong lay at the heart of it, and the sides of the rocky hollow it dominated grew thick with greenery. Plants clung to the vertical surfaces, their roots grabbing hold of anything they could, and vines coiled downwards towards the water's surface. Trees grew around the shore, their trunks long, slim stalks that reached towards the circle of sunlight above.

He stood at the entrance of the billabong for a long time, still as he could manage, his human body the only thing giving his presence away—the rise and fall of his chest as he breathed and the beating of his heart.

As he beheld the billabong, Kyne remembered. He knew this place, felt the memory of it in the reality he'd left behind. He understood the path he was supposed to walk now...the path he would lead Eloise down.

A shimmer appeared before him, distorting the oasis as it moved. A creature had come to greet his unexpected arrival...as it had then.

A face shone through the invisible mirage, revealing a man with translucent skin that shone like a pearl—white and cream, with ghostly patches of green, purple, and blue.

"I see you," Kyne said to the elemental, never once breaking his gaze from the translucent creature. "I know where you are...and now, we're coming for you."

Kyne felt his body wrench backwards and the billabong rushed away. He flopped through the air like a rag doll, flying through the sapphire sky, then through the flimsy veil that protected life from the vacuum of space. He gasped as the air was sucked out of his lungs, his vision erupting in a rainbow of colour.

Kyne fell to his knees and heaved, throwing up clear liquid onto Vera's shaggy rug. He was in the witch's dugout again, the strange, fractured world buried in his memories, gone.

"Well, better out than in," the witch declared, grimacing.

"Tastes like saltwater..." He gagged again and Eloise rubbed his back.

"Yeah," Vera murmured, "the Brinewold will do that to you."

Eloise sat beside him, carefully avoiding the danger zone on the rug. "Did you see?"

"Yeah," he rasped, wiping his mouth with the back of his hand. "I saw enough." He leaned against the couch, too weak to crawl onto it, and closed his eyes. "I feel like I've been turned inside out."

"What happened in there?" Eloise asked.

Kyne grimaced and looked up at Vera. "What did *you* see?"

"They really did a number on your mind," the witch said, sitting on the couch. "They seemed to have taken some memories and messed with others. That's why the things you can recall are scrambled like a kaleidoscope."

"I'm not surprised," he managed to say. "Coen had said they were supposed to be broken themselves."

"Kyne..." Eloise took a deep breath. "While you were in there, your skin..."

His heart skipped a beat. "My skin what?"

"Well, it was turning this odd shade of white," she explained. "Just patches of it, but it was all pearlescent...kinda like the inside of a shell, you know?"

"Don't forget the hair," Vera added.

Kyne swept his fingers through his overgrown locks. "My hair?"

"Oh, it's back to normal now," the witch added. "But it was matching your skin for a while."

He pressed his cold fingers against his fevered brow. He was getting one hell of a tension headache.

Eloise rubbed her palm over his thigh. "Kyne?"

"It sounds just like the elemental I saw at the billabong," he murmured.

Vera glanced at Eloise, her expression hopeful. "You *saw* one?"

"I know where to go now, but first..." he grimaced and rubbed his temples, "I need some ibuprofen."

CHAPTER 7

Finn picked his way through the scrub, wandering aimlessly towards the flat horizon.

Bulbous, bruised clouds skidded across the sapphire sky, grazing to the north of Solace as they tracked east en route to the coast. It was a reminder he didn't need—his dreams had done enough of it without his waking hours weighing in.

In the dark, he saw the echo of the muddy green and black pulsing energy that was the Old One itself. He saw it rising out of jagged fissures across the outback. He saw the poison reaching into the sky, tearing away the atmosphere. He saw Siora fall into it, her hand reaching towards him. He saw her silver eyes and the fleeting moment of clarity right before the current swept her away. He saw—

Finn scowled and continued, burying the memory along with all the rest. Was it a vision of the future or his own fears playing tricks on him? If he listened to Coen, then maybe the reason he was seeing it all mixed up like that was because of the Dreaming. The Dreaming was everything existing all at once, and it was strong in this land.

Maybe.

If only he still had a job. If only he could pay off his potato debt to Blue, then he wouldn't have to think about all the rest.

Since all the food had rotted, the publican had decided to stop serving lunch and dinner to customers other than the Exiles, rendering the fae's employment over before it'd even begun. It meant they had little to eat other than pasta and rice cooked in water laced with Vera's witchy additive. No wonder he was grumpy. Anyone with a brain would be in a constant mood with that diet.

Finn kicked a stone, sending the pebble flying across the red sand. It'd been his first job, and he was looking forward to flipping his first burger. *Stupid tentacle monster.*

Following the skipping rock, he kicked it again and tracked its path. It was on the third kick that he realised that the dull throb behind his right eyeball was gone. He'd gotten so used to the annoying stab of pain that he was suddenly lonely without it.

That's it, then, he thought. *That's how far it goes...*

He'd finally come to the edge of the Old One's

reach, the corruption vanishing from the land beneath his feet. It also meant he felt the absence of magic and his body was now running on reserves. He had time to wander and explore, but he'd have to return to Solace by sundown if he wanted to avoid getting one hell of a migraine.

Free from the poison, his mind cleared and he was able to think clearly for the first time since returning from the Black Mountain.

It'd spread so far.

He shook his head and picked up the rock. Turning it over in his palm, he rubbed the dust from the surface, then hurled it with as much force as he could muster.

The rock soared through the air, turning over and over as it flew. Finn's silver gaze followed its arc as it descended back towards the earth. After all these years, he still had one hell of a throwing arm.

In the distance, the sun reflected off a mirage. He paused as the rock sailed through it and disappeared.

What's going on here?

The gossamer curtain reflected as he pressed his magic towards it, and it shimmered faintly against the mottled sky. Something was hidden there, and it wasn't a fae illusion...

So it could only belong to one other person.

It seemed the paths that ran deep in this country had guided Finn to yet another destination he didn't know he needed to visit...or perhaps it was the other way around.

Finn scoffed and walked towards the veil. Who knew why anything and anyone did the things they did in this place? They just *were*. Frustratingly so.

It wasn't long before the karsts Kyne had told him about rose out of the illusion, the vast field of beehive-shaped rock formations shimmering into existence.

Some magic, he thought. *But her power shouldn't have crumbled so easily.*

A track lay at his feet and wound through the scrub. It was nothing more than a scraggly divot that looked like it'd been scratched out by wandering kangaroos and other critters, but the symbolism was so obvious, it made him roll his eyes.

He set his right foot onto it and immediately sensed magic deep within the rock. She was here...waiting.

Following the trail into the shadow of the karsts, he walked until he found another path leading upwards, so Finn climbed, reaching the top with little effort.

The stone was smooth and shiny—people had passed through here often, but these days it was only Andante who called this place home.

He was wondering what happened to the mob who lived here before the druidess arrived to hide it all way when he heard her voice echo behind him.

"Took you long enough," she said in a haughty tone.

Finn turned and glared at the old woman. "I had stuff to do."

She had nothing witty to snap back, so he sat and dangled his feet over the cliff edge. Beholding the field of banded rock formations before him, he shook his head. *To think she hid all this beauty away... This country...*

Feeling her gaze burning into the back his head, he glared up at her. "*What?*"

"You have something to say, so say it."

Finn ground his teeth and sat sullenly for a while. Out of all the Exiles, he'd suffered the most. He had just cause to be angry, didn't he? No one could fault him for being offended. *Right?*

"If Eloise is successful, I'll have to leave Solace."

"And?" Andante asked.

"This place has become my home," he told her. "More than my birthplace."

Andante stared at the view before them, closing off her expression. She remained still and silent for so long, Finn almost got up to poke her just to make sure she was still alive.

"My people are travellers," she finally said. "We wandered through the veil that separates all, exploring and learning."

Finn rolled his eyes. "And look what it got you. Near extinction."

"After all we endured and after all we saw, my

people returned to their ancestral home." She turned to stare at him. "And so could you."

"I could never go back there," Finn snapped.

"Because of what you did?"

"No." He shook his head. "Because I am so far removed from it. If I went back, the world I'd find wouldn't be the one I remember."

"Stop looking to the past," Andante told him. "There is fear in freedom, but also hope."

"What good is hope?" He swept his arm across the horizon. "I wish for Eloise to fail so I won't lose my home, and if she does, then everything will cease to be. Maybe not today, maybe not tomorrow, maybe not for ten thousand years, but the Old Ones will erase all of this. *I'm selfish*."

"At least you admit your faults," the druidess drawled. "The first step is always the hardest."

"If the Old Ones are sealed away for good, then Solace won't hold any magic. I won't be able to stay here."

"Then go back to Ireland."

"And beg the witches to let me through their precious portal?" he scoffed. "Like they'd let me. I'm a known criminal and exile. The fae *never* forget."

"Always so dramatic, always so dire." The old woman chuckled. "Unseelie fae make for good tragedies."

"What's that supposed to mean?" Finn felt his anger rise and resisted the urge to fling the old bat off the side of the cliff. "If we lose, *I die*. If we win, *I die*."

"There is another solution," she told him. "One my magic can reveal to you...if you choose. Think of the *why*, Finn."

"You're impossible!" Fed up with her blathering, he stood and began to climb back down to the path below. "Crazy old bat!"

"You have a path laid before you, Finn Oreah'anza," Andante called after him. "It is up to you whether you walk it or not."

"Screw the path!" he shouted as he tore through the druidess's illusion. "Screw it to hell and back!"

The sound of a drill whirred out of the roller door of Wally's garage and echoed through the stillness of Solace. The place had been an unusual hive of activity for the last three days as work continued on Kyne's Troopy, and that morning was no exception.

Dull murmurings vibrated from the radio, filling the garage with the monotonous meanderings of a national talkback show. People rang in and complained about the government, their neighbours, the weather, and all manner of things that got on their nerves. Wally loved listening to it, but in an ironic sort of way. He found most of the complaints hilarious.

Kyne usually did his best to tune it out and always

failed. He'd leave the garage annoyed at the human race, heading back out to his claim where he'd spend the rest of the day smashing rocks underground...but not today. Today they were working on the Troopy with Hardy, who had nothing better to do since there was no opal left to cut and polish.

Wally tinkered underneath the hood, checking to see if the engine was up to handling a four-thousand-kilometre trip across Australia. Metal clinked against metal as he worked, punctuated by random chuckles as he listened to the radio.

The floor was littered with rubbish—old cabinetry and insulation from the interior, cardboard packaging and wire scraps from the electric work Kyne had been trying to wrangle, even scraps of material from the newly upholstered memory foam mattress Hardy had whipped up on Vera's dusty sewing machine. The vampire had shown an unexpected flair for the craft, which had everyone cracking jokes at his expense. He didn't seem to mind. They all needed a few laughs.

Kyne's stomach churned and he leaned against the side of the Troopy. The back doors were open, and the interior was a mess of sawdust and insulation scraps, but he didn't see any of it. His thoughts were still occupied with his scrambled memories, but it wasn't just that; it was also what'd happened to him in the real world.

His hair had returned to its usual colour, the strange silvery-white Eloise said it'd turned nowhere to be seen—along with the patches of pearlescent colour on his skin.

Vera didn't understand what she'd uncovered, and neither did he. There was no easy way to describe his vision, but he wondered if the truth of what he was, what both he and Eloise were, had been revealed to them—the true form of the elementals, the people from the dark places between the stars.

"What's the matter?" Hardy asked, breaking through his troubled reverie.

"Nothing." Kyne pushed off the side of the Troopy and dusted off his hands. The solar panels weren't going to wire themselves.

"I know that look on your face."

"I have to get the Troopy finished," Kyne told him. "We have to leave as soon as possible."

The vampire frowned. "Since when?"

"Since Vera unscrambled my mind."

"You're that sure of where to find the elementals?"

"It's not that exactly..." Kyne picked up the solar panel and leaned it against the rear wheel. "I've felt restless since that day, like I set off a countdown the moment I put my memories back together."

Three restless nights had almost made him believe he hadn't simply been walking through his memories. He felt as if he'd actually reached out to the elemental at the billabong and announced his imminent arrival. *Way to give them a chance to call the movers.*

Hardy picked up a spool of electrical wiring and handed it to the miner. "What did you see, exactly?"

"Vera led me through my subconscious to where the elementals messed with my mind," Kyne explained. "The whole thing was strange. I knew they were my memories, but they were broken apart, and when I tried to piece them back together... Well, the pieces didn't quite fit. It was...clumsy."

"So, they're not all-powerful mystical beings from a higher plane of existence?"

"Maybe not in this dimension."

Hardy chuckled.

"It felt like they were glitching," Kyne added.

"How so?"

"Their physical form seemed to shift and change. Like..." he frowned as he tried to find the words, "like they were here and someplace else at the same time."

"Stands to reason."

"We're going to have our work cut out for us," Kyne murmured, looking out of the garage at Solace. "They're..."

"Broken?" the vampire prompted.

"Yeah. *That*." And they weren't human, so it was difficult to tell how things would go. "What if it's another trap?" Kyne wondered aloud. "What if the reason they couldn't complete the job was because they were corrupted, just like everyone else who's tried to crack those seals open?"

"That's a risk we're going to have to take," Hardy

replied. "The Old Ones aren't a tangible enemy we can fight. Darius, the Dust Dogs, the Nightshade…they were easy in comparison. Finding the elementals is the only way forwards. At least, the only one I can see."

He was right. Everyone was right. Kyne was the only one still trying to fight it. It didn't matter how many times he tried to unravel the mystery, it always had the same solution…the elementals.

They held all the answers and not just to the ultimate question of the survival of the reality, but to why he was born in the first place. It was the question he wanted answered the first time around and maybe… Maybe it was the key to everything.

"I'm going to take the coral key to them," he said to the vampire.

"Really?" He looked out of the cool garage to the outback beyond. "I'd almost forgotten about that thing."

"You and me both."

"I always thought it was a red herring," Hardy went on. "A false trail laid by the mountain to trigger the Dust Dogs into action."

"We all thought that, but it's too coincidental. It's made out of coral, and Andante called the Old One here the heart of the ocean. The whole area used to be a coral reef… It's got to mean something."

"And you didn't have it last time you met the elementals."

Kyne grunted. That was his exact thought. Give

them a present, and maybe they'd be more open to hearing what they had to say. It was worth a shot.

"So, do you think Eloise is going to like the Troopy?" Hardy asked.

It was a relieving change of conversation and Kyne shrugged. "It's not exactly as roomy as her van, but it'll get us to where we need to go."

"But it's not self-contained."

"I installed an outdoor shower," the elemental complained.

"You're such a bloke." Hardy laughed and began clearing up the rubbish strewn around the garage.

"Who's a bloke?" Wally asked, emerging from underneath the bonnet.

"Kyne," Hardy said. "He thinks an outdoor shower's going to cut it."

"Eloise is adventurous. She won't mind."

"Mind?" Wally exclaimed. "After travelling in her fancy motorhome? *Boy...*"

"You two have issues," Kyne muttered as he began unspooling electrical cable. "And they're entirely human."

"*Gimme that.*" Hardy snatched the spool out of the miner's hands. "Go get your bit of coral. You're not going to be happy until you do."

"What do you know about wiring solar panels?" He tried to take back the wire, but Hardy yanked it out of reach.

"I know enough."

"And I know the rest," Wally added.

"All right, all right." The miner picked up his hat and made his way towards the roller door. "If I'm not back by dinner, send out a search party."

"Another one?" Hardy shouted.

"Watch out for goop!" Wally called after him.

Without turning, Kyne lifted a hand, made a rude gesture, and continued across the highway.

CHAPTER 8

Kyne clutched the steering wheel of his battered ute as it bounced along the rutted track.

The trail led out to an old opal claim a few kilometres outside of Solace, though it was rarely used since the last owner had given up the chase a few years prior. Opal was a tough game, especially in the remote reaches of the outback.

The storm had changed the landscape in subtle ways, and it was just enough to throw his memory off the scent. If it wasn't for his elemental powers, he'd have a hard time finding the location again, let alone the track.

The ute crashed over a pothole, the ground banging against the underside. Kyne cursed and kept going, hoping nothing had been damaged. It was a long walk back to Solace.

Finally, the claim came into sight, or what was left of it—a few sheets of rusted corrugated iron and the shaft leading down to the abandoned diggings. The law stated that all mining sites had to be rehabilitated, which included backfilling and removing unwanted rubbish, but the last owner hadn't bothered. He probably assumed no one would come check, and from the state of the track, Kyne knew he'd been the only person out here since.

Parking the ute in the clearing, he climbed out. Tossing his hat into the front seat, he slapped on his battered hardhat and turned on the headlamp.

He lifted the sheet of iron he'd placed over the shaft and moved it aside, then looked down into the dark hole. His headlamp lit the way, the light illuminating the seven-metre drop.

It looked dry enough down there with no goop in sight.

Good, he thought. *It ought to be a fast turn-around.*

Kyne flung his leg over the edge, and as his boot settled on the first rung on the ladder, he hesitated.

He usually liked being underground. His affinity with the earth made it a comfortable place—well, as comfortable as standing in a hole with hundreds of tonnes of rock above his head *could* be—but ever since the seal had cracked, a lingering apprehension plagued the back of his mind.

At least the corruption hadn't seemed to have spread this far...if it ever did. There was a limit on the mountain's sphere of physical influence, so it stood to reason the same would happen here.

Wishful thinking, he thought as he continued down the ladder.

He lingered at the bottom, both his feet planted firmly on the ground. Listening to the earth, he felt the coral key at the end of the tunnel, just where he'd left it all those months ago. Had it really been that long? It was almost a year since Eloise had arrived, right at the end of the last mining season.

Kyne ventured down the tunnel to the void where the last miner had been chasing the reef line through the soft rock. He'd been hoping to find potch imbedded in the wall but had never seen the illusive flash of colour that meant opal was near—and he never would have. There was nothing to be found in this part of the landscape, not now and not ever, which made this site the perfect place to hide something valuable.

He stood before the wall and placed his hand on the chiselled earth. Sensing the treasure buried within, he let his power trickle forth.

The rock parted like butter, melting away until the coral key was revealed. The palm-sized sphere glowed a soft pink in the light cast by his headlamp, the flecks of coral and quartz glittering as he picked it up.

But an acrid smell filled the air the moment the key parted from its resting place. Black sludge began to pool in the hole, bubbling out of the earth like tar.

"Shit," Kyne cursed, covering his nose with his forearm.

He took a step back, the light bobbing and casting long shadows around the tunnel. The key was holding the Old One's corruption back, and now he'd broken the dam.

Kyne backed away as the goop rose faster, only to find his boots sloshing through an inch of the stuff underfoot.

Turning, he ran down the tunnel, buttoning the coral key into the breast pocket of his shirt as he went. His foot caught on a rock and he stumbled, his shoulder slamming against the rough wall, the jagged surface cutting into his flesh.

Black tar splashed and seeped over the top of his boots, soaking his socks and working in between his toes.

Kyne's stomach lurched and his lungs filled with the potent fumes. He dry-heaved, his shoulders shaking as the corruption began to leech into his body.

He looked back the way he came, the light from his headlamp darting around the tunnel. The goop only seemed to be rising faster, the liquid soaking through his clothes up to his knees.

A rumbling sound reverberated deep within the earth and Kyne cursed, his panicked voice echoing through the mine. His powers had dulled the moment the corruption had burst forth, though he still had enough control to feel the rush of goop that was gushing out of the hole the coral key had lain in.

He ran as fast as he could. The black goop

thickened, dragging his legs and weighing him down. His headlight flickered and died, plunging the tunnel into darkness, but a sliver of light pulled him forwards...

The shaft was in sight.

He was going to make it. *He had to make it.*

Slamming into the ladder, his sticky hands scrambled at the rungs, slipping and sticking as he heaved himself up and out of the thickening tar, but the goop surged, filling the tunnel and rising up the shaft.

He reached towards the light as the corruption reached his neck and heaved in a deep breath as it covered him completely.

Finn stormed across the outback, his mood souring with each sullen footstep.

Stupid druid. What does she know, anyway? She doesn't know me. She hides in her stupid cave like a crazy person. She—

Finn stopped and looked down at *Marlu*. The kangaroo stared up at him with her big brown eyes and twitched her nose.

"What?" he snapped, his foul mood souring even more. Where the kangaroo was, Coen certainly followed. And he certainly wasn't in the mood for more introspection from yet another vague resident from the outer reaches of Solace.

The kangaroo rose up on her hind legs and bounced past him, leaping a little too close for comfort. Her tail swished and clipped his leg, turning him around.

"Hey!" he shouted. "Watch yourself!"

The kangaroo stopped and looked back, waiting for him to follow.

"Forget about it."

The kangaroo continued to stare, and Finn was almost certain he felt his insides liquefy. *Marlu* was special—he knew that much from her constant companionship with Coen—but how special was she exactly? Could her gaze turn him inside out? With all the magical nonsense this town attracted, he wouldn't be surprised.

"Fine," he muttered, waking towards her. "You win. *Happy?*"

As soon as he moved, *Marlu* bounced away, leading him through the patchy scrub to the west of Solace. They were headed back into the middle of nowhere, away from human habitation. Where was the kangaroo taking him?

Finn had nothing better to do, and he wasn't ready to head back to the pub, so he sucked up his self-pity and followed. Not far ahead, *Marlu* jumped through a patch of thick bushes and disappeared.

"Talk about a wild 'roo chase," he muttered,

pushing through the dry scrub. "When I get my hands on you—"

Stepping into a clearing, Finn jerked to a halt, his spiralling mood forgotten.

He saw a ute parked by an abandoned mine shaft, saw a hand sticking out of a hole filled with Old One sludge, and knew it could only be one person.

Kyne.

Finn sprinted, calling on his magic to propel him across the clearing. Lunging as the hole bubbled over, he grabbed Kyne's hand and pulled. His power flared, coursing through his veins as he dragged the miner out of the shaft.

Kyne emerged from the back tar, the hole making a gross sucking sound as the last of his body came free, and they tumbled to the ground. The miner heaved in lungfuls of air, gasping and spitting sludge.

Luckily for them, the goop stopped at the surface and didn't continue to rise.

Finn looked down at the blackened miner. "How are you not dead?" He pinched his nose as the wind changed direction. "You stink by the way."

Kyne spat and wiped his mouth, but only succeeded in smearing more goop on his face. "Buggered if I know."

He screwed up his nose, feeling a little guilty he didn't listen to *Marlu* sooner. "What were you doing down there anyway?"

Kyne unbuttoned his shirt pocket and took out a small, round disk. "Getting this."

"And what is *that*, exactly?"

"The coral key."

It was the first time Finn had laid eyes on the mythical key and he squinted at it. It wasn't much to look at really; a small disk about an inch thick, made of pink coral, dusted with salt and a vein of blackish quartz—the latter probably a result of the high iron content in the earth.

He curled his lip and snorted. "This is what those biker dingoes went so crazy about?"

"It was a just a tool used by the Black Mountain to corrupt them," Kyne said. "I don't think they really knew why or what they were so worked up about."

"And you went down into that hole to get it, *alone*, knowing there was goop about?" He shook his head. "Your logic astounds me."

"There wasn't any goop until I took the key out of the rock."

"*You don't say.*"

"There's a tank of water in the tray," Kyne said, pointing to the ute. "I've got to get this stuff off before it corrodes my mind."

"Are you sure it hasn't already?"

"I'm sure. I don't even feel sick."

He eyed the elemental. *Expect the unexpected* was his motto in all of this.

Kyne clicked his fingers. "*Finn.*"

"Whatever." The fae looked over the edge and saw a hose coiled up beside the tank, which ran the width of the cab, and there was a whole slew of equipment besides. "*Wow*. You really come prepared."

"It's the outback, mate. If you don't think you'll need it, you're a fool to leave it behind."

Finn brandished the hose and pointed the nozzle at the miner. "Can I hose you down? It's turned to 'jet'... Is that gentle or will it rip off your skin?"

"Give it here." Kyne scowled and went to snatch the hose out of his hands. "This isn't *Girls Gone Wild*."

Finn tossed the hose at him, dodging contact with the goop. It was the worst stink he'd smelled in his life, and he'd smelled some pretty rank odours. There was no way in hell he was getting it on his skin.

Kyne's fingers slipped on the plastic and the hose clattered to the ground. Cursing, he picked it up and leaned over the try of the ute. He fussed with the tank, then flipped a switch, and something mechanical began to hum.

Finn stepped back as the miner hosed himself down, the black goop diluting with the ochre sand as it pooled beneath him. He took off his boots and socks, hosing both, then tossed them into the back of the ute.

"Do you think there was something similar to go with the seal under the Black Mountain?" Kyne asked.

"Probably."

He grunted and turned his attention back to the hose.

Over forty thousand years, there were plenty of opportunities for something to go missing. If there was a talisman like this coral key, then its existence was long-forgotten. Besides, it wasn't needed anymore. Eloise had seen to that.

"It could come in handy back in town," Finn stated. "Keep things habitable."

"*Theoretically*." He peeled off his shirt and scowled. It was beyond saving, so he tossed it into the tray with his boots.

"It's stopping you from throwing up your internal organs right now," Finn went on, "and you want to give it them as a peace offering?"

"Yes. Yes, I do." The miner looked down at his jeans and sighed.

"You're not going to get naked, are you? You can't make me ride back to Solace with your bare arse, you know."

"No one asked!"

"You know, you haven't said thank you for dragging you out of that stinking tar pit yet."

"*Thank you*."

Finn smirked and glanced at the mine shaft where goop bubbled and popped, sending a waft of something unimaginably stinky into the air. "That stuff could be constituted of Old One excrement, you know."

The blood drained from Kyne's face. "Old One crap?"

Finn laughed, his meeting with Andante well and truly on the back burner as far as brain power went.

Kyne gagged and picked up the hose again. The coral key sat on the edge of the ute's tray, sparkling in the sun. The little disc's value had risen exponentially, and Finn eyed it with new interest.

"You think the elementals saw this coming?" the miner asked as he began hosing off his jeans.

"Sure. They seem like a crafty bunch, don't they?" It was clever really, to create a talisman to patch up their shoddy craftsmanship. "They can't finish a job, so supply a puncture repair kit."

Kyne snorted. "Everyone knows those things are temporary."

"My point exactly, but our water content is currently rotting away. That's why we feel sick..." he eyed the key, "some more than others."

Kyne closed his hand around the disc. "Finn, we have to take it to the elementals, otherwise we risk them tossing us out again. We can't take that chance... not with the entire universe on the line."

Finn snorted. "You do understand what's going to happen to me, right?"

Kyne's expression softened. Of course, he knew. Everyone knew but had said nothing. Was it that terrible? Sure, it was. It felt like he was bartering his life for an entire reality just as he was beginning to like living again.

"I'm such an Unseelie," he muttered.

"We'll do whatever it takes to help you, Finn. You know that." Kyne set the hose down. "Vera can make another talisman, and we'll keep recharging it for as long as we can. We'll find another place of power, and—"

"*No.*"

Kyne blinked as if he'd been punched in the face. "No?"

He looked at the circle of black goop and sighed. "I'll find my own way back."

"Finn?"

He didn't reply as he walked into the scrub.

The stupid old bat was right. His path hadn't ended yet. Another trail had opened before him, and he was already walking it. It would be the greatest path he'd ever follow, but would it ever end? And if it did, would it be in a happy place?

There was no way to know.

CHAPTER 9

Eloise slid the last of her clothes into a storage compartment inside the Troopy and let the lid close with a dull *thunk*.

Kyne had done a wonderful job fitting out the interior and hooking up the electrics, but it was Hardy's sewing skills that'd impressed her most. The vampire had upholstered all the cushions in a basic —but outback friendly—material in the colour of graphite, *and* had made matching curtains. There was even a magnetic fly screen fitted to the back door, and those fancy insulated covers for the front windscreen.

Topped off with Wally's mechanical knowhow, the Troopy was ready to hit the road for the four-thousand-kilometre trip to the Pilbara.

Climbing out through the front cab, Eloise vaulted onto the ground. The 4WD was a beast compared to her van and Kyne's 4x4 ute. It was borderline as to whether she needed a stepladder to get into the passenger seat.

Kyne poked his head around the rear of the Troopy. "All set?"

"As I'll ever be." Eloise looked down over Solace, the presence of the Old One looming over her head as the sun rose, the last sliver rising above the barren outback horizon. They sky was clear, making the dawn a little chilly, but it wasn't the only thing that made her shiver.

The corruption was invisible as always, but it was everywhere now.

The boab was fading, the once enormous tree withering as the sludge leaking from the seal seeped into the water table. Even the birds had fallen silent. The usual morning screech of the thousand parrots and budgerigars that soared overhead on their way to their local billabong was absent.

First, people stopped coming—the road trains had detoured a fortnight ago, and it'd been just as long since a traveller had passed through—and now the wildlife had gotten the memo.

Solace was becoming a ghost town, and soon, it would be full of malevolent spirits drawn by the Old One for protection.

"I thought we could head west and stop in Bourke to pick up supplies," Kyne said. "We have to backtrack a little, but it's the only major city for a good while, and they have a good supermarket there."

"Huh?" She blinked.

The miner frowned and stood before her. "Where were you just then?"

"Just wondering where all the birds went."

He followed her gaze and breathed in deeply. "It's eerie without them, isn't it?"

They stood for a moment, the gravity of the situation hanging over them like the blade of a guillotine.

"Are you sure you're all right?"

Kyne's eyebrows rose. "Why wouldn't I be?"

"Well, you *were* submerged in that black goop…and you still smell a little funky."

"The coral key protected me."

"Yeah but—"

"I'm fine."

"But we don't understand what the Old Ones are," she said. "Not really."

"Vera checked me over," Kyne replied, smoothing a hand through her hair. "Even Drew had a sniff. They didn't find anything."

Eloise couldn't help the smile that crept onto her lips. "Sounds kinky."

Kyne chuckled and closed the back door of the Troopy. "C'mon. Let's head down to the *Outpost*. It's getting late and I want to get on the road."

"It's only six a.m.," she complained.

"Yeah, and the sun's already up." He pointed to the horizon.

"*Barely.*"

"You're stalling..." Kyne hesitated, his brow creasing. "Don't you want to go?"

"I do, it's just..." She flexed her fingers. "I-I'm scared."

"About?"

Suddenly, she felt like crying. "All of it."

"Me, too."

She looked up at him and sniffed. "You are?"

"Of course I am. That mind thing Vera did on me...?" He let out a low whistle. "That was some freaky shit." She laughed as he placed a swift kiss on her cheek. "What do you say? Shall we head down to the *Outpost* and see the others?"

"Okay," she replied, feeling bold once more. "Let's go."

Eloise climbed into the passenger seat as Kyne took the wheel. The Troopy rumbled to life and they were bumping down the hill on the rutted out gravel road—one of the many reminders of Siora and the fae's passage through Solace—towards the highway.

The Exiles were waiting for them on the *Outpost's* verandah—Wally, Blue, Finn, Vera, Hardy, Drew, and even Clarke—and they stepped onto the road as the Troopy approached. Andante, Coen, and *Marlu* weren't there, but they hadn't expected to see them. All the advice they could have imparted had long been given.

Usually there wasn't much reason for anyone to check for traffic, but even more so these days. There was no threat of being squashed by a road train, so they spread themselves out as the Troopy pulled up outside the store.

The elementals hopped out, twilight long gone as dawn shone over the little township. Golden rays of sunlight poured over the top of the ridge, though the highway remained in shadow. The whole scene was beautiful, though the desolation hiding just under the surface saddened Eloise.

"You got your path mapped out?" Wally asked.

"We're going to head down to Bourke first," Kyne told him. "Fill up on supplies, then turn north to Longreach."

The old wolf let out a low whistle. "That's a good ten hours."

"Yeah, well… The sooner we get there, the better. We'll aim for Mt. Isa after that, then into the Territory."

"Just don't go killing yourselves beforehand," Blue said. "Watch the road."

Kyne clapped the publican on the shoulder. "Will do."

"Take care." Clarke reached out his hand towards Eloise, but she gave the police sergeant a hug instead.

"Look after Vera, okay?" she whispered into his ear.

Hardy caught her eye over the sergeant's shoulder and winked.

"Of course," Clarke replied, letting her go.

Drew practically elbowed him away to get to Eloise.

"Are you sure you don't have room for one more? I shrink down real good, you know."

"Oh, I know," Eloise said with a laugh. "A dingo with a backpack...a sight I'll never forget."

"We need your sight around town," Kyne told him. "You're the only one who can see and sniff out the corruption."

"You make a great guard dog," Finn announced.

Drew growled and turned to the fae. "Lucky for you we're mates now, otherwise—"

"Otherwise, what?"

"Oh, cut it out, you two," Eloise exclaimed, hugging Finn before he launched himself at the shifter. "I'm going to miss you most of all."

"You're only saying that to placate me," the fae complained. "Aren't you?"

"Of course not."

Finn let out a sigh as they parted. "You're lying. I've always been a tough pill to swallow."

"Sure, but that's just one of your many charms." She smiled up at him. "I guess you'll have to trust me on that one."

Finn narrowed his eyes. "Are you sure you want to take that rubbishy bit of rock with you?"

"*Finn*," Kyne said. "We've already talked about this."

"The risk is worth the reward," Vera added. "The elementals need to know who they are and why they've come. The key is the key to that."

Drew snorted. "Say that ten times fast."

"They can't refuse us this time," Kyne added. "Once they understand why we've come, they'll have to listen. If they don't, we'll make them."

"Don't go doing anything silly," Vera said with a sniff, wrapping her arms around Eloise. "You take care, okay?"

"Of course," Eloise replied. "I plan on coming back in one piece."

"We believe in you," the witch murmured in her ear. "All of us. No matter what."

Eloise felt another wave of tears prickle her eyes as she drew back. "Vera... I don't know how I ever survived in this world without you. You're my best friend."

She wiped at her eyes. "*Aww...*"

"And what was I to you?" Hardy coughed loudly, though he was trying his best to hide his silly grin.

"All of you," Eloise declared, looking around at the Exiles. "You're all my best friends and my family." She took Kyne's hand in hers and squeezed tightly. "We're going to come back and when we do, we're going to save the world."

"That's our little desert pea," Finn quipped.

"Go on," Wally said. "You better hit the road if you want to make it to Bourke by the time the shops open."

Vera sniffed and clutched Clarke's arm. "I hate goodbyes."

"This isn't goodbye," Drew said. "It's see you later."

"See you later..." the witch murmured. "I like that. *See you later.*"

Before she could chicken out, Eloise climbed into the passenger seat of the Troopy as Kyne got into the driver's side.

The engine rumble to life once more, and he waved one last time as he pulled out of the spot in front of the *Outpost* and onto the highway. He thumped his fist against the horn, tooting as they departed on their mission to find the elementals. After talking about it for so long, they were now on their way...

Eloise leaned out the window and looked back at the Exiles. The wind tore at her hair, whipping it across her face as she waved. She saw her supernatural family return her 'see you later', each waving frantically as the Troopy sailed down the highway.

Then Solace faded into the distance...and it was gone, leaving nothing but the red heart of the Australian outback surrounding them.

Vera stood beside the highway, digging her toes into the warm ochre sand as she watched Clarke, Drew, and Finn unload a stack of barriers from the trailer hitched to the sergeant's police 4WD.

They were those gaudy orange things that lined the sides of annoying roadworks, and he'd brought enough to span the width of the highway. Wally, Blue, and Hardy were on the north side setting up a cordon to match the one they were haphazardly piecing together at the south end.

It seemed like a flimsy blockade, but with the magic leaking from the seal already keeping people away, it was part of their cover story in case anyone with immunity or supernatural leanings came looking.

Finn wiped his brow as he stepped back, letting Clarke and Drew do most of the work.

"Finn," Drew exclaimed. "We could really use a hand, mate."

"Those things are heavier than they look!" the fae cried. "Are they filled with rocks or something?"

"Sand," Clarke replied. "And not that much of it, to be honest."

Finn snorted. "Just enough to be annoying."

Vera sighed and looked south towards the horizon —the same direction Eloise and Kyne had gone. She already missed them.

"That oughta do it," Clarke said, dusting off his hands. "Let's call it."

"Thank God," Finn declared.

Drew elbowed the fae. "And what do you know about God?"

"I know it's something people say when they're relieved."

"That's a little sacrilegious," the shifter fired back.

"Hey, I'm from another world, okay? Give me a break."

"Like the one you took while we did all the work?"

"Vera didn't do anything, either."

"Vera doesn't have enough upper body strength."

"Now you're the one being sexist."

"When were you being sexist? That has nothing to do with being sacrilegious."

Clarke shook his head as the men gathered in the shade. Vera had already lost track of their back and forth, but she was used to it by now.

"Here." She handed them each a water bottle. "Tastes like crap, but it's drinkable...and cold."

Clarke took a sip and made a face, but downed half before he came up for another breath. "Thanks. It's bloody hot today. Hot and *dry*."

"It's the tentacle monster," Finn stated. "Sucks up moisture like a sponge."

"If you need someplace to stay..."

The fae scrunched up his face. "Thanks, but I don't like you like that."

"That's not what I meant," Clarke replied. "I've got a perfectly good couch, though I'm sure you'd be more comfortable at the motel."

"If it's all the same to you, Sergeant, I'd much prefer to stay in Solace."

Vera leaned closer to Clarke. "Actually, he can't leave. He needs the magic from the seal—"

"I can hear you, you know," Finn declared. "Lightning Ridge is too far to go without a battery."

"And I need to stay to watch the goop," Drew added.

"And I need to keep an eye on those two." Vera said. "But I can take turns with Hardy."

"Good," Clarke murmured, kissing her on the cheek. "I don't like the idea of you being here if that thing is making you sick."

She shrugged. "Honestly, I can't even feel it anymore."

"*Still...*" He leaned in for a deeper kiss.

"Gross," Finn exclaimed, breaking them apart.

Clarke rolled his eyes and turned back to the bright orange barrier. "Now what?"

"Illusion time." Finn clapped his hands and cracked his neck. "If anyone comes looking, all they'll see is a giant sinkhole, not an intact town besieged by tentacle monster goop."

"What happens if they get too close?"

"Well, if they keep walking, they'll pass right through the illusion," Finn explained. "It's not an impenetrable wall."

"That doesn't sound good," Clarke muttered.

"If anyone is silly enough to try to get a closer look, we'll be here to stop them," Vera assured him. "And Hardy will compel them to forget and send them back to wherever they came from."

All they had to do was buy time until Eloise and Kyne returned. Hopefully, they'd have the secret to ending their Old One problem once and for all, then they could set things back to the way they were. That was the ultimate goal, anyway. Back to business as usual...until another magic threat tried to destroy the world.

"Stand back!" Finn boomed. "Or else you will be caught in my illusion!"

Drew rolled his eyes. "God help us."

The fae stepped forwards and made a show of holding up his hands towards the sky and began to twist his fingers in artful patterns—something Vera knew he *didn't* need to do. He'd always had a flair for the dramatic, but Vera knew he was only doing it for Clarke's benefit—the ultimate 'rub it in, why don't you'.

The air shimmered before them as Finn's thin, gossamer illusion spread outwards, covering Solace as it went. It shone like the surface of a soapy bubble, flickering with subtle colours—the purples, greens, and blues of Unseelie magic—before settling into the landscape.

Vera blinked, and Solace disappeared before her very eyes. All that was left of the town was...well, *nothing*.

The vast expanse of the outback stretched before them, brilliant red, blue, and green as always. But the highway twenty metres north of the cordon fell away into a jagged sinkhole wide enough to swallow an entire road train—a whole truck with three laden trailers—and then some.

"*Wow...*" Clarke stared at the gaping hole in the highway. "It looks so real."

"You've seen me cast before," Vera said, feeling a little jealous with how easily Finn had summoned such a detailed illusion.

"But the whole town is just...gone." The sergeant shook his head. "I've seen you do stuff, but nothing like this. This is...*wow*."

"I'm starting to like you now," Finn drawled. "But don't let it go to your head."

Drew laughed and clapped Clarke on the shoulder. "Don't stroke Finn's ego. He's hard enough to deal with as it is."

Vera smiled, but no matter how hard she tried, she couldn't feel it. It felt like they were saying goodbye.

"It's bittersweet, don't you think?" she murmured. "Like we're turning off the lights and locking the doors...not knowing if we'll be able to come back."

"You're not leaving," Finn said.

Drew nodded. "Yeah, we're still going to be here."

"Oh, you know what I mean," the witch said, waving her hand at them.

"Yeah," Finn murmured. "We know."

"C'mon," Drew said. "Let's go see how the others got on."

"If they can find their way through that illusion," Clarke added.

Finn grinned and puffed out his chest. "Because I'm *that* good."

At least someone's in a good mood, Vera thought as the men walked towards the 4WD. *And at least Clarke is finally fitting in amongst the Exiles.*

Everything was going according to plan, but she couldn't help but feel like something was coming to break it apart. Something that would happen before the bit at the end. Not just for Eloise and Kyne, but for Solace, too.

Vera turned towards town, where Finn's illusion had all but erased it from the map. The whole thing gave her the creeps.

"I guess we'll just have to wait and see," she whispered.

CHAPTER 10

The Troopy rolled out of Bourke, New South Wales, laden with food, water, a full tank of fuel, and an extra canister slung on the roof.

Bourke wasn't the largest town going. It had flat, wide streets, ample parking, and a pretty river with a park—a thick layer of greenery over the rust-coloured earth. It had all the essential amenities, plus historical markers, a caravan park, and even a small airport—everything they needed to get by.

Then they headed up the Mitchel Highway towards the border into Queensland, the second of four states they'd have to drive through to get to the Pilbara.

Eloise watched the buildings fade into the flat landscape as the two-lane highway curved a little to the east, then angled at a straight shot north. They passed a few patches of farmland, and then it was nothing but a flat expanse of low-lying scrub, scrappy gum trees, and the never-ending sky.

Eloise pushed her sunglasses up her nose and looked down at the coral key, turning it over in her hands. She hadn't let it go since they'd left Solace, and so far, she couldn't make heads nor tails of it. There was nothing magical about it, really—it was just a perfect circle of coral, salt, and quartz.

"You know," Kyne said, glancing at her before turning his gaze back onto the long stretch of road before them, "I always thought it was chalcedony, not coral."

"I think I remember you saying that," Eloise murmured, holding the key up to the window. Light glowed softly through the stone, illuminating the rich pink colour.

"Chalcedony is similar to quartz. It's made up of silica, which is the same basis of opal, but is formed out of agate."

"Who in the what now? You may as well have spoken gibberish."

Kyne chuckled. "Long story short, they have the same origins in silica. Chalcedony is usually blueish-grey, though."

She turned the key over and studied the vein of blacked grit running through the centre. "Why is it pink, then?"

"It's a supernatural bit of crystal that was holding back magical goop. How long is a piece of string?"

"You've got a point." Eloise sighed and slipped the

key into her bag, which she stowed in the footwell in front of her.

They had a long way to go, so she settled in and rolled down the passenger side window. The wind billowed into the cab, cooling the interior better than the struggling air conditioning.

She held her hand out the window and let the air float through her fingers. Twisting her wrist, she felt the currents pull at her skin. It was as if she could grasp the threads and weave them into whatever she desired.

Kyne's hand came to rest on her thigh. "Careful. You might actually make us take off."

She pulled her hand back into the Troopy and sat up, blinking. "Huh? Was I...?"

"Let's add air onto the list of elements you dabble in...not that I'm jealous or anything."

"Sorry." Eloise wound the window back up and shoved her hands under her legs.

"Don't worry about it."

A flush of embarrassment heated her cheeks. "I guess I'm more powered up than I realised." Ever since she was able to tap into her deeper power to help Hardy fight Darius, she'd been growing. It was like she'd opened some sort of supernatural flood gate, and her power was still unfurling.

She glanced at Kyne and wondered why he couldn't do the things she could. If he tapped into his deeper abilities, could he have the same potential?

"Here," Kyne handed her his mobile phone, "I updated the head unit so we've got Bluetooth. I made you a road trip playlist."

Eloise grinned and opened the music app. "Seriously? You made me a playlist? That's so romantic."

"Don't get your hopes up. I'm not exactly a music type of guy."

"That's because you've got rocks in your head."

Kyne laughed and shook his head. "Ladies and gentlemen, we have ourselves a regular comedian."

"Regular?" Eloise rolled her eyes. "Give me a little credit."

Finding the playlist, she hit play, and the first song ebbed through the speakers. It was 'Dreams' by Fleetwood Mac. and she sank back into the seat with a sigh.

"This song reminds me of the moment between night and the first light of dawn," she said. "That dreamy time when everything seems so small and humanity is so far away. Like you're alone with the entire universe."

"Twilight?"

She clicked her fingers. "That's the one."

"I'm glad you like this one, at least. I reckon I've peaked too soon," he told her. "It's all downhill from here."

"I have faith." Eloise began scrolling through the list, smiling as she saw the next few songs. A few tracks reminded her of her school days, and her expression started to fade. "Kyne?"

His gaze didn't leave the highway. "Hmm?"

"We, uh... We've never really talked about... Well—" The words caught in her throat. They'd been through so much together, and she'd shared more painful things than this, so why was it so hard to ask?

He looked at her, his brow creasing. "Hey... What's wrong?"

"I was just wondering about... Well, you never talk about your childhood. You know most of mine, and I feel a little selfish for not asking. All this stuff with the seal has been about me. And I'm not usually comfortable being the centre of attention. I've always made myself small, you know? I didn't mean to not ask, it's just—"

"Eloise." Kyne's hand covered her mouth and he chucked. "It's fine."

"It is?" Her voice was muffled. "Because—"

"I grew up with my real mother." He moved his hand back to the wheel. "We lived in a few places, but the longest was in Adelaide."

Eloise worried the hem of her T-shirt. "Oh...I thought you were adopted."

"I just don't like to talk about it, is all." Kyne shrugged. "She raised me on her own and never talked about my dad; he was a forbidden topic. I wanted to know, but I never asked—I had no reason to. We had a good life. We weren't rich or lived in a fancy house, but we had all we needed. He was just... Well, he didn't matter."

"When did you find out about your powers?"

"I'm not sure, exactly," he murmured. "I think I always knew they were there, but I didn't understand, not until..."

"Until?"

"My mum passed away when I was eighteen," he replied. "Cervical cancer. She didn't know she had it. When she was finally diagnosed, it was too late to do anything. It'd already spread."

"Kyne..." She slipped her hand onto this thigh. "I'm so sorry."

"The shock of it triggered something inside me..." His hands tightened around the steering wheel. "The whole hospital shook. They called it a once in a century earthquake, but it must've only been a one or two on the Richter scale. Nothing, really." He scoffed at the memory. "I figured it out and began working for a bloke in Coober Pedy. He had an opal mine he needed a hand with. Shifting dirt, mostly. Back breaking with crap pay, but he gave me a small cut of any opal we found...and we found a lot."

Eloise smiled. "I bet you did."

"That mine was how I learned to use my powers to find opal. After the claim dried up, I moved on and traveled for a bit. Eventually, I found my way to White Cliffs in New South Wales where we dug up white opal pineapples—these beautiful apple-sized specimens covered in spikes. They can sell for more than half a million dollars if you get a good one, but they're delicate things that shatter if they're hit the wrong way. Then I went up to Lightning Ridge looking for black opal. I built myself a reputation along the way and made money surveying claims, and eventually, I settled in Solace." Which, with all its unique residents and guardianship issues, had put a stop to his travelling. "Meeting the others... That's when I began asking questions. It took me a long time, but I finally asked the right one." He fell silent and Eloise knew he was thinking of his first trip to the Pilbara.

"Your mum never remembered anything about the elementals?" she asked.

"If she did, she never told me." His expression closed over and he glared at the straight stretch of flat highway. The road just kept coming, long and lonely.

Eloise set the phone into the cup holder, suddenly lost for words. She'd struck a nerve, but she understood his past hadn't been all sunshine and daisies. Just like her own, it'd been full of unexpected awakenings, loss, and a listlessness that'd driven them both to a life of wandering...until Solace and the seal had caught them in its gravitational field. Now they both orbited the town, caught in the legacy of a forty-thousand-year-old plan to save the universe.

Kyne tensed and shifted in the driver's seat. "There has to be a reason why we exist, right? Why the elementals cast us out. It can't all be for nothing, can it?"

Eloise shook her head. "No."

Kyne's scowl deepened. "There *has* to be a reason."

Finding meaning in life was a human condition, and at that moment, she felt it keenly. With all they were facing, and after travelling clear across the outback to find the elementals, what if they learned it was all for nothing? That their fight was futile and it was only a matter of time before all things ceased to be?

"There is a reason," she murmured, "for all of it." She just hoped it was the one they wanted to hear. "Hey, do you want me to drive for a bit?"

"Yeah, nah. I've got you." Kyne smiled and flashed her a wink. "Maybe you can do a stretch tomorrow."

———

Drew wandered through Solace, his dingo feet silent as he padded over the warm outback sand.

The sun had set, but the heat of the day forever lingered in the earth and air. It was always like that, though—even this time of year never quite made it to 'long sleeve weather'.

Above, the plume of magic leaking from the seal glowed brighter, the blue more radiant as the cloud billowed higher into the sky, its fingers stretching farther into the outback. The bioluminescence rippled as it mingled with Finn's illusion, but it carried past the boundary and dissipated into the night.

Now that Eloise and Kyne had gone, things seemed to be accelerating. It made Drew think that maybe there was something in Coen's story about the great emu after all—the only thing the emotionless Old Ones reacted to was the people from the dark places amongst the stars.

The elementals.

Drew continued through the silent town, past the darkened *Outpost*, and stepped onto the trail at the rear of the building. He had his patrol route down pat and walked it without much thought. If something changed, magically or not, he'd *see* it.

Rounding a curve in the trail, he spotted a shadowy figure sitting in the middle of a clearing. He recognised Vera instantly. She had a particular smell about her, one that'd changed when the Nightshade left her, but he'd know it anywhere. Witches had a certain fragrance that carried notes of sandalwood and talcum powder, with undertones of their legacy. In Vera's case, it was the ocean. Not that it was unpleasant, but he wouldn't bottle it anytime soon.

The witch sat in the dark before the little totem Finn had carved her, watching the sky with a sad gleam in her eyes.

"*Hey*," he said, moving off the trail.

She jumped and twisted around, her magic

sparking steely blue through her aura. "Drew! You scared the crap outta me!"

"*Sorry*," he said. "*It's difficult to be noisy as a dingo.*" He sat beside her, thumping his tail onto the ground. "*What are you doing out here?*"

She shrugged and turned back to the totem. "Clarke went back to the Ridge, and I couldn't sleep."

He nipped at her knee. "*Is that all?*"

"No, of course not." She swatted him away. "It's the Old One. Whatever its magic is, I feel connected to it… like it's a part of me."

"*It's probably just an echo from when it corrupted the Nightshade.*"

"Yeah, maybe." A soft smile ghosted across her lips, but it was gone almost as swiftly as it'd arrived. "I feel like we're standing on a precipice overlooking a gaping maw of nothingness, and there's nothing we can do about it."

"*That's* exactly *what's happening.*"

"Drew!" She slapped his shoulder blade. "You're meant to say something reassuring, not state the obvious."

"*It's hard not to be a disillusioned smart arse when the sky is full of glowing Old One juice.*"

The witch worried her bottom lip, and Drew could almost see the cogs turning in her head. "I think I have a spell that can help me see what you see." She held out her hand. "Can I?"

He lowered hie head and glared at her. *"As long as you're not going to zap me. You know I hate being zapped."*

She rolled her eyes and grasped the rough of his neck. "I promise I won't zap you."

"So you'll just try to dominate me instead?" He tried to shake himself free, but she tightened her grip. *"I always knew you had a thing for—"*

"Shh. I need to concentrate."

Drew felt warmth spread from her touch, but that was it. Relieved at the lack of electrical current, he waited to see if her spell worked.

Vera looked towards the night sky, waiting as her spell wove into being.

"Did it work?"

"Just a second... I think so." Her eyes widened as the spell revealed his sight to her. "Wow..." She took in the breadth of the Old One's magic for a long time, her gaze darting back and forth as the bioluminescence billowed lazily. Finally, she glanced down at him, her eyes glowing with the scope of the universe above. "You see this all the time?"

"Yes," he replied. *"It's getting brighter, too."*

"I can't believe something so beautiful is making everything so sick."

"It's nature," Drew told her. *"Anything bright blue in the ocean is highly poisonous. Blue bottle jellyfish, blue ringed octopuses..."*

"I guess so." She sighed and let her hand fall away. "That's better. The spell has run out of juice. I mean, the corruption has a beauty to it, but I can do without the constant reminder."

He let out an annoyed sigh. "*Thanks a lot.*"

"Do you see it when you're not a dingo?"

"*No,*" he replied. "*Only now.*"

Whatever had transformed his ancestors had come from the spirit of this country, and thus, tied his dingo side to all that happened within it. That's why he could *see*, why Coen had chosen him to teach, and why he saw the corruption twisting Solace.

Drew had come a long way in the past year— evolving from a troubled shifter to a powerful guardian. He didn't know what it meant or what his role in the coming battle would be, but maybe that was the point. It wasn't for him to know all the secrets of existence...only to guard them from harm.

"*It's frustrating,*" he admitted. "*Being able to see what's killing us, but not being able to do anything about it.*"

"Yeah," Vera murmured. "Being powerless sucks."

No, he realised, they weren't powerless. Their supernatural skills were just incompatible with their current circumstances. The story of the Old Ones was for the elementals to finish, not them. Drew, Vera, and all the others were just along for the ride.

The truth behind everything—of their place in the universe and the meaning of their existence in the face of its entire erasure—was up to each of them to reconcile on their own. Whether it was erased or not wasn't for them to decide.

"Drew?" Vera asked. "Are you okay?"

He waited a moment, collecting his thoughts. Maybe this was the most important thing he'd ever say —it certainly felt like it.

"*Maybe that's the lesson*," he told her. "*The greatest battles we'll ever fight are the ones we fight with ourselves.*"

CHAPTER 11

The journey across Australia's north was a fleeting affair; Eloise and Kyne's quest was not one for stopping to see the sights along the way.

The highways were long, straight, and lonely. They did pass a bit of traffic the closer they got to the major cities—trucks, caravans, utes, 4WDs—but mostly, they were alone. It was a long way between drinks in the outback, as the saying went.

After hitting their first map marker in Longreach, they had eight hours to Mt. Isa. From there, they crossed over the border into the Northern Territory and stopped at a small campground just north of Tennant Creek. On the fourth day they had another ten-hour drive through the Territory to the Western Australian border, where they camped near Lake Argyle. Finally, they drove another seven hours to Fitzroy Crossing, which they'd make their home base for their search into the depths of the Pilbara.

It was five hard days of driving, which could've been cut in half if Kyne had let Eloise take the wheel for some of it. He'd muttered something about being able to handle the fatigue and that she'd need all her strength for the trail into the wilderness, but it annoyed her more than it should've. Since she'd returned from the mountain, he seemed to have put her on a pedestal, and she didn't like it. Eloise preferred to look him in the eye from the same level, not from above.

Fitzroy Crossing was a small place, sitting on the banks of the Fitzroy River. Normally Eloise would find it pretty, but there were too many other things occupying her mind.

She leaned against the window of the local IGA supermarket, watching wisps of orange backlit clouds skid across the sky.

To think the future of all this was up to *her*.

The automatic doors slid open, and she blinked as Kyne came out carrying a calico bag full of food.

"I got you a present." He held out an ice cream in a gold and brown wrapper.

She smiled and took it without complaint. "A Magnum Ego? *Premium*. You must've paid a pretty penny for that out here." The wrapper crinkled as she opened it. "And you got the one with the caramel sauce inside? *Aww*."

"What can I say? I'm a romantic."

"What one did you get?"

He chuckled as they strolled across the empty car park. "I'm lactose intolerant."

"What?" She blinked, the ice cream hovering just before her mouth. "You are?"

"Just kidding."

"Kyne!" She jabbed her elbow into his ribs. "That's not funny."

"It is...*kinda*," he replied as they approached the caravan park. "It's my way of saying don't worry about it. Exchanging our life stories wasn't the first thing that came to mind, what with everything going on. I barely asked about yours, so I reckon we're even."

That wasn't entirely true. As a newcomer to Solace in the grip of an already tense situation, of course, there'd been questions. He knew she'd been adopted, he knew about her parents, and about her life since. She'd been so bent on proving herself that she hadn't stopped to think about his past at all.

Through the trouble with the Old Ones, she'd learned about Vera, Drew, Hardy, Finn, and even a little about Wally and Blue, but not Kyne. It didn't seem to bother him, but it bothered her. A lot.

"We've got everything we need," Kyne said. "I figured we could get a good night's sleep tonight—"

"Good luck with that," Eloise complained. "Who can sleep in this heat?"

Technically, it was the middle of winter, but the Pilbara had missed the memo. From what she could tell, after her almost year of experience in Solace, there were only two distinct seasons—wet and dry—and both were stinking hot. She took another bite of her ice cream, only to find it was down to the stick, so she licked the last bit.

"Yeah, *nah*. It gets cold at this time of year, you'll see," Kyne told her with a smirk. "So, we get a good night's *rest* tonight, then head out just before dawn. We'll escape the heat of the day and be on the trail at sunrise."

"Sunrise?"

"I know we've barely had time to gather ourselves, but I figured the sooner we find them, the better off we'll be."

Kyne had been there before, but the truth was they couldn't know what they'd find this time. The elementals hadn't been expecting him before, but now the tables had turned. All kinds of trouble came to mind—traps, magical attacks, illusions, and even ordinary human dangers like getting lost, dehydration, *sunburn…*

When they got back to the Troopy, Kyne began fussing with the groceries. Seeing his mobile phone sticking out of the back pocket of his shorts, Eloise grabbed it.

"Have you heard anything from the others?" she asked. The screen lit up, showing the time and date, and no notifications. He didn't keep any photos on the lock screen, so it was just a plain black background.

"Nothing. I've messaged Vera, but she hasn't replied."

A pang of worry twisted her heart. "Do you think something's happened to them?"

"I'm sure they're fine. Reception was always patchy at best, and the corruption probably distorts any signal there might be, not to mention Finn's illusion probably acts like a giant buffer."

She felt sick, knowing they were there with the corruption seeping into everything that made Solace, Solace—the earth, the water, the boab, *the people*. What if it corrupted them before they could make it back? What if it killed them?

Her hands trembled and she turned away from Kyne, but he tugged at her hand. She didn't want to show him her fear, not when they were about to face his. She had to be strong for him. This was as much his journey as it was hers, maybe even more.

"Eloise, it'll be all right." Kyne wrapped his arms around her. "The best thing we can do now is to finish what we started."

"I know," she whispered.

"Hey, I'll make a campfire, I'll cook, *and...*" He let her go and rattled around in the calico bag, finally emerging with a bright pink packet. "I got marshmallows."

Eloise felt her shoulders lighten a little and took the packet of sweets. "Ice cream and marshmallows? What did I do to deserve you?"

"You don't have to do anything," he murmured, caressing her cheek. "You're perfect just the way you are."

At sunrise, Kyne and Eloise found themselves on a trail headed towards a lookout point off the highway.

They had left the Troopy parked to one side of the pullout, partially hidden in the bush, loaded up their backpacks, and headed out. A hundred metres in, the trail opened up to a beautiful view of the landscape.

The sunrise made the whole scene come alive, revealing a breadth of colour Eloise hadn't fathomed before. A series of gorges threaded through the rich, burnt orange rock like veins, millions of years of erosion deepening their paths into the earth.

Kyne simply smiled and nodded towards the bush. There was no trail where they were going, but he felt one within his blood.

They weren't long on the trail before Eloise felt a steady stream of sweat dripping down her spine. The back of her T-shirt was soaked, and every time her backpack moved, she felt the gross dampness. She wouldn't say she hated exercise—she was up for adventure, for sure—but she didn't go out of her way to hike through the outback in the heat of the day, either.

"How far is it exactly?" she called out to Kyne, who was setting a brisk pace through the patchy bush.

"If we keep it up, we should arrive by lunchtime," he replied. "Not too fast, or the heat will get us. We need to follow this old creek bed for a bit, then veer off to the south."

Eloise raised her eyebrows and looked down at the sandy ground beneath her feet. This was a dry creek bed? It looked just like every other bit of bush around, but she supposed that's what made it so dangerous out here during the wet season—the unpredictability of flooding.

When they finally left the creek, the ground became rockier, the uneven surface slowing their progress. They weaved around slices of hard rock, clambered around ledges, and ducked in and out of patches of shade amongst the growing rubble.

It hadn't seemed this rough from the lookout, but now they were amongst it, the sheen had worn off the beautiful vista—along with the first layer of skin on both of Eloise's palms, forearms, and knees.

Through it all, Kyne led the way, his inner compass pointing him towards the elemental's billabong. He didn't stop to get his bearings once; he just kept walking as if he'd been here a million times.

Ahead, Eloise spotted a drop off where a gorge began to cut rough the rugged terrain. Kyne headed towards it, his head lowered as he picked his way over the rocks and through the scrub.

"Kyne," Eloise called. "You're getting too close to the edge. Come back a bit."

He didn't seem to hear, continuing through the brush at the side of the gorge.

"Kyne?"

He ducked under a branch, the eucalyptus leaves brushing his shoulders, and turned towards the void.

"Kyne!" Eloise shrieked as she lunged towards him.

Her fingers wound around the strap of his backpack, and she heaved, digging the heels of her boots into the earth. He cried out as he fell backwards, landing on her hard.

They lay in a silent heap for a long moment, Eloise's leg stinging from a new scrape—just another for the collection—and wincing as a sharp rock poked into her left arse cheek.

Luckily, Kyne had fastened the clip at the front of his backpack, otherwise the whole bag would've come off and he'd be tumbling down the side of the cliff.

Eloise managed to wriggle herself from underneath Kyne and sat beside him. She grasped his face and turned it towards her, checking his pupils. "Bloody hell, are you all right?"

He blinked, his lashes batting furiously, and shook his head, dislodging her hands. "I don't... What just happened?"

"You almost walked off the edge of a cliff," she said, pressing her palm against his forehead. She knew he should've let her drive. "Are you sure you got enough sleep last night?"

"Yeah, I..." Kyne looked at the drop before them

and swallowed hard. "I didn't even see it. How could I not see *that?*" He pointed to the gaping void of air. "It —" The words died in his throat. "It's *them.*"

Eloise glanced at the gorge. "The elementals?"

"They're testing us."

"Some test," she muttered.

"Did I hurt you when I fell?"

"Just a little scrape. It's nothing."

Kyne ran his hand over his face. "I should've seen this coming."

"*We* should've," she corrected. "And we know to be on the lookout now." She pushed to her feet and held out her hand. "C'mon. We have to keep going."

"Are you sure you're all right?"

"You're asking me?" She sighed and wiggled her fingers. "On your feet. They're going to have to try harder than that if they want to stop us."

Kyne nodded and took her hand.

They continued along the rim of the gorge, keeping a safe distance from the edge, venturing deeper into the northern reaches of the Pilbara.

Eloise's feet felt like they were going to fall off, but she kept putting one boot in front of the other, lured forwards by the faint sound of trickling water deep within the rocks. For all the dryness and radiant heat on the surface, below them was a hidden oasis.

Her powers flared as she imagined plunging her feet into the cool water, feeling the drag of the lazy current between her toes. After a morning of hard hiking, it sounded like *heaven*.

Kyne came to an abrupt halt in front of her. "Do you feel that?"

Eloise almost smacked into him, but was glad he'd picked a sliver of shade to stop in. "Feel what?"

"The air is different here." He looked around with a frown. "We're not far from the gorge, but..."

"But what?" She let her magic pulse around them and felt the elements call out to her. Earth, air, water... not the elementals themselves, who seemed glaringly absent from it all.

A faint breeze ruffled his hair as his gaze met hers. "Eloise—"

The words were torn from his mouth as a violent tornado of wind whipped around them. Eloise stumbled, gasping for air as her breath was ripped from her lungs.

Magic crackled all around, chaotic and sharp, its source unknown. It was everywhere—up, down, left, right, inside... It was all things in all directions.

Her eyes widened. *The currents.*

The elementals had summoned the rivers to guard the billabong, and they'd stepped right into their trap. This was worse than falling down a gorge; they could end up anywhere and any-*when*. She might have some hope of controlling it, but Kyne—

"Kyne!" she shrieked as she reached towards him. "*Kyne!*"

"Eloise!" He reached desperately for her, his eyes wide with fear.

Their fingertips brushed for the slightest of moments before she was torn away, cast amongst the currents of time and space with no way to stop herself.

The outback faded, shrinking into a pinpoint of red and blue light...then it was gone.

CHAPTER 12

"Finn."

A boot nudged Finn's side and the fae snorted, swatting aimlessly through the air.

"Finn, wake up."

He rolled over, groaning as he was jerked out of deep sleep and glared up at Drew.

A dark sky and a twinkle of stars remained above, just as it had when he'd closed his eyes. The fire had died down, which meant he'd had a few good hours before being rudely awoken by the dingo's worn-out Blundstone boot.

"This better be good," he drawled, rubbing his eyes. "I'm still fried from that illusion, you know. I need a good week to recover."

"No, you don't," Drew said, "and it *is* important." The shifter held up his mobile phone, a human device Finn saw as entirely annoying, wasteful, and useless. "Vera called."

"This better not be goop-related."

"It's goop-related."

Finn sat up and rubbed his face. "Where is it now? In her undies drawer?"

"Worse. Seeping through the walls." The shifter kicked dirt over the glowing colas in the campfire. "She needs help getting her stuff out before it all goes under."

Groaning, he lurched to his feet and followed Drew down the hill to Solace. When they arrived at Vera's, the witch was already running at a frantic pace, carrying a box of books up the stairs.

"Oh, good," she said through a heavy breath, "you're both here. Hardy's already inside."

Finn wandered past and ventured into the dugout. It was the first time he'd been in Vera's home, and given the fae's history with the witches, he should probably feel weird about it, but the stench of corruption was already thick in the air. There was no time to poke about.

He curled his nose as he peered at the walls, watching as droplets of blackish goop oozed from behind the cracked paint. It moved slowly, not yet coating the floor to any worrying degree. It was probably hampered by all the magical witchy things Vera kept down here.

"Don't worry about the furniture," Vera said, hurrying down the hall. "Grab as much stuff from the altar room as possible. I've already got my grimoires and tarot cards."

"What about your undies?" Finn asked as Hardy hurried by, the vampire blurring as he used his super speed to expedite the process.

"I'll get my undies, thank you very much," the witch said with a sigh.

"I'd hurry then," Finn told her. "Once you take out the crystals and magical bits and bobs, there'll be nothing holding back the goop."

Vera's eyes widened.

"You may not have a coral key, but all this junk is the next best thing."

Hardy appeared in the hall, his man-bun askew. "Pack all the crystals and talismans into the tubs I brought over from the workshop. We'll carry them out last."

"Why hasn't anyone else's house flooded?" Finn wondered.

"Elevation," Hardy replied. "They all sit up on the ridge. Vera's is the only one down in Solace. I assume we'll all face the same issue given enough time."

"Hopefully Eloise and Kyne will be back before then," Drew said, hurrying by with an armful of clothes.

Finn grunted and stepped into the room with the altar. Crystals, herbs, and all kinds of trinkets hummed merrily, their magic reacting to his presence.

He put things into a plastic tub, dismantling the

altar. *No wonder the craglorn sucked this stuff up.* It was like handling drug-laced nectar.

Over the next few hours, they carried out as much of Vera's belonging as they could before the goop completely covered the walls. When it began to seep through the floor and turned the rugs into squishy sponges, they retreated outside to sort through the jumble beside the road.

The sun had already begun to rise, the first light of day casting long shadows across the chaotic pile.

"It looks like we're having a garage sale," Drew said as they surveyed Vera's belongings.

"What doesn't fit in the *Outpost*, we can put in my shop," Hardy said, starting to pick over the furniture.

"There's goop on the couch," Finn stated.

"*Great*," Vera groaned and pinched the bridge of her nose. "Put it on the incinerate pile."

"Don't worry," the vampire murmured, placing a hand on her shoulder, "it's all replaceable."

"Hey!" They all looked up at the sound of Wally's voice as the old werewolf hurried across the highway. "What's going on? Why is all your furniture outside?"

"Goop," Finn stated. "What else?"

The old timer looked annoyed. "Why didn't you call?"

"It was three a.m.," Vera told him. "I didn't want to bother you."

"You can give us a hand moving some of this junk

into the *Outpost*," Drew said. "But the couch has to go on the burn pile. It's got goop on it."

Finn's stomach squirmed and he looked towards the highway. "I'm going to check the boundary."

"Typical," Drew exclaimed. "Rack off once the real work starts."

"Real work?" the fae scoffed and jabbed a finger at Vera's dugout. "Have you seen those stairs?" He rolled his eyes. "Anyway, no one's been watching the barrier."

Hardy nodded. "He's got a point."

"*Thank you.*" Finn mock bowed and backed towards the highway. "*Rilae*, have fun."

Leaving the Exiles to sort through Vera's belongings, he made his way past Blue's pub, following the lead of his nausea. His gut was rarely wrong, but lately, it could just mean he had a case of Old One gastro...or it was the abrupt change in diet. He missed potatoes most of all.

Finn felt his illusion was holding strong based on the looming benevolence of the Old One and the lack of animal and bird life, but nothing else seemed amiss. Still, he watched and waited. If there was something out there, it'd reveal itself soon enough.

A faint breeze ruffled the leaves of the great gum tree by the pub, a mirage shimmering on the horizon. The warmth of the early morning sun was already heating the asphalt of the highway as he walked towards the bright orange cordon, and he knew it was going to be a hot day ahead.

His thoughts went to his meeting with Andante as he balanced his way along the white line in the middle of the highway. Spreading his arms, he placed one boot in front of the other, edging south one step at a time.

Go back to Lor'Iyslar? Really? Maybe he could go someplace else. Travel with her to her mysterious Darklands and help her reach the Druids in their home world. That'd be an adventure...but could he survive there?

He reached the edge of the illusion and stumbled, his gaze fixing on a shadow in the distance.

Someone was approaching.

Finn lingered within the safety of his boundary, watching as the figure ventured closer. Step after step, the distance shortened until he realised it was a woman.

She wandered along the road, loose strands of her long brown hair trailing in all directions as the breeze caught it. She had no car, no bag, no sunglasses or hat, no water bottle...and by the looks of it, no shoes.

Finn's hackles rose as she approached the bright orange barrier. She stopped before it, hesitating a moment, before stepping around the blockade and continuing towards Solace.

Lingering at the edge of the illusion, he waited, feeling his magic tingle down his spine—a warning.

At first, he didn't realise who he was looking at. Her features were so plain, she didn't appear real, but it was her.

It was her.

He stepped through the illusion. "*Siora?*"

Finn couldn't believe his eyes. He'd seen her fall... He rose as his entire body shook and approached the cordon, his gaze never leaving her.

Her blue-green hair had turned into the mousey brown of the *De'ashlide*—the non-magical fae—and the silver of her eyes was long gone. Green looked back at him now...green with flecks of chestnut.

Finn took an unsure step towards her, his heart thrumming a painful beat in his chest. He'd watched her fall and the Old One take her. The luminous green essence of the entity had swept her away, dragging her into its depths.

He'd seen it.

Siora stared right through him, and it wasn't until he placed his hand on her arm that she jerked into existence. She blinked furiously, shying away from him.

"It's okay," he murmured. "*Hush...* I mean you no harm."

Her gaze met his briefly, then darted away again, but it was undeniable... It was her.

"Siora?" He held out his hand. "What happened to you?"

Her lips moved as if she was trying to speak...or trying to *learn*. He waited a moment, then she said, "W-who... Who?"

"You're Siora," he told her. "And I'm Finn."

She stared at him, her eyes wide and confused. She didn't remember him.

He wiggled his fingers. "Here. Take my hand. I'll show you."

Siora looked down and reached towards him, edging forwards. "Hand?"

"Yes. *Hand.*"

Her skin was cold as she slipped her fingers over his.

As their palms connected, he instantly knew the Old One had stripped away all her magic. It wasn't just the colour of her eyes or the ordinary hue of her hair; he couldn't feel anything familiar inside of her.

Whatever had happened when she'd been taken by the Old One, it'd rendered her human. *De'ashlide*...the only thing she'd hated as much as the Seelie.

It was as if she'd been wiped clean. *Reborn.*

Finn felt a sudden pang of boundless hope. The possibilities she had were now endless compared to the end he faced. All the hatred, hurt, and fighting of her past could be left behind, leaving her with a future that had a real chance of being peaceful. She wasn't tied to magic anymore. She could go anywhere. This world, their own world...*anywhere.*

"I thought I had lost you forever," he murmured.

"You did?"

"Yes." He wanted to wrap his arms around her and hold her tight, but her confusion held him back. "Where did you come from?"

Her brow creased. "I don't know."

"How did you get here?"

"I-I don't know."

Sensing her panic, he pointed towards Solace. "Never mind. Let me take you someplace safe."

"Safe?"

"I'd like you to meet a friend of mine. You'll like her." Not that she had the first time around, but there was only one person he could think of who could help at a time like this. "Vera."

Siora tilted her head to the side. "What is... Vera?"

"A woman," he told her. "Vera is a woman. A really nice one."

"*Nice*." She smiled, the childlike emotion a strange thing to see on her usually hard features.

Finn raised his eyebrows and tightened his grip on her hand. "Yes. *Nice*."

Vera watched the fire consume her couch, her arms crossed over her chest.

She loved that old thing—the cushions had softened in all the right places, and even the gaudy floral pattern had grown on her over the years. It hurt to see it go up in flames, but it wasn't so much the loss of it that had her down in the dumps—it was the principle of the thing.

She had no power. It was a realisation she was still

having trouble coming to terms with. She was corruptible, annoyingly mortal, and not spiritual enough to understand the goings-on. Vera Walsh, one of the most powerful witches alive, had been benched.

"Who's that with Finn?" Drew asked, breaking the morose silence.

Vera turned, her heart skipping a beat. For a moment she hoped Clarke had come back from the Ridge, but he and Blue had promised to stay away until Eloise and Kyne returned. In its current state, Solace was no place for humans.

But it wasn't Clarke.

A woman walked beside the fae, their hands clasped together as they approached.

"I don't know," Vera murmured. Who'd be out here, of all places? If the Old One magic didn't keep humans away, then the cordon and the illusion should've done the job.

"Bloody hell," Hardy cursed. "It's Siora."

Vera blinked and glanced at Drew.

"Siora?" the shifter asked. "She looks..."

"Human," Vera whispered.

Her coloured hair had faded into a plain mousey brown, and her silver eyes shone dull green as she stared at the bonfire like it was the first time she'd seen fire.

Finn tugged her hand, coaxing her towards the Exiles. "Siora? Come. This is Vera."

She turned, her gaze searching for the witch. "Vera?"

Siora looked like she'd been dragged through a hedge backwards and needed a decent shower and a brush. Her clothes didn't look much better, though they didn't seem to be in the loose-fitting bohemian style that she'd preferred. Her white blouse was stained a reddish-orange from all the dust in the air, her blue jeans had been ripped across both knees, and her feet were bare. Wherever she'd come from, she'd had time to change.

"Yes, I'm Vera," she said, frowning.

"I found her on the road," Finn told them.

Vera nodded and picked up a crochet blanket from one of the piles and wrapped it around Siora's shoulders. "Come and sit. You must be tired."

Siora stared at Vera, her eyes wide as she was guided to an armchair they'd placed on the keep pile.

"Finn said you are nice," the fae stated.

She snorted as her gaze flickered to Finn. "Oh, he did, did he?"

"She doesn't seem to recognise any of us," Drew murmured in the background. "What's with that?"

"You saw her fall," Finn told him. "Your guess is as good as mine."

Vera sighed and took Siora's hands in hers. Drew had told her how Finn had used his true magic to obliterate the shadow fae at the Black Mountain, but Siora... Her corruption had run a different course.

She'd retained her body and mind, twisted as they were, and fought to stop Eloise from sealing the Old One back into the mountain. But Finn had been there to stop her, and during the struggle, she'd fallen into a fissure filled with strange green magic—the essence of the Old One itself—and was swept away.

How she'd come to be here, where the second Old One was causing havoc of its own, was worrying.

She let her magic warm her hands, the tendrils of the Brinewold reaching out towards the fae...but they didn't find anything supernatural. Siora was completely human, and whatever power she'd held as an Unseelie fae was gone.

But it was more than that. Siora felt...vacant. There was no other word Vera could think of to describe it. The fae had the outer shell of her body, but everything inside was empty, as if she'd just been born.

Vera stood, her brow creasing.

"I'll sit with her," Wally said, picking up on the vibe in the air. "I'm no good at that stuff, anyway."

"Who are you?" Siora asked, staring up at him.

"I'm Wally," he told her, taking off his hat. "Pleased to meet you." He nodded towards the Exiles. "Go on, we'll be fine."

Siora was still staring at him, her eyes wide. "What is a Wally?"

"Wally's my name."

"Oh..." She worried her bottom lip. "There's two of you."

He scratched this head. "Uh...I suppose there is."

"Who is it?"

"Well, it's more of a what than a who..."

Vera turned away from the puzzling scene and crossed the road with Drew, Hardy, and Finn. They stood in the shade cast by the opal workshop, watching Siora and Wally discuss the finer points of werewolves.

"She doesn't seem to remember anything. She's like a child, learning everything for the first time," Vera mused. "It's as if the Old One erased all but her most primal instincts."

"As if she was just born moments ago," Hardy said, echoing her earlier thoughts.

"She's not supernatural anymore," Finn told them. "I can't sense any magic in her at all."

Vera nodded. "Neither can I."

"Then it's possible she can be compelled," Hardy said. "Maybe I can get something out of her."

"That's providing she remembers anything," Drew stated. "Look at her." They turned to watch Siora, who was now hypnotised by the flames consuming the couch. "Does she look like someone who remembers a thousand years of living in another world?"

"Severe trauma can bury memories," Hardy murmured. "It doesn't mean they're erased."

The shifter snorted. "What happened on that mountain was pretty unforgettable."

Vera lightly touched his arm. "And traumatic."

"Where did she even come from?" Drew asked,

reminding them of her completely ambiguous arrival. "Did she emerge from the goop? Fall out of the sky? Step through a portal?" He waited, but no one had any theories to offer. "My point exactly. How do we even know it's Siora?"

"*I know*," Finn snapped.

"You've all said it," the shifter went on. "She's like a shell. A child who was just born ten minutes ago."

"It's Siora," Finn growled. "I've known her my entire life. When I look at her...there's no one else it could be."

"What are we going to do with her?" Hardy asked. "Solace isn't exactly a human-friendly place right now."

Vera glanced over at the bonfire. She wanted to take Siora in—it was the kind thing to do—but what if Drew was right? They couldn't afford any mistakes, not with the whole universe on the line.

"She'll stay with us," Finn snapped. "No matter what she's done in the past, she's still a victim of the Black Mountain, just as much as any other supernatural being who was corrupted by it."

"Finn, she was swallowed whole by the Old One's essence," Hardy said. "There's no telling what it could've done to her."

"If you're that scared, vampire, I'll take sole responsibility for her," the fae replied, narrowing his eyes. "She'll stay with me. I'll take care of her."

"Finn, that's not what I meant," he added.

"Wasn't it?"

"I only mean for us to be wary."

"He's got a point," Vera said. "This isn't the mountain, Finn. We don't know how this Old One will manifest." It may have already begun.

"I brought her here because she needs help," the fae hissed. "I brought her to you, Vera. You know what that means to our kind."

She nodded. "I do, but this goes beyond old blood feuds, Finn. Way beyond."

Hardy turned to Finn and cocked his head towards Siora. "What do you think? Give compulsion a try?"

The fae shrugged and curled his lip. "*I suppose so.*"

Returning to the bonfire, the Exiles gathered around the armchair where Siora and Wally were talking about the full moon.

"What do you reckon?" the old werewolf asked. "She seems sweet to me."

"That's because she's interested in all your old man ailments," Drew stated.

"Smart arse," Wally cursed.

"Siora?" Hardy knelt at her feet and her gaze met his. "How did you come to be here?"

She stared at him, and it almost looked as if his compulsion had worked, but she blinked and glanced at Finn.

Hardy looked up and shook his head.

"Either she doesn't know or she can't be

compelled," Drew said, rolling his eyes. "Which means she's still supernatural—"

"She's *De'ashlide*," Finn interrupted. Turning to Siora, he smiled and held out his hand. "You'll stay with me. I'll take care of you."

Siora grinned and took his hand. "Yes."

"That solves that, then," Drew stated with a snort. "Let's just ignore the month she spent marinating in Old One juice."

"Drew," Vera hissed. "Not now." She turned and smiled at Siora and Finn. "We have some cleaning up to do here, but I'll come by later to see you both. Okay? Give you some time to settle in."

"Settle in," Siora echoed.

"I'll bring some things with me," Vera told Finn. "We'll figure it out."

"I trust *you*," he murmured. "Just you." Finn shot the Exiles one last warning look and led Siora away from the bonfire.

Vera watched them walk along the road hand-in-hand and sighed. How far they'd come...and how little they'd moved.

"Are you sure about this?" Drew asked, standing beside her.

"Not entirely."

The shifter grunted. "I'll make sure to check her out later tonight."

Vera nodded and turned back to the piles of her belongings. "Let me know what you see."

Drew chuckled behind her, the sound carrying through the silence. "I knew you didn't trust her."

It wasn't about trust, Vera thought. It was about something much deeper than that. She just wasn't sure what that *something* was.

"C'mon," she called. "Let's get the furniture inside. I don't want the sun bleaching the fabric."

CHAPTER 13

Eloise felt herself spinning, even though the world was dark.

Her hair flew in all directions as the currents of time and space flung her in an uncontrollable arc. She reached out to grab something, anything, but all her fingers felt was rushing air. Air that felt like silk, but air, nonetheless.

Points of light exploded around her, popping into existence like miniature fireworks, sparkling and crackling. The current was casting her out, but where?

Before she had time to try to course correct back to the Pilbara, she felt herself being flung into reality and pulled downwards by gravity. She landed hard, rolling across uneven, rocky ground, her body bashing painfully with every turn. With no control over her trajectory, she had to ride the landing out.

Crying out, she coiled her arms against her chest, then finally began to slow. Rolling to a complete stop, she lay still for a long moment, disorientated and rattled.

"*Bloody hell*," she finally managed to curse. Her voice reverberated around her, deepening as the sound faded.

Gasping, she managed to sit up. Her head swam and every part of her body stung, but she seemed alive. Reaching up, she pressed her palm on her throbbing arm, her hands shaking.

Her stomach squelched, and she almost hurled up her breakfast. It took a few deep breaths until the urge passed.

It was in this moment that Eloise realised she wasn't on Earth anymore.

Looking up, she saw the purplish blotched sky and knew she'd been here before. It was the same place she and Drew had travelled to when they'd followed Finn on his walkabout.

There was an 'otherness' about it that had her on edge. It was in her reality, but apart from it—a dream world, a vision, a prophecy.

Above, the great arm of the Milky Way cut the whole sky in two, stretching from horizon to horizon. The landscape carried the colours of the outback, though they were tinted purple. It looked like the Pilbara, but it could easily be anywhere in the thousands and thousands of square kilometres that made up the Australian outback.

The sound of a footstep crunching on rock

vibrated lazily through the thick air and Eloise looked around.

"Kyne?"

Coen emerged from the folds of space and time, his aura shimmering with a soft pearlescent glow.

"I had a feeling they'd send you here," he said. "Predictable as always."

Eloise stared up at him, still dazed from her rough landing. "Coen?"

The Indigenous man smirked and sat beside her. "They hide behind illusions and trickery, just like Andante."

"The elementals?" She stretched out her twisted legs and winced as her battered body protested.

"Sit and be calm. You will heal, given enough rest." Coen pointed to her arm. "See?"

Eloise lifted her hand to see the impressive graze was already shrinking. "*Oh…*"

"It's this place," he told her.

"What is it exactly?"

"A place between." He pointed to the ground, then the sky.

"Why would they send me here? It felt like we'd gotten too close and triggered a trap… The moat around the castle, so to speak." Suddenly, she felt exhausted and rubbed her face. "Was it an attack?"

Coen shrugged. "Yes and no."

"Then it's a test?"

"Maybe."

Eloise scowled, annoyed at Coen's vague answers. "Then where's Kyne? Why did they separate us?"

"He is still out there, looking."

"You're not answering my question," she said, her temper rising. "Is it because you don't want to tell me... or because you can't?"

Coen tapped his forehead. "They won't let me in unless they open the door."

Eloise sighed and turned her gaze onto her boots. This whole thing would be a hell of a lot easier if they were fighting a regular bad guy, not some ambiguous celestial entity without a solid body. And Coen was definitely the 'Gandalf' character—the wise, magical mentor—but he didn't have any of the answers because... She tensed, making her scrapes sting.

Because he didn't remember.

"Coen?" She looked up at him, but he was staring up at the Milky Way with a dreamy smile on his face, not paying any attention to her at all. The question died in her throat before she could formulate it. Even if he knew, he still couldn't tell her.

"The elementals threw me out, but not Kyne," she said instead.

"They didn't bring him here."

Bring... Throw... She mulled over the two words. "They didn't cast me out at all, did they? They brought me here for a reason. Almost all of us have seen this place in one way or another."

Her heart skipped a beat. Kyne had seen it when

Vera had gone into his mind to unravel his memories, and that meant Vera had seen it by proxy. Finn had come here on his walkabout when he'd been lured by the mountain, and Drew had when she'd brought him along.

Only one thing connected them all to it—the elementals.

"This is where they came from," she murmured. "The dark place amongst the stars."

"I always thought it might be," Coen said. "But if returning home was that simple, they would have gone thousands of years ago."

Eloise's temples throbbed as she tried to make sense of it all. Maybe it was a kind of way station, a kind of limbo where souls would be tested before they rose higher. The elementals came down from the stars, so she'd always thought of them as ascended beings— lifeforms who'd had physical bodies but had risen to a state of pure energy.

If she was in this place, then maybe they wanted her to ascend.

"But I'm not ready," she blurted. "*Coen...*"

"I can send you back to Kyne," he murmured. "You must make contact with the elementals. Only then may I join you."

"You'll help us?"

"When you are inside, you can open the door for me," Coen told her. "Together, we will find the answers we seek."

Eloise reached out and grasped his hand, finding comfort in the warmth of his skin. He was real. He was *solid*.

All at once, everything hit her and she began to tremble. Tears gathered in her eyes and she tightened her grip on Coen.

"I don't understand how I've gone from accidentally scrambling people's minds to this power to sitting in this place and not thinking it's weird." She shook her head and breathed in the thick, soupy air. "I never freaked out about any of it, not even once. But—"

"It's because deep down, you always knew this is the truth."

"I'm terrified," she managed to rasp.

"You understand the gravity of what has been placed on your shoulders," he told her. "Much has been asked of you, and more will be asked still. Have faith, Eloise Hart." He began to fade, the dreamy world of purple iridescent shadows dissolving into a trillion tiny flakes.

Her fingers slipped through his. "Coen…"

"Find them," his voice echoed from far away. "Show them the key…"

This time, when the rivers carried her away, they were gentle, and at their end, she saw a golden light guiding her home.

As the wind roared around them and the world faded in and out of blackness, Kyne reached desperately for Eloise. Her feet lifted off the ground and the current carried her into the air.

"Kyne!" she shrieked. "*Kyne!*"

Their fingers brushed for the briefest of moments before she was torn away, disappearing into the sky.

The wind died down as suddenly as it'd picked up, taking the thick layer of reality he'd felt pass over them with it, and he was alone.

Eloise was gone. Just...*gone*.

Her backpack fell to the ground with a *thud*, the water bottle popping free from the side pocket.

"*Eloise!*" His voice echoed back to him, the panic rebounding off rock after rock. "*Eloise!*"

His only answer was his voice being thrown back at him, fading into the distant Pilbara until that too was gone.

He fisted his hands into his hair and tugged, his heart racing. The air crackled with the remnants of an all too familiar magic.

They'd taken her.

He picked up a rock and hurled it into the air with a cry of rage. It clattered into the gorge, tumbling down until it too was silent.

The currents were gone, but could he reach out to them himself?

Eloise had told him about the rivers—the currents that flowed through space and time—but he'd never walked them himself. Somehow, the elementals had pulled her onto them, which meant she could be anywhere or any-*when*.

Kyne had never been able to tap into the other elements, not like Eloise. He'd tried over the years but had never found a way to connect with anything other than the Earth. At the thought of losing her, he felt his powers flare hotter than he'd ever felt them.

Maybe he just didn't have the right motivation.

Turning, he faced the place he'd last seen Eloise and reached out towards the sky. His anger simmered, binding with his anguish at her loss, as his elemental abilities coursed through his veins.

"I'm not going to let you take her without a fight," he rasped. "You have no right."

For the briefest of moments, he almost believed he burned with the same silver-threaded gold that Eloise had burned with that night in Solace. He could see it in his mind's eye, binding with the stars themselves, and for the first time in his entire life, he felt powerful. Like he had control amongst the chaos of life.

But then it was gone, and he wasn't sure if it had been there at all or if it was just a delusional fantasy.

His magic spent, he fell to his knees and let out an exhausted whimper.

It wasn't enough. *He* wasn't enough.

"*Eloise...* I'm sorry. I'm—"

She appeared out of thin air, pushing her way

through a gossamer curtain of translucent light, as if she'd floated down from heaven.

He stared up at her, his eyes wide. "Eloise?"

"Don't look so shocked," she replied, falling into his arms.

Kyne held her tight, breathing in the tangy scent of her citrus shampoo, his entire body shaking in relief.

She was solid. She was *real*.

"I thought they'd taken you from me," he whispered.

Eloise clung to him despite the uncomfortable heat. "Was that you?"

He blinked. "What?"

She drew back and ran her fingers over his lips. "The golden light. I saw it on the way back, and when I stepped out of the river, there you were."

"I tried to follow you," he said. "I didn't think it worked…"

"Kyne, there's more to you than a bit of earth," Eloise told him. "I saw it when Vera helped uncover your memories." She handed him her water bottle. "However I'm wired, I think I'm just able to access it easier, that's all."

He sighed and shook his head, letting his fingers play across her face, memorising every inch. "Trust you to make an attempted abduction about everyone else but yourself."

She hesitated. Apparently, the thought of being kidnapped by the elementals hadn't crossed her mind.

"What happened?" he asked. "Where did you go?"

Eloise told him of a place with a purple hue, where the sky was the universe with no atmosphere to make it blue. She was describing the strange world he'd seen when Vera had gone into his mind.

"I saw the same place," he told her. "I thought it was a warning."

"A warning?"

"Of what would happen to the Earth when the Old Ones began dismantling our reality. Taking away all the plants, animals, humanity... Pulling away the atmosphere until nothing but space remained. Like hitting *rewind*."

"I don't think it was a vision," she murmured. "I think... I think it's the place we go before we ascend."

Kyne frowned but saw the sense in it. The elementals had come down from the dark places between the stars, but why take Eloise there?

As he put two and two together, he looked away, his stomach turning over.

If he was to believe the memory Vera uncovered, then he'd been there, too. Where he'd been deemed unworthy and thrown out, and Eloise had been welcomed.

Was she destined to ascend to a higher plane of existence? Was this how their story was going to end? Was that the price she had to pay to save the universe? A thousand questions tumbled through his mind, each worse than the last.

"Don't," Eloise murmured, reading his expression. "Don't even go there. Not until we've spoken to the elementals."

He swallowed hard, all his past insecurities resurfacing.

"Kyne, *promise me*."

"I promise," he rasped. He trusted her, but them...? Not in a million years.

"Coen was there," Eloise went on. "He found me in that place and sent me on my way, but you were the one who guided me back."

"Coen was there?"

"Yes. I think..." She worried her bottom lip. "When we find the elementals, he'll be able to meet us there. Their magic is keeping him out, but we can let him in."

It was becoming clear that the elementals had their own agenda, and whatever their end game was, it didn't necessarily align with the Exiles. What if all this —the currents, the place with the purple hue, his scrambled memories—was a test? If so, he was failing. *Miserably*.

Kyne swallowed his pride, his anxiety, his self-consciousness, and his fear. They were still on the journey to the bit at the end, and they didn't know all the facts. He had to keep his head screwed on or he could lose the battle for everyone before they even began fighting it.

"If there's another way, then Coen will help us find it," he said, running his hands over Eloise's arms. "Are you hurt? Can you keep going? Those elementals have got some serious explaining to do."

"I'm fine." She smiled and began untangling herself from his arms. "Let's find our bio-parents and hold them accountable, huh?"

CHAPTER 14

It was the fourth day since Siora had appeared on the highway outside of Solace, and she'd been learning at an incredible pace.

For Vera, it'd been a mad scramble to sort through her life before it'd drowned in goop in her dugout. Her belongings were now stored in various places all over town—her furniture sat in the aisles in the *Outpost*, her herbs and potion making supplies were at Hardy's, and she stored her crystals and clothing at Drew's.

Needless to say, she had *a lot* of clothes. Her wardrobe had taken over half of Drew's dugout—the sparsely furnished home now resembled little more than a fashion warehouse.

And that morning, Siora stood in the middle of it all, looking at the ceiling as if it would collapse on her head.

"Are you sure?" the *De'ashlide* asked.

Vera looked up from the box she was sorting through. "About the clothes or the roof?"

"Both?"

"The roof won't fall in. Kyne built it."

"Kyne?"

"Don't worry." Vera laughed. "He's good with rocks." She held up a cute T-shirt. "This one looks your size."

Siora's gaze flickered around the room. "I have clothes."

"You can't go around wearing the same thing all the time."

Siora picked at her blouse. "Why not?"

"Well, you have to wash those eventually," Vera said, reemerging from the pile with a cute green floral dress. "So, you need at least one change for when the others are in the wash. I'm more than happy to give you some of mine. As you can see, I've got plenty to go around."

"There are so many colours..."

"Clothes help show off your personality and besides, putting outfits together is fun." She held up the dress against the *De'ashlide* and nodded. "Nice! I think green suits you. It's natural, earthy... This dress tells the world you are a beautiful, carefree woman who's in touch with nature."

Siora blinked. "Clothes can say all that?"

"Sure!" Vera rummaged in the pile and took out more pieces she thought would work with Siora's complexion. "A fantastic outfit can do wonders for a woman's confidence."

"I'm not sure who I am."

Vera looked up, and when she saw the despair on Siora's face, she sighed. "Don't worry. We'll figure it out. We'll start by seeing what kind of clothes you like. Superficial, I know, but it's only been a few days." She placed a reassuring hand on Siora's shoulder. "Don't be so hard on yourself." She held up the floral dress again. "Yes, no...maybe?"

"Yes!" Siora grinned, the sudden change in temperament giving Vera a little whiplash.

"Okay, this one goes on the yes pile." Vera looked her over thoughtfully, noting her tangled, but long, straight, mousy locks. "I can braid your hair like mine, if you'd like."

"Will you?" The idea seemed to excite her. "Please?"

"Of course." She sat Siora down in front of the mirror they'd saved from her bedroom and combed her fingers through the *De'ashlide's* hair.

As she worked, it gave her time to think and study the one-time Unseelie fae. Her reappearance was a shock, and the timing *was* suspicious. Hardy was right to be wary, but after spending time with her, Vera couldn't find any red flags.

She was a human who'd been through a traumatic experience and needed help. Vera, being Vera, was determined to do whatever she could. If that began with clothes and a hairstyle, then that's where she'd start.

"You know, you don't have to stay out in that tent with Finn," she said. "You can stay here with me and Drew until you figure out what you want to do."

"Thank you, but I like being outside," Siora replied. "I don't know why, but the sky comforts me. Being underground..." She bit her bottom lip. "Drew has a lovely home, but I don't like being here for long. I feel...caught."

"That's okay." Vera nodded as she wrapped the end of the braid with a black elastic. "The fae like being outside. We tried to get Finn to move into town, but he wouldn't budge, not even an inch."

"Why would you ask him to move if he was happy?"

"Finn was alone out there," Vera replied. "After all he went through, we were just worried about him being on his own."

Siora smiled, catching Vera's eye in the mirror. "That was kind of you."

"Okay, I'm finished. What do you think?"

As the *De'ashlide* turned her head from side to side, studying her new hairstyle, Vera watched closely. The Exiles had decided to keep the truth about what was happening in Solace a secret from her. They didn't want to confuse the situation any more, and the last thing any of them wanted was to needlessly frighten her, especially since everything was so new. But it seemed her understanding of the world was rapidly catching up regardless—her speech had improved dramatically, and Vera felt like she was talking to an extremely well-read adult. It gave her hope that Siora could find a place to start anew, away from all the hurt the Old Ones had caused her and from her troubled past in the fae world.

"I like it!" Siora declared. "It was so tangled."

Vera chuckled and held up her finger. "Hang on a sec. I've got an idea..."

She dove back into the pile of her belongings, taking a plastic tub down off the stack in the corner. Inside was a tiny fraction of her crystal collection.

The raw quartz points clacked together as she fossicked, moving polished fluorite and selenite towers aside until she found what she was looking for—a small bracelet made of gemstone chips and threaded onto thick jewellers elastic.

Vera held it in her palm for a moment, feeling the essence of the minerals, then turned to Siora. "Here. This is for you." She slipped the bracelet over the *De'ashlide's* hand.

Siora held up her arm and stared at the brilliant blue stone, her gaze taking in the threads of white and black through the chips. "It's beautiful."

"This stone is called lapis lazuli," the witch explained. "It's known as the wisdom stone because it helps bring forth the inner-self and guides truth, honesty, compassion, and self-expression. Maybe it can help."

"Thank you."

Vera bit her bottom lip and wondered if she could help in another way. "Did Finn tell you what I am? What I can do?"

Siora nodded. "He said you are a witch. That you can perform magic."

"I can." She glared at the lapis lazuli. "I use it to help people. To heal and guide. I work with plants to make medicines and crystals to guide and protect."

Siora held up her arm. "Like these?"

"Yes, like the lapis lazuli, but I can do other things, too. I recently helped another man find some lost memories, and I think I can help you regain some of yours, too."

Siora let her hand fall into her lap, her green eyes staring blankly at Vera. The witch shivered, feeling as if the *De'ashlide* was staring right into her soul. She didn't have any magic left, but her subconscious certainly remembered having it.

"No, thank you," she finally said.

Vera raised her eyebrows. "You don't want to remember who you were?"

"I can sense the reluctance in Finn," Siora replied. "It makes me wonder if knowing who I was before will be too difficult to bear."

"What *do* you know?"

"I know I was fae, like him. Whatever happened to

me, I cannot remember, but it has taken the magic he says I used to possess. He says..." Siora trailed off, her forehead creasing.

Vera frowned, knowing what Finn was like. "What did he say?"

"He says I'm free. Why would he say that?"

"The fae aren't from this world," Vera explained. "They come from a place that's seeped in magic. They rely on it to survive. The same magic isn't as common here, so it makes life difficult. He would struggle to survive if he were to leave Solace."

Siora turned to the mirror and studied her reflection. "There is magic here? In this place?"

"A little," she replied. "My magic is compatible too, so I can help him...if he'd only accept it."

"Why wouldn't he want your help? He said you're nice and that you would help me. You *have* helped me." She held up her arm, showing off the lapis lazuli. "You've given me wisdom."

Vera shrugged. "Finn is proud and a little stubborn. He wants to do the right thing, and he does, but I think he believes it goes against his nature sometimes. He struggles with it."

"Why?"

"He's an Unseelie fae. He reckons the Unseelie are predisposed to evil, but I think he's wrong. No one is born evil, not the fae or any other creature. Our choices make us who we are, nothing else. There is potential for goodness in all of us...if we choose it."

Siora had been listening intently as Vera spoke, as if she was absorbing every word and mulling over them. Finally, she touched her fingers to the gemstone bracelet around her wrist and smiled. "A new beginning," the *De'ashlide* said. "A new choice."

Vera looked down at Siora, her frown returning. The things she came out with felt a little chilling. Siora had become articulate and thoughtful, calm and reasonable...all in the span of four days.

She shook her head and reached back into the pile of clothes. It was probably just her nerves acting up.

Taking out a pair of beige strappy sandals, Vera offered them to Siora. "Here, try these on. I think we're the same size."

The *De'ashlide* grinned and immediately strapped them to her feet. "Do they complete the outfit? Is that how the saying goes?"

Vera laughed. "Yes, I think they complete the outfit perfectly."

Eloise was exhausted by the time they found the gorge, and the sun had already passed the point of midday.

Kyne led the way down into the earth, finding a safe path through the loose rock to the ancient riverbed. Eloise was close behind, careful to put her boots when he'd put his...and to never let him out of her sight.

Out of the light, the air was cooler, though the surrounding rock radiated with the heat of the day. Everything in the Pilbara seemed to be supercharged by the sun, whether it was in its direct path or not.

No wonder it was a sparsely populated part of the country.

They stopped for a quick lunch on the shore of the dry river, sipping on their water bottles as the cloudless sky hovered above. Silence found them—there was nothing to talk about and they were both tired. Besides, now they were literally on the elemental's doorstep and the gravity of their journey was finally hitting home—they'd discussed their next steps plenty.

Thankfully, their path was easier than it had been above. The river had carved the way over millions of years, eroding the rock until the climate had caught up with it, drying most of the water out of the entire region, turning it into desert. The best part was that there were no craggy rocks to clamber over. All they had to do was follow the river to its source, so that's what they did.

The farther the two elementals went, the closer the cliffs became, until they were forced to walk in a single file. With each twist and turn, Eloise's anxiety and hope grew in equal measure, her tired feet throbbing in her boots.

"It should be just ahead," Kyne said behind her, the

sound of his voice bouncing back and forth. "A turn or two…"

Eloise pressed her hands against the rock face, steadying herself as she slipped around the tight bend…and came to an abrupt halt.

They'd reached a dead end.

She pushed against the rock, expecting to find an illusion, but the wall was solid.

"No. No, no, *no*…" Frustrated tears gathered in her eyes. "Are you sure this was the right river?"

"Yes, I'm sure. Let me see," Kyne said, squeezing past. They pressed together in the tight space, the air hot and thick.

He put his hands on the rock, using his elemental power to reach out. A moment later…nothing happened.

"But you should've been able to… But…" Eloise felt like crumpling into a ball and ugly crying. She was so hot, tired, and through with all the mind games.

"I should have…" Kyne told her. "Which means this is all of them."

"Another test?"

"Yeah, nah, it's probably more to do with me telling them we were coming," he reminded her. "I thought I was speaking to a memory, but the more stuff that happens out here, I reckon it was more than that."

Eloise let out a frustrated cry, the sound echoing back at her. "After everything we've been through to get here… They can't shut us out like this! They made us and threw us out into the world with no one and nothing to guide us. *They owe us.*"

"I don't disagree."

She felt the weight of the coral key in her pocket and raked her gaze over the walls, but they were smooth. It wasn't that kind of key then, so what use was it?

A stab of anger hit her heart like a red-hot poker. "They almost sent you off a cliff; they made us climb over all those rocks in forty-five-degree weather, and they sent me to another plane of existence..." She pushed past Kyne and faced the dead end. "*Let's give them a taste of their own medicine.*"

Her hands slapped down on the rock, and she let go of her powers, forcing them into the wall. Kyne placed his hand on her shoulder and his magic flowed into her, giving her the courage to push forwards.

Their combined will slammed into the rock like a sledgehammer and the path began to open. Cool air hit Eloise's face, instantly taking the edge of the heat in the gorge behind them.

"Talk about ringing the doorbell," Kyne murmured.

Rock melted away under the force of their combined powers, revealing an opening beyond. The scent of water and growing things filled her senses, and she breathed deeply.

It was the billabong Kyne had told her about.

Stepping out of the gorge, she dropped her backpack onto the sandy shore and gazed up at the vines and greenery lining the banded rock formation. Her anger was doused by the sight.

Above, light pooled in through the circular hole, casting a thick ray of warmth onto the greenish water. Several trees had taken root at the base of the billabong, their trunks stretching abnormally high to reach the sun.

Kyne set his bag down and stood beside her. "They're here," he whispered. "Can you feel them?"

Eloise nodded, the tingle of what felt like a thousand pairs of eyes focused on her, shivering down her spine.

The air shimmered across the billabong on the far shore. Eloise stared, transfixed as a human figure appeared out of the haze, and gasped as her magic responded.

It was one of them. An elemental.

She saw it now, why they deemed themselves broken. The figure seemed to have trouble manifesting, its form flickering in and out of reality as it approached. Hovering over the water, it took on the shape of a man with white, pearlescent skin before dissolving into the strange clear ripple in the air.

The elemental's bare feet touched the shore as he emerged from his half-state. His hair mirrored Kyne's in style—swept back and brushing his collar—and was so white, each strand appeared clear. His matching skin shimmered with ripples of purple, blue, red, and green as the light touched him, and his eyes appeared blue with flecks of steely grey that carried a haunting echo of something more.

He stood before them, clad in a simple cream-coloured shirt and trousers, unblinking and silent, waiting.

In that moment, Eloise was struck with a strange calmness and a familiarity that made her think of Hardy. Why would she think of the vampire now? Her memory took her to the tent north of Soalce, as Darius stood over them, her friends and the world on the brink of destruction, and the moment when she understood what flowed through her veins.

She hadn't realised what it meant—not until her gaze had connected with the elemental. It was spirit. Truth. Her journey.

Kyne grasped Eloise's hand, breaking the spell.

"I told you I was coming," he snarled. "Here we are. We're done with your tricks."

The elemental's expression came alive, his face twisting into a mask of anger. As he lifted his arms and the air filled with magic, Eloise lunged forwards.

"No!" she shouted, thrusting the coral key out in front of her. "You will listen to what we have to say. *You will listen.*"

The elemental jerked backwards at the sight of the key, his gaze fixed on Eloise. He lowered his hands and glared at Kyne. Whatever the circular cut of coral represented, it meant something to the man.

Across the billabong, the air came alive, rippling

like the surface of the ocean until it finally parted. Body after body manifested on the shore, ten men and women, all as beautiful and translucent as the next.

Then the man spoke for the first time. "We have waited a long time, *daughter*."

CHAPTER 15

Drew sat beside the fire at Finn's camp, watching Siora, who was watching him.

Above, the sky was darker than usual, despite the cloudless atmosphere. The stars shone as if they lay behind a sheer curtain of blackened netting, their light nowhere near strong enough to break through.

A log crackled and popped, sending sparks spiralling upwards.

In the last twenty-four hours, Siora had braided her hair and found a change of clothes. It made her look more human than ever, as if she hadn't just gone through a miracle supernatural rebirth five days ago.

It was clear Vera had a hand in dressing her. From her sandals, to her dress, to the gemstones she wore around her wrist, all Drew saw was a clone of the witch. He realised she missed Eloise, being the only other woman in town, so it wasn't that much of a surprise. None of the men understood or took much notice of clothes and hair, which probably wasn't the most sensitive thing he could've thought about at that moment.

Drew knew all about the supernatural, and even a little about the spiritual realm, but human social issues…? Forget about it.

"It's incredible." Siora stroked her hands over Drew's fur and traced the outline of his pointed ears. "You are a man inside."

Drew glanced at Finn, who just smirked at him from the other side of the fire.

"*I don't do tricks*," the shifter retorted.

"I've never seen a man turn into a dog before."

"*Dingo.*"

She blinked. "Dingo?"

"*I'm not a dog; I'm a dingo. There's a difference.*" He shook his head, dislodging her hands. There was something cold in her touch he didn't like. Cold and…colourless.

When he looked at Finn, he saw the change in his aura—before he'd gone on his walkabout, it'd been purplish-red, but now it was a mix of blues and yellows. His friend had changed for the better, and the things the fae had seen had set him on a course of redemption.

But when Drew looked at Siora, all he saw was shadow. There was no colour surrounding her, not even a trace of black. It was as if she didn't have a soul at all.

The thought troubled him, and he stood, shaking out his fur. "*I've got to go.*"

"Will you come back?" Siora asked.

"*Maybe tomorrow.*"

Putting her out of his mind, he padded away from the fae's camp, melting into the shadow of night.

Drew made his evening rounds, his dingo shape seeing past the limitations of his human sight. He skirted around the borders of Finn's illusion, tracing the edges of the Old One's influence until finally, he stood on top of the ridge overlooking Solace and sniffed the night air.

There was no doubt about it...the corruption was growing.

The electric blue bioluminescence now stretched past the town limits, over the top of Finn's illusion, and dissipated into the outback. Instead of a lazy cloud billowing in the sky, it now resembled a growing storm—patches within it darkened, while others glowed brighter. He even saw the blue light in the plants. The veins in the long, thin, gum leaves glowed as if the trees had sucked up the corruption through the ground water, giving them an alienesque, yet beautiful appearance.

The whole goopy mess had seemed to have sped up in the last few days, as if the crack in the seal had widened. Maybe it had. No one was game to go down and check, let alone open the hatch to the tunnel.

Drew was afraid the whole thing was filled with sticky black tar, and no one needed to smell that.

It didn't matter, anyway. He saw the truth in the sky every night.

Drew sighed and began the descent down the side of the ridge to his dugout. There was nothing he could do but watch...and wait for Eloise and Kyne to get back.

When he nosed his way into his dugout, the lights were on in the front room.

Vera was stretched out on the couch, leafing through one of her fancy grimoires. She didn't look up as he slinked by and he flicked his tail, whacking it against the side of one of her plastic tubs full of crystals. It made a loud cracking sound, but all she did was raise an eyebrow as she turned the page.

He padded into his bedroom and shifted, morphing from dingo to man in one fluid motion.

Changing used to be a nightmare when he was younger. It was all cracking bones and stretching tendons that gave him a headache and a bad back for days. He'd hated it so much, he had tried to go for as long as he could before his body forced him to shift, but ever since he'd been training with Coen—who'd disappeared *again*—it was easier on him.

Maybe this was the way it was always supposed to be, he thought. *The dingo is as much me as I am it.*

Tugging on a pair of shorts and an old Nirvana T-shirt, he shuffled out into the lounge where Vera was still draped over his couch.

"It's getting worse," he said, lifting Vera's legs so he could sit.

She drew her knees up and grunted, turning the page of her grimoire.

"Is that all you have to say?"

The witch looked up and shrugged. "What *is* there to say? There's nothing we can do about it."

"It's showing in the plants now."

"Like I said," she snapped the grimoire shut, "just more doom and gloom. Did you see Siora?"

"I saw her earlier when I went to see Finn. She was all dressed up in a pretty dress, sandals, and crystal jewellery. I wonder where she got all that from?"

Vera pouted and nudged him with her bare foot. "She looks lovely."

He rolled his eyes. "You've turned her into a mini-Vera."

"What do you expect? I can't exactly take her into the Ridge, can I? Besides, the shopping there is quite thin on the ground. The closest Kmart is three hours away, and the nearest Target is in Tamworth. That's five hours! And they're not exactly high fashion shops, either!"

"No one lives in the outback for the shopping," Drew muttered.

"No, they come here for opal."

"Or to capitalise off the people looking for opal."

Vera scoffed and slapped his arm with her grimoire. "Capitalise? It's good business sense! You might want to get yourself some!"

Drew leaned back against the soft couch and sighed, wishing someone had the foresight to invent a non-corruptible beer. It was going to be a *long* night.

"The point is, there's something different about Siora," he murmured.

"Of course there is," Vera retorted. "She's had her magic stripped away and her memories wiped. She'll never be the same person she was. She's human now, or at least, the fae version of human. What the Old One did to her was the ultimate violation. They changed the essence of her soul."

"I get all that." He shook his head and scowled, wondering if there'd always be a part of Vera that still saw him as an angry kid who kept getting mixed up with all the wrong people. A poor little dog who needed a good brush and a flea bath. "I just can't shake the feeling that there's something else going on there. Something we've all missed."

"Then it has to be the corruption you're sensing," Vera said. "We know it messes with humans, so it probably has some kind of effect on her."

Drew narrowed his eyes.

"Which means she can't stay here," the witch added. "It's not safe."

"I don't even understand how she can be here at

all," he said. "She's not supernatural anymore; she shouldn't have been able to walk up to the illusion."

"It's probably her body's memory of her fae magic. When it left her, it likely left a mark on her spirit of some kind. Magic like that is not easily forgotten. Like calls to like, you know."

"And what proof do you have?"

Vera sat up. "What?"

"What proof do you have?" he repeated. "Everything you've said is just conclusions you've drawn from ambiguous evidence about something we hardly understand. That Old One is the mother of all icebergs."

She stared at him, her mouth hanging open.

"Yeah, I know big words."

"Of course you do... Drew—"

"The green stuff at the mountain is exactly like the blue stuff here," he went on. "But what is it, exactly? We're calling it corruption, but what if it's something else? What if it *is* the Old One? Siora fell into it. She fell into it, and it swept her away, only to spit her out a month later in Solace." He raised his eyebrows, but Vera had nothing to say. "How is that not connected?"

Vera worried her bottom lip for a full minute before she spoke. "When you look at her as a dingo, what do you see?"

Drew scowled, his memory going back to earlier that night, when he sat by the fae's fire. Siora had been smiling and laughing, hanging on every word Finn had said. She'd stroked her fingers through the fur around the rough of Drew's neck, tracing his ears, thinking he was the strangest thing she'd ever seen in her life.

And what had he *seen*?

"Nothing," he told Vera. "Nothing at all."

"Then why are you so worried?"

"You don't get it." He sat up and turned to face her, his gaze drilling into hers. "Everyone has something. A colour, an aura...but Siora had *nothing*."

Vera sat up, her expression troubled. "Nothing?"

"*Nothing*."

"Well, it could be for a lot of reasons..."

"'Reasons' isn't hard proof," Drew said. "I'm not prepared to take any risks or give any benefit of the doubt. There's too much at stake."

"Fine. All I can promise is to watch and wait," she told him. "I can try my magic, but she already refused my help. Anything I do now would be a betrayal of her trust."

"And what about the universe, huh? Isn't the continuation of life for everyone and everything worth the risk of hurting her feelings?"

Vera hugged the grimoire to her chest and closed her eyes. "I guess..."

"This was never going to be easy," he told her. "We might have been demoted to guardians, but we still have to be prepared to fight."

"I know. It's just... I like her, Drew. When I look at her, I see an innocent victim."

"Despite her past? Despite what she did when she brought that storm down on Solace?" As far as Drew was concerned, Siora was the reason the seal had cracked in the first place.

"She was corrupted," Vera fired back. "I know how it feels, remember? It corrupted the Nightshade, which corrupted me. I still feel the violation of that, Drew. *I still feel it.*"

"I know."

"Do you?" Her scowl deepened. "Besides, Finn's right. She has a chance to start over, to rid herself of her past. How can we deny her that?"

"I'm not denying anyone anything. I'm just making sure there isn't an Old One still pulling her strings."

Vera sank back and sighed, her brow still creased.

"It's what we promised Eloise and Kyne," he reminded her.

"Shut up. *I know.*"

"Call it due diligence."

Vera's scowl softened as she rubbed her thumbs across the leather cover of her grimoire. "Due diligence?"

"So? You'll look into it?"

"*Yes.* I'll keep my eyes peeled, but I'm telling you, I've not seen a single malicious Old One bone in her body."

Drew rolled his eyes and got up. "It's late. I'm going to bed." Pausing at the door, he turned. "Don't tell

Finn… If my gut is right, losing her for a second time will probably kill the poor bastard."

Vera shook her head, looking up at him with soft eyes. "Damn… You really have levelled up, huh?"

***

As Drew's sleek dingo form disappeared into the shadow of night, Finn shifted to take his place by Siora's side.

"He is a curious thing, don't you think?" she asked, watching where the shifter had left the circle of firelight.

"Depends on your definition of curious," Finn retorted. "What story would you like to hear?"

They had been passing the evenings with stories about Lor'Iyslar, of the fae and the magic found there. It was a welcome distraction, given the decline he felt in the land around Solace. Stories of their homeland brought them together, but he was careful to tell her nothing of the rebellion or both their roles in the senseless slaughter, only choosing the grandest tales.

From the remote frozen north of An Valran to Lor As'tuann—the Celestial Palace—and the City of Stars, Sil Astrad. He told her of the Silver Stag of Un Alari, and the mythical Heart of the Forest. There was more, but not enough lifetimes to tell her all the history of the fae. Five nights was simply not enough.

"I feel as if something is worrying you," she said.

"That's not a story. What about the Mountain of Glass? I haven't told you that one yet."

"No." Siora shook her head. "Something is amiss with this place."

Finn picked up a stick and poked at the fire, anything to keep his hands busy. "What makes you say that?"

"I feel it," she murmured. "I see it in Vera's eyes. I see it in Hardy's. In Wally's. I saw it in Drew. And I see the sadness you try to hide from me, Finn." She pressed her hands to the sandy ground. "There is no sound here, no life. It bleeds away, drawn into darkness."

Frowning, Finn looked up. Did an echo of her magic still live within her? It had to; otherwise, how would she know?

Her gaze met his. "What is it? What is wrong here?"

"Are you sure you want the truth?" he asked. "It's the thing that changed you."

"Tell me." The firelight reflected in her eyes, and for a moment, it was as if their silver sheen had returned. "I need to understand why."

Finn knew Siora deserved to know the truth, even though the Exiles had all agreed to keep it from her. He knew they were only trying to protect her, but she was living amongst the corruption, just the same as them. If she wanted to know, then he would tell her.

So, Finn gave her the truth. The story of the seal, their struggles with it, the corruption that came from the mountain, the fae's journey to the east, and their demise...

"You fell," he whispered. "I saw you fall. I reached out towards you, but it was too late..."

Siora blinked, but her features showed no recognition at all. Nothing he'd said had triggered anything in her, and not one memory resurfaced.

"There was a moment..." he continued, "a moment just before the Old One swept you away, where I thought I saw a flicker of recognition in your eyes. But you were gone so fast—"

"I'm sorry, Finn," Siora whispered. "I don't remember. I cannot tell you what you want to hear."

He reached out and grasped her hand. "You don't need to."

"And Solace?" she prompted. "Is it like the mountain?"

"What happened there is happening here," he confirmed. "The seal is breaking and corruption is spreading. The magic from the Old One is poisoning the earth, the water, and driving all life away. Soon, the entity will bring the shadows of the dead to guard it as it struggles for freedom."

"And when it is free?"

"Everything will cease to be."

"Why?"

"Because the Old One's purpose here is to destroy this entire reality."

"Why?"

"How do I know? They have no feelings; they do not care," he spat as he jerked his hand away. "They took twelve fae and twisted them beyond recognition. They took you and made you into a monster, all in the name of setting them free. The Siora I knew was stubborn and proud, but she would not—" He closed his mouth and glared into the fire. The Siora he knew *would* sacrifice an entire universe so she could go home, he realised. After all they'd been through, after all the bloodshed and betrayal, he still held affection for her, and now it was clouded by the shell the Old Ones had returned.

Vera was right. They knew nothing of why she was here, let alone *how*.

Finn sighed, gathered his emotions, and pushed them back down. "They do not care about the people and creatures who live here...but we do. We think the world and universe are worth saving, so we fight for it."

"I see." Siora cast her gaze downwards. "But Vera said you need magic to survive."

Finn hesitated, his heart twisting. "Yes, I depend on the very thing that destroyed you," he managed to say. "It troubles me, but what can I do? I can't change what I am."

"If you could return to your world, would you?"

Finn thought of Andante's offer and shrugged. "I still have things to do here."

"I understand."

"I did bad things there," he admitted. "I was exiled

because of them, sent here to live a life starved of magic...but you could go back. It's your home, too."

"Perhaps...but I couldn't go without you."

"I don't think I have the courage." It was the first time he'd admitted as much, and his heart felt lighter for saying it. "But if we went together... A thousand years is a long time and the fae have longer memories, but perhaps that's where my path leads. If we succeed in our battle against the Old Ones, then I will have to leave Solace regardless. I could finally take you home. That was all you ever wanted, and I would give it to you if that's what you truly desired now, as a *De'ashlide*."

Siora smiled, her eyes lighting up. "A world of magic. I should like to see it." But as soon as her happiness had appeared, it faded. "But... Whatever happens in this reality, you have a guaranteed place there because of the creature you are. Would you extend the same courtesy to the other Exiles to save their lives?"

Finn hesitated. The thought hadn't occurred to him, and guilt flooded his body. Andante could open a portal to another reality, but they couldn't save the entire planet. There was no time, no explanation good enough to convince humanity, no power they could wield to save themselves...but the Exiles? They could all go with him to Lor'Iyslar and pass as *De'ashlide*— Blue and Clarke certainly could. Vera would be elevated as a witch through the covenant her kind made with the Seelie, and he knew Eloise and Kyne would be held in high regard as elementals. Drew's dingo would be thing of renowned magical curiosity at the university. Perhaps they could even find a cure for Wally's lycanthropy and Hardy's vampirism.

Would Andante agree to it? Of course she would, but would it be right? Was it what he truly wanted? He'd still be an exile, forced to live in hiding, forced to forsake his family name and live in secrecy for the rest of his days. Vera's status wouldn't save him, nor would the elementals uniqueness be enough to grant him a royal pardon.

What a selfish Za'adei, he thought. *I would condemn my family to erasure because of jealousy.* No matter what he did, he would lose. Every. Single. Time. But it wasn't right to deny them a chance at life.

"I see," Siora murmured. "You would not."

"I never said that," he bit back.

"But you feel it."

"Of course, I feel it," he cried. "I'm waiting for the moment my story gains a happy ending, but no matter which way I look at it, I lose. I'm destined to sacrifice everything time and time again. No life or a half-life. Neither is living, is it? I'm tired, Siora. I'm so tired of feeling this way."

She slid into his arms and cupped his face in her hands. Her gaze pierced his, rendering him silent, then she kissed him.

He knew it wasn't her the moment their lips

touched. It wasn't the Siora he'd once known. It was her body, but the Old One had taken her memories, erasing all the choices she'd made—the choices that made her who she was.

He drew back, knowing it wasn't fair to force his memory onto her. She had to make new choices now.

Siora gazed up at him. "Will you tell me about the Mountain of Glass?"

He shivered and wrapped his arm around her shoulder. "It is called Si Ithqua in my language, and it lies beyond An Ud Xashri, the River of Bones—the greatest glacier known to all of Lor'Iyslar. It is said that a great tree grows within the mountain."

Siora smiled, entranced by his words. "Tell me about the tree?"

"The fae call it the Heart of the Mountain..."

CHAPTER 16

Eloise grasped Kyne's hands as the elementals emerged from an invisible place beyond the physical world. Her heart pounded as they gathered around them, each reaching out to touch their faces with long, pale fingers.

She counted eleven men and women, all with the same pale hair and iridescent skin as the man who'd greeted them. Each one was beautiful—tall, elegant, without a blemish to be seen. Even a supermodel would feel inadequate standing beside them, but it wasn't their beauty that drew her to them.

Her magic came alive as they touched her cheeks, flowing into her, then through Kyne, and back again. It was a greeting, a homecoming...a return to family. Their blood was her blood, and they were all her parents.

A woman emerged from the group—tall and willowy, with bright blue eyes and crystalline hair—

and took Eloise's hands in hers. "I am called Ilyana," she said. "I speak for all."

Eloise was enraptured as the woman guided them to the edge of the billabong. She sat by the water, folding her limbs into a graceful pose, and they sat before her, flopping onto the sand in an uncoordinated tumble in comparison.

The other elementals watched them settle by the water before walking away, fading in and out of sight as they returned to wherever they lived amongst the gorges.

"What are your names?" Ilyana asked.

"I'm Eloise and this is Kyne." She slid her palm onto his knee.

"We have seen this one before." The elemental stared at Kyne, her expression giving away nothing.

"It was an unforgettable experience," he replied tersely.

Her blue eyes flashed with a glint of annoyance. "And yet, you persist."

"We have to. We want to know..." Eloise took a deep breath, sorting through the hundreds of questions that'd filled her heart since their trip to the Pilbara had begun, but settled on the most important. The coral key was heavy in her palm, the strange pinkish circular stone warm to the touch. Holding it out to Ilyana, she said, "We need to hear everything."

The elemental looked down at the key, but didn't

take it. "We are born of the stars... A place beyond the body."

"Pure energy," Eloise said, unable to look away. "Free from the constraints of biology."

"Yes. We exist not just in this reality, but in all reality." Her body faded before solidifying again. "We have been given many names in many worlds. You have called us elemental, and perhaps we are in this form we are bound to, but we prefer to be known as Celestials. Our kind was once as your humans were... until we became something more."

Hope sparked in her heart, and she felt herself lean closer. "And how did you come to be here on Earth?"

"We answered a call for help long ago and descended."

"But why would you help us if you were safe?" Kyne asked. "Our universe is just one grain of sand."

"The entities you call the Old Ones...we exist alongside one another, but they have no connection to the universes they lay claim to. We originated amongst the pages of reality, and understand what it is to be..." she looked him over, "*creatures.*"

Eloise worried her bottom lip as Ilyana spoke. It appeared as if the Celestials had their own struggles with the Old Ones, just in a higher dimension. Even though they'd shed their human bodies, it seemed they still retained some of their emotions. They remembered their beginnings and their influence in the continued existence of all things.

"However," Ilyana continued, "when we undertook the descent, not all went accordingly. Something went wrong." She held up her hand as it faded in and out of existence, her skin shimmering as if it were covered in a fine layer of pearlescent glitter. "We were forced into a half-life, neither in the higher realm nor at peace in this reality. Our powers were diminished, and all we could do for the people here was to seal away the Old Ones and hope."

"But why are you still here?" Eloise asked. "After all this time, why haven't you gone home?"

"They can't," Kyne murmured. "She said they're bound."

"He speaks the truth," Ilyana said, her eyes narrowing. "We should have ascended once our task was complete."

But they couldn't finish what they started, so what had they done? "The children..." Eloise murmured.

"Are necessary."

"Necessary?" Kyne demanded. "Are you serious?"

"Entirely," Ilyana replied, her voice cool.

"Kyne," Eloise murmured, "we knew the answers we got mightn't be the ones we wanted to hear. What's done is done."

And the truth was the Celestials had hybrid children in hopes of creating ones who'd be 'unbroken' enough to complete their task. They sent them out into the world, alone and helpless, hoping that one day they'd be paid a visit by someone like...her?

"It was cruel," Eloise went on, "the way we were left in the world, but I think I understand now."

Ilyana smiled, even as Kyne bristled beside her. "Many will never know the blood they possess," the Celestial murmured. "Few will discover it, and fewer still will understand its true purpose."

Eloise felt her heart swell with the thought of how many elementals must be out there, living amongst humans. How many knew they were different and struggled just as she and Kyne had? How many had destroyed their lives by accident? They were out there alone and afraid, without anyone to guide them.

"All this time, though?" Eloise asked. "There must be thousands of us. Why did it have to be this way?"

"Tell me," Ilyana murmured. "Why have you come?"

Eloise hesitated, the blatant refusal to answer her question taking her aback. "We told you, we need to know everything."

"No." Ilyana's expression hardened to something that looked like annoyance, or a Celestial approximation of it. "You have brought the stone."

Eloise held up the coral key. "This?" She glanced at Kyne, who looked like he was about to erupt. "Would you have seen us without it?"

"We would have seen you."

"See?" Kyne murmured with a shake of his head. "It was always you, Eloise."

"Speak your truth, not your heart, elementals,"

Ilyana snapped, her blue eyes turning to ice. "It does you no favours not to."

Eloise's heart twisted. Had they come all this way only to piss off the Celestials, get thrown out, and condemn the entire universe? She couldn't bear the thought of another set of parents hating her.

"We want to finish your quest," she blurted, desperate to keep the Celestial's favour. "Kyne and me...we want to lock the Old Ones out of this reality forever."

"You and him?"

"Not just us." Eloise shook her head. "The other people who live in Solace, too."

The Celestial gazed at them, her body shimmering in and out of focus. "Is that all?"

Kyne glanced at Eloise, his features hardening. This conversation wasn't going the way they'd planned, but they'd already gotten a lot of answers. They wouldn't learn how to defeat all-powerful cosmic entities in an afternoon.

"We don't have much time," Eloise replied. "The Old One in the mountain almost broke free, but I sealed it away again, but the second seal beneath Solace is cracked. Corrupted magic is seeping out—it's in the water, the air, the plants, and driving away humanity. It's happening fast, almost like this Old One is more powerful. We don't know how long it'll hold."

"I see." Ilyana stood abruptly and swept her arm

towards the opposite shore of the billabong. "Come. I will show you where you can rest."

Kyne stood, his anger flaring. "I don't think you understand—"

"I understand perfectly," the Celestial interrupted. "Forty thousand years ago, it took twelve Celestials to bind the Old Ones." Her eyes narrowed as she looked him over. "It will take more than two half-cast elementals and a mere hour to banish them for eternity."

Kyne raised his eyebrows and remained silent as Ilyana turned and walked around the shore of the billabong. At least the Celestial had the foresight to realise they couldn't walk on water.

Eloise took Kyne's hand and smiled. "We'll work it out," she whispered. "We have to gain their trust, then they'll show us what we need to do."

The elemental grimaced and looked across the water. "I hope so."

"They will," she told him, following Ilyana towards the opposite side of the gorge. "You'll see."

***

Kyne had barely caught his breath by the time the sun set that night.

He lay atop his sleeping bag, one arm behind his head, the other stretched out for Eloise, who nestled beside him. The Celestials seemed to have disappeared into another plane of existence for the night, so they were alone by the billabong.

Above, a spattering of stars glimmered through the circular opening, each silver dot mocking him. These people—people who'd admitted to parenting him, Eloise, and countless others over tens of thousands of years—were barely tolerating his presence.

Eloise seemed to be enamoured, but he found them flighty, vague, and aloof. One wrong word, one wrong look, and it'd be all over. They held all the cards, and he didn't like it, and if he was being truly honest with himself, Ilyana was an epic bitch.

And he didn't trust epic bitches.

But at least they understood the concept of food, having left them an assortment of plant-based native leaves and roots—a strange Celestial charcuterie board of sorts—that tasted like newspaper. Thankfully, he'd had the foresight to pack some muesli bars and—he slapped at a mosquito that landed on his arm—some of Vera's magical vanilla bean bug repellant.

The sound startled Eloise awake. She lifted her head and blinked until her gaze focused. "*Hmm*," she mumbled. "I almost forgot..."

"Where we were?"

She rolled over and slid her arm over his waist. "Can't sleep?"

"No. I'm over-tired, I guess." After a full day walking in oppressive heat, almost falling off a cliff, expending the limits of his elemental abilities, *and* listening to Ilyana's tall tale, it was no wonder.

"Kyne?"

He turned his head and brushed his lips across her forehead. "*Eloise.*"

"You haven't said anything about... Well, about what Ilyana told us."

"What is there to say?"

She raised her head, fully awake now. "A lot."

"What do you want me to say?"

Her eyes narrowed. "*What's on your mind.*"

"Ilyana doesn't like me very much," he said. "None of them do."

"No, she doesn't," she agreed.

"You wanted me to tell you what was on my mind. That was on my mind."

"It's not about liking each other," Eloise went on. "It's about finding out where we came from and why."

"It's exactly what this is about," he told her. "You're unbroken enough for them to accept you, but I'm not. Knowing I was close enough to find them, but still damaged...? It's a kick in the guts."

"Have you forgotten they almost threw us both out this afternoon?"

Kyne didn't reply. It was only because he'd been with her. If Eloise had come alone, they would've accepted her the moment she set eyes on the billabong. It was she who'd save the universe, not him. He'd just driven her here.

Still, the abandoned and rejected boy inside him was skeptical. No one did anything out of the goodness of their hearts. Even the purest of them all still carried a grain of selfish pride, even if it was just a desire to feel good in the wake of a selfless act. It was the hardest lesson he'd learned in the wake of his mother's death and the awakening of his power—everyone wanted *something*...no matter how insignificant that something was.

Besides, Ilyana hadn't told them why they'd created the elementals. Eloise had come to some unknown conclusion, voiced it, and the Celestial had gone along with it. But who knew if it was the truth? Was any of her story real?

"Kyne?" Eloise prodded.

"Don't worry about it," he told her. "I just have to find my own way to reconcile it all. The truth is hard to hear when it's not the truth you were expecting."

"Or hoping for."

"That, too." He looked back at the circle of sky. "Go back to sleep. I have a feeling tomorrow's going to be another big day."

"Are you sure you're all right?"

"I'll be fine after some sleep."

Eloise frowned, but she settled back onto her sleeping bag. "Okay...love you."

"Love you, too."

When he was sure Eloise had drifted off, he sat up. Looking down at her, he was struck by her beauty. In this light, she almost looked Celestial herself. Her golden, sun-kissed hair shimmered with strands of silver, and her skin looked so pale she could've been made of star dust...and she had chosen him to love.

Maybe he was too broken to see, but none of this felt right.

Sleep was far beyond his reach, so he stood and began to follow the edge of the billabong. His bare feet sunk into the soft, pinkish-red sand, the coolness of the water soothing his heated skin.

On the opposite shore, he looked back over at Eloise. She still slept soundly, her body unmoving on the sleeping bags.

Kyne sat on a rock and dipped his toes into the water. He watched the ripples spread across the glassy surface, and he knew he wasn't alone. It was a deeper sense that told him—one linked to his elemental magic, one he hadn't felt before.

Looking up, he saw the air shimmer.

"I can see you lurking there," he murmured.

The outline began to solidify, and he saw it was Ilyana.

"You cannot rest," she said.

"No." He wanted to roll his eyes and say, 'No shit, Sherlock', but he held his tongue.

"What troubles you?" Her lip curled, making him wonder if she could read minds.

"There's just one thing I want to know..." he said. "What's the catch?"

"Catch?" The Celestial blinked, the fluttering of her white lashes casting minuscule sparks of magic into the air. Everything she did emitted some kind of otherworldly power, as if she was trying to bewitch his mind and twist his perception of her. Or maybe it was just his natural human skepticism at work—his 'brokenness' manifesting.

"Your *price*," he stated.

"We have no price. We offer our gifts freely to those who make the journey."

"I made the journey once before."

"You were not ready," she stated, her tone a hairsbreadth away from snapping at him.

Kyne steeled his resolve and met her gaze. "I think the word you meant to say was *right*."

Ilyana's expression hardened.

"You said it took *twelve* Celestials to banish the Old Ones, but I only counted eleven today," he continued, gesturing at the billabong. "Where's the twelfth?"

The unpleasantness melted away from the Celestial's face and she smiled. "You are preceptive, Kyne, but you still cannot control all the elements. Your path has not ended, and it will not end here tonight nor tomorrow."

"My path doesn't matter...but you wanna know what does?" He was treading on dangerous ground, but what was the true price for saving the universe? He wouldn't let Eloise unknowingly damn herself in order to complete a task the Celestials failed to do. "The truth. *All of it.* You've lied to us."

"I have not lied," Ilyana spat. "I have no cause for it."

"You just did it again!" Kyne exclaimed. "Your story may be true, and it's all very sad, but it's the part you didn't tell us that's the lie, Ilyana. It's called a lie of omission." He stood and faced her, determined to be unafraid, even though she was infinitely more powerful. "You never said you would help us. Did you ever intend to?"

Ilyana rose, her body unfolding gracefully as the petals of a lily in full bloom, and she smiled up at him. "You are close to the path, Kyne, but you have strayed too far from it. I'm afraid it's time for you to leave."

She raised her hand, and with an absent flick of her wrist, he was sent flying through the air.

Kyne cried out, but he didn't have a hope in hell of stopping her.

He landed in a heap, the impact jerking his entire body and rattling his teeth. A second later, his backpack, boots, and sleeping bag fell out of thin air and scattered noisily across the ground. His left boot smacked his forehead, the impact so hard it stunned his senses for a full minute.

Rubbing his temple, Kyne jerked upright and looked around the dark landscape. The Pilbara stretched from horizon to horizon, and not even a single light or sound penetrated the night.

The billabong was gone, Ilyana was nowhere to be seen...and Eloise was AWOL.

There was only one word he could've said in that moment, and even though there was no one around to hear, he told the wind.

"*Shit.*"

CHAPTER 17

Eloise rose from sleep, her body awakening as her energy returned.

Giddy with the proximity of the Celestial's magic, she smiled and stretched her arms, arcing her back like a cat. It was the best sleep she'd had in months. All her worries seemed so far away...well, at least more than four thousand kilometres far.

She sat up and paused when she saw Kyne and his sleeping bag were both gone. A slight dip disturbed the sandy earth where he'd lain, but that was it.

"Kyne?" she called, looking around the billabong. "Kyne?"

Her voice echoed back to her, paired with the lonely drip of water falling into the billabong from far above, but there was no reply from the miner.

Eloise scrambled out of her sleeping bag, kicking her legs out of the fabric. He'd been right here. He'd been—

"You're awake." Ilyana's voice floated across the water as the Celestial appeared out of the ether. "You slept for so long, we weren't sure you would wake."

"I was more tired than I thought," Eloise replied. Her frown deepened as she looked around the clearing. "Did you see where Kyne went? It's not like him to disappear…"

Ilyana sat beside her and picked up the small circle of black opal that hung around her neck. "This is a pretty jewel."

"It's black opal," she said. "Rare—"

The Celestial smiled and cupped her cheek, silencing any thought she had about Kyne.

"You are perfect," Ilyana murmured, stroking her cheek. "Unbroken. Unblemished. You are the one we have been waiting for."

"I'm far from perfect," Eloise told her. "I've made mistakes. I've hurt people. I'm not pure at all."

"All creatures make mistakes, it is part of learning. It is our journey."

"I suppose so…"

"We have been here for forty thousand years," Ilyana went on. "Living half in this life, half in the other, never ageing, never moving forwards. This is no way to live."

Eloise shook her head. "No, I guess it's not."

"We now have the chance to return home, to ascend once more. We have done enough to help this world, and another will come forth to finish our work."

"Yes, that's why I came." To protect her reality from the Old Ones. To save her friends, her home, and...and what?

"First, we need to help ourselves," Ilyana murmured, her magic swirling. The silver flakes caught in the air, billowing around them as if the billabong had become a snow globe. "There will be another to take up the mantle of saviour."

Eloise blinked, her gaze catching on the flakes. It was stardust... Her magic was stardust.

"Another elemental like me?"

"Yes. All our children have the capacity to become Celestial, but you are the first to reach the pinnacle. There *will* be another."

"But what if there's not enough time? This reality doesn't have another forty thousand years."

"You will transcend reality, Eloise," the Celestial told her. "Time will not matter."

She thought of Kyne, the elemental she loved. He could transcend, too. They could go together. "But what about..." She blinked as her mind fogged. "There was something I was supposed to do."

"You are overwhelmed." Ilyana took Eloise's hands in her own. "It is understandable. The human part of your physical body chains you to this place."

Chained? No, she didn't feel chained.

Glancing across the billabong, through the shimmer of magic, she saw the faint outline of the other ten Celestials gathered on the shore. The empty space amongst them conjured a name…

There was something she was supposed to do, wasn't there?

Ilyana's grip tightened, bringing Eloise's attention back to her. "Let me show you the truth, then you will feel peace."

The stardust swirled, brushing against Eloise's bare arms, fluttered over her chest, up her neck, and tickled her face. Its touch was light as a feather, but the power within was undeniable. It called to her and ignited her blood, and she transformed.

Her skin came alive, the beige undertones of her Caucasian colouring fading as the white pearlescent hue of her Celestial blood came forth. Holding out her arms, her eyes widened as she watched the blues, purples, and pinks shimmer along her flesh. It was beautiful, but she'd never seen herself that way.

She picked up a lock of her hair, finding it'd lost its blonde sheen. In fact, it'd lost its colour entirely. A memory triggered at the sight of the translucent strands, and she knew she'd seen the struggle between human and Celestial happen before, but she couldn't place where. What she did know was that to learn her true potential and complete her quest, she had to become more like them. Could she do it without losing herself?

"This is your true nature, Eloise," Ilyana

murmured. "Do not fight it. It will serve as your guiding light."

Comforted by the Celestial, she allowed her magic to suppress her humanity, but it didn't help with the biology as her stomach growled.

"Oh," she muttered, her cheeks heating as her skin faded back to its usual ivory pallor. "I'm sorry."

Ilyana laughed. "Never mind. Soon you will not have to worry about such things. Come." She held out her hand. "We have much to teach you."

***

The clatter of pots echoed across the remote northwestern corner of the New South Wales outback, the sound fading into the distance as Finn cleaned up the dishes from yet another mediocre breakfast.

Gritty porridge boiled in metallic water. There wasn't even a blueberry or slice of peach to sweeten it, and even if there were, they'd be the furry kind of rotten. Finn never thought he'd see the day when he missed a berry.

He tossed the pot onto the ground and sighed. *Where are you, desert pea?*

But it wasn't Eloise who answered his forlorn thoughts. He turned as the crunch of footsteps pushed their way through the scrub—two sets, if his hearing was correct—just as his stomach growled. *Stupid porridge.*

Drew and Hardy appeared through the trees, and Finn already felt exhausted. It wasn't the right kind of weather for a social call.

The dingo craned his neck, looking towards the camp. "Where's Siora?"

Finn's eyes narrowed. "She went for a walk."

"Great. He's *hangry*," Drew muttered. "Maybe we should give it another day."

"Everyone's hangry," Hardy told him. "Blood is ninety-two percent water, FYI. Besides, we don't have another day."

"What's hangry?" Finn demanded.

"Hangry," Drew said. "You know...so hungry, you're angry?"

"Angry with the letter 'H' attached to it. *How clever.*" The fae snorted. "Should be *rangry*, then."

Drew screwed up his nose. "Huh?"

"Rage," Hardy said with a shake of his head. "Further evidence to support the fact that there's never a good time to give someone bad news. The longer we wait, the harder it'll hit."

"What's so bad that you can't say it in front of Siora?" Finn demanded. Maybe he should pick up the pot again, but it'd do him no good. Hardy had the advantage of speed, after all.

"Well, there's no easy way to say this..." the vampire replied.

Finn scowled. He felt like he was the subject of one of those annoying human conventions known as an intervention. His unpleasant Unseelie side rose, and it was all he could do not to lash out at his Exiled brothers, speed or not.

"You know how I can see things when I'm a dingo...?" Drew asked.

"Spit it out, dog," Finn exclaimed, throwing his hands into the air. "I'm tired of you all treating me like I'm on the verge of a breakdown all the time. I have zero fu—"

"All right," the dingo said with a shrug. "You asked for it... Siora doesn't have an aura."

Finn stared at him, his heart sinking. Deep down, he knew something was wrong, but he'd done the one thing he was best at, *ignoring it*. This time with an added side of 'hangry'.

The one glimmer of hope he'd had flickered, then went out entirely. After what'd happened at the Black Mountain, he'd hoped this was his chance at finally helping Siora free herself from her past. But if what Drew was saying was true, then she was damned and there was nothing anyone could do.

"We're not saying she's corrupted or anything," Hardy added a little too hastily, "or that she's not in control of her own actions. But you have a right to know."

"Me?" Finn scoffed. "It's not my life."

Drew scuffed the toe of his boot into the dirt. "I asked Vera to look into it, but—"

"Oh, so when Vera didn't do anything, you went

and whined to the vampire?" he exclaimed. "Thanks for having faith in me!"

"Finn, this isn't a slight against you," Hardy said. "With everything that's going on, we're worried about Siora's welfare." The vampire took a step towards him. "Being around the Old One in the state it's in can't be good for her."

"Maybe we should send her over to Lightning Ridge with Blue and Clarke, away from the corruption," Drew added. "Just until this thing is over."

They had a point, but if things went bad and Andante was still willing to take him when she left for her mysterious Darklands, then there wouldn't be time to grab Siora from Lightning Ridge. The town was over an hour away by car, and he barely knew how to change gears, let alone outrun the erasure of a universe.

But none of it was right. He was already losing faith in Eloise and Kyne, and he felt like a failure. His thoughts were a betrayal to them, to Soalce, and to the people he claimed were family. After all she'd done for him, especially after what he'd seen her do at the mountain, would he turn his back on her? On all of them?

"Let me talk to her," Finn murmured, his anger fading. "If she truly has no soul, then my magic will reveal it."

Drew winced. "I didn't want to say the S-word. It sounds..." He shrugged.

"Whatever," the fae drawled. "Don't follow me."

Hardy held up his hands. "Of course. You do what you've gotta do. Come find us when Siora's decided what she'd like to do. No judgement."

Finn nodded and turned to follow the trail she'd taken through the scrub. She was probably searching for treasure again.

All week she'd been collecting little flowers, little sprigs of all the outback plants, rocks, and other precious things. Curiously, all were absent of corruption, like some part of her remembered the magic she once held. Who knew why she wanted them, but if they made her happy, who was he to question it?

Finn found her amongst a copse of gum trees, the cream blouse Vera had given her billowing around her waist in the dry breeze.

She was picking gum leaves, scrunching them in her hand, then smelling the eucalyptus.

"Hey," he said, stepping into the shade beside her. "What have you found?"

"These leaves have a beautiful scent." She held out her hands. "Smell."

Finn cupped her hands and breathed in the potent eucalyptus, his lungs filling with the warmth of the bush. It was the perfect moment, so he let his magic flow down his arms, through his fingers, and reached towards her...but the delicate threads found nothing.

His gaze met hers and Siora dropped her hands,

her expression blank. Not even a hint of anger tainted her beautiful features.

When she'd kissed him, he'd assumed the feeling her touch evoked was the result of her absent memories. The Siora he'd once known had been reborn; thus she was an entirely new person.

But it was an assumption, not the truth, and the truth was too terrible to bear...so he'd ignored it without even knowing. And now, standing before her, he couldn't put it off any longer...and neither could she.

"Siora was never here," Finn whispered. "She died on that mountain."

"Only her memory remains," she whispered.

Drew was right—her soul was gone, *erased*—but he didn't suspect even a grain of the truth Finn now felt.

"You've made her body a shell," he murmured, tears welling in his eyes. "Why?"

"To see with eyes that were blinded."

"To judge?"

"This reality is full of selfishness," she replied, monotone. "It's ugly, wrong, and a blight. It must be eradicated."

Finn jerked away. "What? That's it? You're not even going to give us a chance to change your mind?"

"You had that chance, Finn," Siora replied. "For seven days, you've shown nothing but contempt for this reality. Given the opportunity to return to whence you came, even you would not save your family from their fate. Why should we spare them?”

“You would make me the spokesperson for an entire universe? I’m not even from here!” he scoffed and took another step back. “Either you’re completely daft or you planned it this way. Do you answer to a higher power, I wonder? Do you need to justify ripping a page out of the multi-verse? You went to the one person who’d tell you what you wanted to hear. You’re a real piece of work.”

“The decision was made long ago, Finn,” she replied. “We need no justification.”

“Well...” Finn called on his magic, opening the floodgates to his deeper power. “If you think this was going to be easy, then you’re sorely mistaken.”

Siora smiled, the motion twisted now that he knew what resided in her body. “We have existed longer than you can perceive, Finn. The only power you have in this place is the power we allow you to have.” She raised her hand and closed her fist, the motion cutting off the flow of magic to his body. “You are a parasite feeding off what you can never comprehend.”

Finn gasped and fell to his knees as she twisted the oxygen out of his lungs.

“We are beyond all that will ever be in this place,” she went on. “And knowing this, you still wish for them to be judged?”

Finn was not beyond begging in that moment. “*Please.*”

"Then you will *all* stand before us."

"Siora..." he managed to rasp, "I'm sorry... *I'm*—"

And all was black.

CHAPTER 18

The sun rose lazily over the Pilbara, lighting the cloudless sky to the first shades of midnight blue—bold tones that hid all but the brightest stars from the naked eye.

Kyne sat amongst his scattered belongings as he laced up his boots, seething.

Tossed out on my arse by a translucent woman. Not the smartest move, but at least I know she's lying.

The rough landing had made his bad leg flare up, and he rubbed his thigh, cursing. The wound he'd suffered during Siora's storm all those months ago had never quite healed. The fae's magic had suppressed his elemental abilities, and when that tree had fallen on him, it'd been impossible to get himself out of trouble. *Thank God for Finn.*

Looking out across the rugged terrain, knowing he was dozens of kilometres away from human habitation and separated from the love of his life, he felt a pang of loneliness so profound he felt his magic stir.

The reverberations fluttered through the earth, bumping against all the precious rocks and minerals hidden within the ochre stone. Gold, quartz, iron... they were just the tip of the iceberg, but none of them could help him find his way back to Eloise and the Celestials' hidey-hole.

They were up to something, and it had nothing to do with saving the universe, that he was sure of. Whatever it was, they needed Eloise, whereas he was disposable, like the rest of their so-called 'children'.

Kyne swallowed, his throat already dry and raspy. First, water. Then he could plot his next move against Ilyana.

His eyes focused as a shadow appeared behind him, the rising sun elongating the outline of a man. Jerking around, he saw Coen standing atop a rock, glowering down at him.

"You didn't let me in," the Indigenous man said.

"I didn't know we were supposed to."

"And so, the path winds," he mused, looking towards the rising sun.

Kyne blinked as the dawn illuminated the Indigenous man. He was sure he'd just seen colour play across his features and down his bare arms. Purples, blues, pinks, and greens, reminiscent of the shimmer on an oil spill or the inside of a precious shell. The same colours that—

"You're one of them," Kyne blurted, his eyes widening. "You're a Celestial."

He had to be—it'd explain *a lot*. His constant comings and goings, his tendency to disappear for long stretches of time, his knowledge of spiritual things, his interest in guiding Eloise.

"I was lost," Coen said, "but I remember now." He sat on the rock, propping one leg up and resting his arms on his knee, swinging his other foot lazily.

Kyne raised his eyebrows. "That's it?" He'd been waiting for more of an explanation.

"Is there more?"

"Uh, *yeah*. About forty thousand years more."

"Ah, you'd like a story." Coen grinned. Kyne knew how much the Indigenous man *loved* to tell stories, though he hoped this one made sense. "After our encounter with the Old Ones, I was separated from the other Celestials. I wandered, my memories fading until they were no more."

"So, what exactly have you been doing since thirty-eight thousand BC?" Kyne asked with a scowl. "Waiting for the Old One egg to hatch?"

"I've been on a walkabout for a long time," Coen murmured, ignoring the miner's irritation. "I've had many days and nights to learn the secrets of this world—the people who walk it, the magic it holds. Even the things I was capable of doing, as broken as I am." He held up his hand, but it wasn't like Ilyana's. It was solid, firmly placed in reality, and very human. "I didn't understand who I was, so I took on the form of the people I observed. Over time, I became part of their community, but they knew I wasn't like them and they were afraid."

"So, that's why you never wanted to live in town with us?" Kyne wondered.

He shrugged. "Now, more than any other time, I have been accepted amongst a community for who I was, despite what I may or may not be."

Kyne nodded, knowing it was Coen's quest to understand his past that had kept him on his path. His walkabout would only end when the Old Ones were gone, and perhaps not even then.

"If you had the chance to ascend again, would you?"

Coen smiled, his eyes holding the breath of the universe within them. "I came to love this country, and when I rediscovered the threat the Old Ones posed, I decided to do something about it."

He guessed the answer to his question was no, and unlike Ilyana's story, Coen's made sense. "Did you know about us?"

"I met many elementals and saw a familiar magic inside them, but you were the first who I believed may be able to help."

Kyne hesitated. "Me?"

"Yes."

"But then Eloise came along and..." He looked up,

suddenly realising how Eloise had truly come to be stranded in Solace. "Her van... That was *you*?"

"What is that phrase...?" Coen grinned, his eyes sparkling. "Happy accident?"

Kyne shook his head and sighed. Why had he never seen it until now? The Indigenous man had his fingers in all the pies, stirring and guiding them all on the path towards saving everything.

"Because you weren't ready," Coen said, reading his expression.

Kyne picked at a strand of dry grass, his emotions rolling around like they were stuck in a tumble dryer. So what now? He wasn't as broken as he thought he was? He didn't understand how it all worked, but Eloise was still the key, regardless.

"Your memories and Eloise's powers..." he murmured. "That's what all this was about?"

Coen nodded. "I knew I'd find the last of my locked memories when the Celestials let you and Eloise in. Now I know the truth, and the path ahead is clear."

"I'm glad one of us knows what to do," Kyne mumbled. "I found my way to the billabong twice now, but I don't think there's going to be a third. I practically told Ilyana where she could shove her half-truths. She didn't like that."

"What happened when they greeted you?"

"They almost threw us out again," he replied. "But when they saw the coral key, their tone changed. Though, the more I think about it, the more I wonder if it was my presence that clouded their judgement. As soon as they realised Eloise was there, they couldn't throw down the welcome mat fast enough." He looked up at Coen. "When they touched her, I felt their magic...but I don't think we felt the same thing."

Coen tilted his head to the side. "In what way?"

"The Celestials never reached out to me, but Eloise was holding my hand. Their magic flowed through her and into me, and it felt...wrong. It sounds strange, but it was porous, like a rock that'd been eroded by wind and rain over centuries—full of holes that were growing bigger and bigger. I wanted to wrench my hand away from hers, but I couldn't." He sighed, his brow creasing. "But Eloise seemed dazzled by them."

"Ilyana," Coen murmured.

Kyne's head snapped up. "You remember her?"

"Yes. I remember a great deal. Ilyana was always...headstrong."

"That's a nice way of putting it." The miner snorted and rolled his eyes. "She had a lot to say. I could see the holes in her story—she slipped up when she said they'd needed twelve Celestials to seal the Old Ones away—but Eloise overlooked all the red flags, believing my personal issues were clouding my judgement."

"Your judgement is not impaired," Coen stated. "I always suspected they never intended to finish our task. Sealing the Old Ones away was always going to be temporary, but they hoped an elemental would come forth one day to lead them home. Their plan has already taken forty thousand years to come to fruition, so they would not take any chances."

"Especially not with the Old Ones on the verge of breaking free."

"Especially not," Coen agreed.

"The ultimate smoke screen," Kyne muttered. "Unbroken enough to help them ascend…only to leave this reality on one hell of a countdown."

Their story finally had an explanation, but it was far from over. Eloise was bewitched by the Celestials, and if they got their way, they'd take her to a higher plane of existence, and everyone and everything in this reality would be left to face complete erasure.

Kyne's jaw tensed and he balled his hands into tight fists. They had to get her back.

But what if she doesn't want to come? a small voice said in the back of his mind. *What if her mind is clear, and she still chooses them?*

That's bullshit, he thought, pushing away his insecurities once and for all. He knew Eloise, and he knew the love they had. He knew her desire to save this universe was strong, and he knew how she loved their Exiled family back in Solace. She would never willingly abandon them to nothingness.

Kyne looked up at Coen, his resolve hardening. "How long do we have until she's out of our reach?"

"It's difficult to say… Eloise must make the final choice."

"Then we need to do something because she's being coerced into making it." Kyne pushed to his feet, his leg throbbing as he put weight on it. "The Celestials need twelve to ascend. Can you help them?"

"I cannot take Eloise's place," Coen shook his head, "nor would they accept me, even if I could."

"Why not?"

"It's not as simple as a choice for me. My abilities are not as fractured as theirs, but I am still impaired. I've spent too much time amongst humans—I like it here—but Ilyana sees it as a betrayal." So, they exiled him for it, locking him out of the billabong and denying him his memories.

For the first time, Kyne saw Coen through new eyes. He was no longer the carefree character who appeared out of thin air, laughing and making jokes, being shadowed by his constant companion *Marlu*. He was now an otherworldly figure, his power beyond anything any supernatural on Earth would ever possess. He'd seen the mysteries of the universe, existed as pure energy in a place beyond the pain and limitations of biological life. He'd known true peace. And if they failed, he'd cease to be with the rest of them, but still, he wanted to remain, no matter the outcome.

Kyne realised that he admired Coen, not for what he was, but for who he'd become as a result of his walkabout.

As the thoughts piled up in Kyne's mind in an

orderly fashion, Coen's smile widened, as if he knew what was happening. Finally, he stood and dusted off his tatty jeans. "Eloise is in danger. We must enter the gorge again."

Kyne grabbed his backpack as the Indigenous man hopped down off the rock and picked his way across the rough terrain.

"Can I just ask one thing...?" He waited until Coen turned before he spoke. "Did you know this would happen?

The Celestial nodded. "I needed my memories and Eloise needed to unlock her true power before we could face the Old Ones."

"That's why you needed us to let you into the billabong. So you could save us from Ilyana. You knew she'd try to use Eloise as the twelfth Celestial."

"There was no other way."

Kyne said nothing as he shouldered his backpack. He'd knowingly put them in danger, not even bothering to warn them.

Despite the betrayal he felt at Coen's deception, there was no rewinding time. He had to believe he had the power to bring Eloise back, and he was going to fight for her...no matter what.

"C'mon," Kyne said, nodding towards the horizon. "Let's go put a kink in Ilyana's forty-thousand-year-old master plan."

The first thing Eloise learned was that time meant nothing to the Celestials.

They were prepared to wait because there was no end to their lifespan. With one foot still in their ascended state, they could remain on Earth indefinitely, not bound by the same biological restraints she was. Food and water were curiosities, temperature was a novelty, and day and night were simple markers.

They had time to wait for someone like her to arrive—the elemental who was unbroken enough to join them.

Eloise stood beside the billabong, fixated on the magic Ilyana had awoken inside her. She now understood why they made her the way they did. She was the bright light that guided the lost through the darkness. The North Star. The Min Min. The Southern Cross. She was the bridge between worlds.

Make paths by walking... She scarcely remembered who'd told her that.

"Is this what I needed to learn?" Eloise wondered aloud. "My blood guided me here so I could become...*starlight?*" She felt silly saying it, but it was the only accurate word she could think of.

"This is the true purpose of the elementals," Ilyana told her. "Your journey is almost complete."

"I can save them," she whispered, staring at the pastel colours playing across her pale hands. "I can see. I can see where they are..."

"Yes, you can save *us*." The Celestial touched Eloise's shoulder, drawing her attention. "Twelve is a sacred number. To return home, we needed a twelfth."

"Me," Eloise whispered.

The Celestial nodded. "With your help, we can finally ascend."

Ascend? Eloise's heart skipped a beat. "But—"

"Eloise." Ilyana's pale hand cupped her cheek. "You will be saving our lives, creatures far beyond humanity, physical being, and reality itself. *Only you.*"

"I have the power to save you?" She looked around the billabong at the other Celestials—powerful creatures with a knowing beyond anyone who'd ever lived on Earth. "All of you?"

Ilyana nodded and held out her hand. "Come. Let me show you."

As the Celestials joined hands, she glanced over her shoulder. A hollow place opened in her heart and mind, and she wondered if there was supposed to be something that filled it.

People. Places. *A quest...*

The Celestial beside Eloise took her left hand as Ilyana took her right and her entire body went rigid. Their power flowed through her, her Celestial blood reaching out towards them.

This felt like home, like she finally belonged someplace. All the struggles she'd faced were melting away, their memory fading until none of it would matter.

Giddy from the rush of what she could only describe as star fire, she looked up at the circular opening in the rock and gasped. The brilliant blue sky shimmered and faded into a purple starscape.

"What's happening?" she asked, unable to tear her gaze away.

"We are ascending to the place between," Ilyana replied, tightening her grip on her hand. "Whatever you do, do not let go."

"Why not?"

"It will take time for all of us to follow you there."

"Oh..." Her mouth formed an 'O' as the limbo reality began to glimmer through the walls of the gorge. "Am I doing this?"

"We are doing this together, but you are our guiding light." The stars brightened, the silver points flaring. "This is the very fabric of the universe," the Celestial explained. "We must pass through it before reaching the higher realities."

"Higher realities...? You mean, there's more than one there, too?"

"Reality, perception, knowing, *being*... They are all layers within layers. No one knows how many there are, for there is no end. Everything is everywhere and every-when. There is no direction, no course to set."

An image flashed in Eloise's mind. A man and a creature walking on red earth under a sapphire sky. Was he a dream?

"Look," Ilyana murmured. "See what awaits you, Eloise. See your true potential."

She followed the Celestial's gaze, and through the shimmering starscape, another layer appeared...and she got her first glimpse of what lay beyond.

"It's beautiful," she whispered, tears filling her eyes. "It's so beautiful..."

CHAPTER 19

As Vera walked around the tiny town she'd come to know as home, a deep sadness filled her heart. Solace had transformed from a sleepy opal mining outpost to an eerie supernatural limbo, all in the span of a handful of weeks.

The giant boab by the *Outpost* was looking more grey than green, and its limbs had shrunken, each branch dropping off in section after section, until each had withered to nothing. The little pieces littered the ground like dark confetti, celebrating the coming downfall of their reality.

Vera's sandals crunched as she walked over the debris, her witch sense ringing out in alarm. There was nothing she could do about it, so she ignored the magic in her blood and continued her patrol. Her eyelids drooped with exhaustion, her shoulders ached, and her heart...well, her heart may as well be broken.

The corruption was taking its toll, not just on her, but on all of them.

Vera looked down the highway, towards a mirage that wobbled on the horizon, and sighed. All that was missing was a tumbleweed.

Drew was right—the corruption was progressing at an accelerated rate—but his revelation about Siora troubled her, too.

Vera could try to look inside her, to see if she had a soul, but the spell was complicated and often affected the caster just as much as the subject. It wasn't a pleasant thing to go through, but it wasn't the pain that kept most witches from performing it—it was the ethical connotations. A spell like that was tantamount to torture.

No, Siora had been through enough, and their current predicament wasn't going to override Vera's sense of right and wrong.

There were other ways of verifying the existence of Siora's soul, but it was the kind of witch-work that needed a full coven of twelve. Twelve was a sacred number; four sets of three to represent the four earthly elements. Rarely did they need the fifth to be represented by a witch, using talismans to complete their spells instead.

The Crescents wouldn't need a talisman or a coven of twelve, Vera thought. *If I were one, I'd be able to do it on my own.*

But she was a Brinewold, her link to the

Nightshade gone, along with her visions. Her connection to the element of water should be enough on any other day...except on the one she needed to stand against the Old Ones.

It seemed ironic to her that her blood carried elemental magic connected to water, and the thing that lived beneath them was referred to as the heart of the ocean. Maybe it had nothing to do with water at all; maybe it was simply what the people living here gave the entity when this land was coral reef.

As Vera continued to stroll around Solace, she considered that Siora might be corrupted like Drew had suggested. She had her own experience with the Black Mountain, and Siora had literally fallen into it. A concentrated dose might be to blame.

Her memories from her time as the Black Mountain's brainwashed soldier were hazy, muted, and far away. The more she tried to grasp at them, the further they retreated into her mind. Without her parents, or any living Nightshades, she had no way of knowing if it was the echo of the Old One causing it or the entity that'd plagued her father's bloodline for centuries.

Maybe that's what'd happened to Siora's soul. After being submerged in the Old One's essence for an entire month, it'd retreated so far within her that not even Drew could see it. If that was true, then it would come back in time...but maybe not in the space of a human life span. Siora's physical body could die before she regained it and then what? Was she doomed to never move on or be reborn?

It was cruel and—

Vera let out a yelp as she smacked into something hard. Rubbing her nose, she cursed and looked at the place the illusion was supposed to be.

There was nothing before her but open space. The highway snaked off into the distance, the trees fluttered in the slight breeze, and the hardy spinifex grass was as pointy as ever. Finn's illusion was doing its job, creating a wall between the outside world and—

"Oh God, please don't tell me…" Her heart clenched, sending a wave of nausea straight to her stomach.

Vera raised her hand and held it palm out. Moving one step towards the barrier, she held her breath, but nothing happened. She took another and her palm smooshed into an invisible wall.

Swallowing a pile of vomit, she pressed her other hand against the barrier and moved across the highway, hoping with every fibre of her being that it was an anomaly. But no matter how far she went, the result was still the same—Finn's illusion was now reality.

It had to be the corruption messing with his magic; there was no other explanation.

Vera wasn't a good runner. She'd avoided it ever since she'd left high school with its horrid compulsory physical education classes. No matter what she did, her arms flailed like wet noodles, and her entire class had teased her mercilessly. Crying in the toilets had become a weekly full stop on the torturous sentence that was educational mandated exercise.

But today, she ran.

By the time she'd made it across town and up the rise towards Finn's camp, her lungs burned.

"Finn!"

She flailed to a halt, sucking in painful breaths as sweat rolled down her spine. Her heart felt like it was nearly exploding every time it beat and her toes… She looked down and saw they were covered in a thick layer of red dust and stung like hell.

I'm never running again.

"Finn," she rasped, staggering the last few metres through the trees. "Finn! We've got a problem!"

When the fae didn't answer, she opened her mouth to curse at him, but the words died in her throat.

The camp looked like a whirlwind had torn it apart. The tent was half collapsed, coals from the fire were scattered across the clearing, and footprints and gouges filled almost every available space in the ochre sand.

"Finn?" she whispered, barely audible over her ragged breathing. "Siora?"

It was no use. The fae were gone.

Propping herself up against a tree, Vera cast out her magic. The steely blue of the Brinewold flared and spread out across the campsite, the tendrils of power filling the scuff marks in the earth.

When her spell was complete, and the last of it had left her body, electric blue light glimmered amongst the sand like a beacon, telling her *what* had happened.

It was unmistakeable, unforeseeable...and far too late to do anything about it.

The Old One had taken them.

No, no, no... They'd been so blind. They'd—

Vera's stomach rolled with a sharp pang of nausea and a fine sheen of sweat beaded across her forehead. She sensed a shadow looming behind her, and the corruption flared around her. The condensed burst of poison almost brought her to her knees, but she managed to regain control, the Brinewold calming the muddied waters.

"Siora," she whispered.

When she managed to turn, her gaze met Siora's, and she froze. The *De'ashlide* stood awkwardly, her expression blank, but her eyes were filled with a depth Vera couldn't comprehend.

"I came for you last," she said. "You were kind, Vera. If I could experience emotions like a human does, then perhaps I would regret my next action."

Vera raised her hand, her heart twisting. "Wait—"

But there was nothing she could do as her world went dark.

Kyne scrambled down a steep scree into the gorge—the third of the day—his boots slipping on the crumbling shale. He almost caused an avalanche with is uncoordinated descent, while Coen skipped and hopped all the way to the shady bottom. *Typical.*

"I think this is a good place," Coen declared.

"How do you know this is the right gorge?" Kyne asked as he dusted off his trousers. "There's a lot of them around."

He waved a hand. "Near enough is good enough."

"Well, that's reassuring."

"Now, let's open a door!"

"A door?" Kyne looked up at the ribbon of sky above. "How are we supposed to get in if Ilyana is blocking the way?"

Coen gestured for him to step closer. "I'm going to show you how."

"That'd be a first," he muttered.

"Call on your power," the Celestial said. "Keep it at the ready."

Kyne felt his elemental magic stir, the familiar threads he used to seek out opal amongst the earth coiling inside his body. "Okay. Now what?"

He had images of smashing their way through a wall of solid rock and running into the billabong, but Coen chuckled.

"Now you peel back the surface within," he said. "Your power travels deep paths inside. There is much more to discover around you than just the earth."

"You mean, I can be like her? I'm not broken?"

"This is the next stage of your journey," Coen told him. "All you need to do is take the first step."

"Sounds simple when you say it like that."

"Go." Coen nudged him towards the rock face. "Make paths by walking."

Kyne staggered forwards a step and sighed. *Walk?* Was it really that simple or was he too daft to see what was right in front of him? As usual, Coen was being vague and impossible. So much for showing him how.

He took a deep breath. Peel back the surface. Okay, *sure.* He knew how to use his magic to manipulate the earth, so all he had to do was focus on what he wanted to find.

Eloise.

The first time Kyne saw her, she'd been at Hardy's. That first glimpse had been a lock of golden hair and one blue eye.

Like a shy wallflower, she'd peeked around the edge of the workshop door, afraid of who she might see beyond. He'd not long been back from his first trip to the Pilbara and had lost his connection to his elemental abilities. He was angry, hurt, and lashed out at everyone...including her.

Then, when they'd gone down into Black Hole Mine together, when the roof had collapsed, Eloise was the one who'd reignited his magic. He didn't realise it at the time, but it was always her. She'd guided him back without even knowing it.

Kyne hadn't known the exact moment he'd fallen in love with her, but now he saw it as clear as day. It was in the dark, while his magic kept tonnes of rock from crushing them. It wasn't the life-or-death situation that had stirred his feelings; it was like calling like. Her path was intertwined with his. His Celestial blood knew it, and so did hers.

"I understand now," he murmured as his being peeled back and a new thread joined the others. The rock before him melted away, creating a window into the Celestials' sanctuary. "I'm coming, Eloise."

Kyne climbed through the window and Coen followed close behind.

The Celestials were gathered in a circle on the shore of the billabong, magic thick in the air. The rock faded in and out of sight—each time it disappeared, it was replaced with a purple-tinged night sky—and he knew...

They were leaving.

Kyne looked for Eloise, finding her amongst the Celestials, and the sight of her stole his breath.

Her hair had gone from golden blonde to silvery white, and her skin was translucent and shimmering with an oil slick of colour. She was becoming one of them, shedding her humanity.

As she became aware they were no longer alone, she turned and her gaze met his...but not one flicker of recognition flashed in her brilliant sapphire eyes.

"*Eloise,*" he whispered.

Ilyana whirled around, dropping Eloise's hand, and hissed as she laid eyes on Coen.

"*You*," she snarled.

"Hello!" Coen chortled. "Long time, no see."

"How dare you. You abandoned us long ago, and now you interrupt our one and only chance to ascend?"

The Celestial shook his head. "It's time to stop," he told her. "This is not the path."

"Thousands of years amongst humans has addled your magic," Ilyana spat. "You are not welcome here."

"Thousands of years confined to a hole in the outback has stagnated yours," he retorted. "I forgot many things, but you forgot the most important part...*on purpose*."

As the two Celestials argued, Kyne edged towards Eloise. Her gaze remained fixed on him, and she blinked, but the man beside her still grasped her hand. Whatever magic they were conjuring seemed to be confusing her.

They'd done the same thing to him—changed his memories, altered his perception. It was their meddling that had caused him to lose his connection to his elemental abilities in the first place. It was a violation, but what they were doing to her was far worse—Ilyana had taken her free will.

"*Eloise...*" He held out his hand and she hesitated.

The Celestial who held her snarled and jerked her back towards the circle.

Ilyana turned to him, Coen forgotten, and snatched Eloise's hand. "You will not take her. She has chosen to help us."

"Because you stole her memories," Kyne exclaimed. "You manipulated her from the very start. *I felt your magic.*"

"You cannot ascend while we are here," Coen reminded her. "I will stop it."

"There are twelve of us now," the Celestial said. "You can try, but you will never succeed."

"I don't think so." Coen smiled and nodded towards Kyne. "I brought back up."

Ilyana glared at the miner, and whatever she saw in him caused her to hesitate.

"Eloise must choose for herself," Coen went on. "It is how it has always been done. You know the uncertainty of ascending under duress, Ilyana. After all we have been through, you would risk it?"

The Celestial tensed, her eyes burning with furious blue ice, and she let go of Eloise's hand. The man to her right followed suit, and Eloise was free from their path to ascension.

Around them, the billabong settled back into its proper reality, the purple world beyond disappearing.

Kyne glanced at Coen, uncertain.

"Go to her," the Indigenous man murmured, touching his index finger to his throat.

He blinked and faced Eloise, conscious that twelve Celestials were staring at him. He had one chance to prove his love and bring her home. Everything hinged on this moment, and for the first time, he realised how hard her journey had truly been. The weight of an entire universe was crippling, but one thing shone through. *Love.*

Eloise stood before him, her Celestial form shimmering like pure starlight.

"Remember who you are," he murmured. "Remember why you came here. Remember what you're leaving behind. Then, make your choice." He cupped her translucent cheeks and pressed a kiss to her forehead. "Ilyana would make you forget everything, but it's only right that you should know the entire truth." Lowering his right hand, he pressed his thumb against the black opal hanging around her neck. "No matter what you decide, I will always love you, Eloise."

Kyne's elemental magic flowed into the stone, following the ripples of colour imbedded deep within the silica. It touched the edges of iron that gave the potch its black hue and ignited the rare, precious flashes of red, green, and purple.

The opal he'd dug out of the red heart of the outback. The opal she's shaped and polished. The opal their power had touched, and the opal that bound them together.

Her lips parted and golden strands shone through her translucent hair. Cream splotches welled up through her pearlescent skin. The blue ice of her eyes melted, and minuscule flecks of brown appeared around her inner irises.

"*Kyne?*"

"Yes," he said, the tears that'd been welling in his eyes spilling over. "I'm here."

She fell into his arms with a gasp, her shoulders heaving with silent sobs.

"I've got you." He held her close, their magic coiling together. "*I've got you.*"

"You lied to me," she whispered. For a moment, Kyne thought she was talking to him, but she extracted herself from his embrace and turned to face the Celestials. "You manipulated me."

"It had to be this way," Ilyana said, holding her head high. "There was no other way."

"Of course there was another way," Eloise exclaimed. She took a step towards them, her anger causing her Celestial magic to pop and fizz, the air exploding with tiny silver and gold fireworks around her body. "You could have helped us save this reality; then there would've been all the time in the world to help you ascend. But you were selfish, Ilyana. You would've condemned countless lives, worlds, and galaxies to nothingness."

"One grain of sand on the surface of a grain of sand," the Celestial said.

Eloise shook her head. "Not. To. *Me.*"

"We were twelves," she hissed. "One cannot stand against the power of the Old Ones."

"I am not alone." Eloise touched the opal. "*We* are going to finish what you failed to complete...and what you're too cowardly to face!"

"You cannot leave. *We will not allow it.*"

"Yes, we can," Kyne said. "Do you really want to try to stop us? It'll end badly, and no one will win. Is that what you want, Ilyana?" He looked at each of the Celestials. "Is that what *you all* want?"

"This is our last chance to go home." Ilyana held out her hands, palms facing up. "The Old One is breaking free, and when it does, we will not be here to suffer your fate, *elemental.*"

The Celestials formed a line, but even as their bodies flickered in and out of reality, Kyne sensed the buildup of power in the air around them. They'd made their choice.

Before they could unleash, Coen leapt in front of them and clapped his hands together. The snap of his palms sent a shockwave through the air and the Celestials staggered.

"Not today, my friends," he declared. "Stay in your hidey-hole!"

Whatever magic he'd used, it seemed to affect Eloise, too. She staggered backwards as the wave rolled over her, and Kyne grabbed her around the waist before she fell.

"I've got you," he murmured into her ear.

"Don't let go," she rasped.

"*Never.*"

A burst of golden magic illuminated her body as she reached for Coen. The Indigenous man turned and took her hand.

"There you are," he said, grinning from ear-to-ear. "Now, fly! Fly like Bunjil, the great eagle!"

Kyne gasped as the air left his lungs and the billabong spun away. He imagined he saw stars, galaxies, and nebulas right before they were sucked into a black hole—that felt more like water spiralling down a plughole—and were spat out into the balmy night air.

For the second time that day, Kyne was flung out of the billabong and into the Pilbara. But this time, he landed on his feet.

CHAPTER 20

Eloise fell back into Kyne's arms, utterly exhausted.

Dawn was still a few hours off and despite the sky being full of glowing stars, the night was dark. The moon hung low, barely a shard of silver on the horizon.

"Are you all right?" the miner asked.

"Yeah, I'm..." she trailed off, unable to finish her thought.

The miner helped her sit and squatted in front of her. "I guess you need another recharge, huh?" He rubbed his palms over her knees, his touch calming as his magic called out to hers. Somewhere along the way, Kyne's elemental abilities had grown.

"They took a lot of your energy to begin the ascension," Coen said, his voice soft in the darkness.

And she definitely felt it. "Where are we? Did we make it?"

There was a pause, then Kyne said, "Bloody hell. We're back at the lookout!"

"I tried to aim for the Troopy," Eloise murmured, pinching the bridge of her nose. The top of her skull felt tight with the onset of a tension headache to end all tension headaches.

"Well, I must say, your aim is impeccable. I was dreading the walk back."

"Me, too." Eloise laughed, the weight of the Celestials finally lifting off her shoulders, hopefully for good.

"Finally, a stroke of luck." Kyne held out his hand. "C'mon. Let's get you in the back where it's more comfortable." He helped her to her feet and the three of them crossed the gravel carpark.

As the miner slid off his backpack, retrieved the car keys, and opened the back door, Eloise realised she was carrying a little less weight than she ought to have been.

"Damn, I left my backpack behind," she moaned. "I'm going to have to replace my driver's licence and cancel my bank card."

"Somehow, I don't think Celestials are into identity theft," Kyne told her. "At least not in the same way humans are." The back door opened, and he helped her inside.

She sat on the back step, her legs swinging over the tailgate. "Yeah, but I'm more interested in some ibuprofen right now."

Kyne frowned. "Headache?"

"A major one." It didn't matter how much magic the Celestials had awoken in her, Eloise would always be part human, and that meant she'd be blessed with all the aches and pains that came along with it.

"Hang on. I've got some stashed in the first aid kit." A light came on inside the Troopy and he fussed in one of the storage compartments.

Coen stood just within the ring of light, shimmering colour playing across his dark skin. When her gaze met his, she knew all she needed to.

"All this time, huh?" she whispered.

Coen chuckled, looking a little sheepish. "I had to play a little trick. I hope you don't mind."

"I mind," Kyne said, handing Eloise two white pills and a bottle of water. "A little."

She felt...confused and disconcerted. The pull towards something beyond her reach had been strong, like she'd stood in the relentless current of a raging river. Something had held her steady, even as the Celestials held her hands. Was it her memory fighting back against Ilyana's deception? Eloise wasn't sure, but the one thing she did know was that the Celestials had inadvertently shown her what she needed to do when they got back to Solace. She just hoped the rest would come when her head ached less.

Kyne tapped her hand. "Get these into ya."

She downed the pills and chased them with water,

the motion giving her a moment to gather her thoughts.

"We have to get back as soon as we can," she told them. "I know what I need to do now, but I need both of you to stand with me."

"Of course," Kyne murmured, taking her hand. "There was never any doubt."

"I must remain for a short time," Coen stated. "I must be sure the other Celestials don't leave the billabong."

"Do you think they'll try to come after us?" Kyne asked.

"Maybe." The Celestial shrugged. "Ilyana covets Eloise. Both ascension and annihilation are within their grasp."

Eloise nodded. "Faced with total destruction, what would any of us do to survive?"

"Absolutely anything," Kyne whispered.

"Which is why I must linger." Coen looked towards the darkness beyond the ring of light. "I will join you as soon as I can."

As he took a step away, Eloise called out, "Coen?"

He paused and looked back at the elementals.

"Thank you," she told him. "For everything."

"You *see* now, Eloise Hart." Coen grinned and she felt his true magic greet her for the first time. "But there is still more to do." He backed away, melting into the night. "I will see you all soon."

And just like that, they were alone.

"You want to hit the road?" Kyne asked, his gaze still fixed on the spot where Coen had disappeared.

Eloise shrugged. They could travel the rivers to get to Solace in a matter of moments, but she needed a little time with Kyne first. He wasn't ready to walk those paths yet, and there were things she needed to help awaken inside him. Once they arrived within the boundaries of the Old One's corruption, there would be no going back. With so much at stake, she had to be sure they wouldn't fail.

Besides, she needed time to recharge her Celestial battery, and the arduous drive across Australia would be enough to do it.

"We both need rest," she said. "Let's set up the Troopy and get as much sleep as we can before morning. We can set off then."

"Are you sure?" he asked. "I thought you'd be keen to get back to Solace."

"I am, but I don't think either of us is up to saving the universe right now. Having power is one thing but using it at the right moment is another."

Kyne studied her for a moment, then smiled. "Sit tight. I'll get everything set up."

"Thanks. I reckon a light breeze would knock me over right about now."

As he stood, she caught her ghostly reflection in the back window and her heart stuttered.

She didn't look entirely human. Her eyes shone bright blue and her hair was streaked with clumps of white. Lifting her hands, she bit her bottom lip as a glimmer of pastel pink and lavender played across her skin. It was only a brief flash before it vanished beneath the surface, but it was enough to startle her.

She fiddled with the cap of the water bottle and drank some more, trying to keep her mind off what'd happened at the billabong.

"We're all set," Kyne said, hopping out of the Troopy. "Give me your foot."

She kicked up her right leg and he unlaced her boot.

She picked up a strand of her hair and glanced at him. "Kyne?"

His eyes narrowed slightly and he shrugged. "Don't worry about it," he said, pulling off her boot. "You're still the most beautiful woman I've ever seen."

She sighed as his words brought a faint smile to her lips and she brushed a finger across the opal hanging around her neck.

He looked up as her touch triggered their elemental connection. "Strange how things work, huh?"

"Strange doesn't even cover it."

Kyne focused on the long stretch of highway before the Troopy, his backside already aching. Flat, featureless land streaked by as they passed a speed limit sign that allowed them to hit 110 kilometres per hour.

Neither of them had slept as well as they'd hoped the night before. Kyne had never been the type to fall asleep easily, even though he could sleep anywhere—in a swag under the stars, underground in a dugout, in the back of a 4WD—his head was always stuffed full of a million and one thoughts.

Soon, the first signs they were coming up on Fitzroy Crossing appeared through the scrub. They wouldn't get back east without food or fuel, so even though going back the way they came felt like they were taking a giant leap in the wrong direction, it was a must.

Eloise sank back into the passenger seat with a sigh. She definitely looked half-Celestial with white streaks in her hair, patches of pearlescent skin, and shining blue eyes. When he pulled the Troopy into the service station, she opted to wait in the car.

Unlike the other Exiles, she'd have a hard time passing as 'normal' now. They might be able to explain her glowing eyes as contacts or a trick of the light, but her changing skin? Translucent hair that looked like fishing line? Long sleeves and a beanie weren't exactly outback-suitable attire.

As Kyne leaned against the 4WD waiting for the tank to fill, he caught her pulling the hood of her jumper up over her hair when a man walked past.

There was nothing they could do about it now. When they'd banished the Old Ones, they'd work it out.

Inside the service station, he stood at the counter, gazing at the display of chocolates and trashy magazines. After their adventures in the billabong, it felt strange to be amongst humanity. The mundane comings and goings seemed foreign. He'd almost forgotten how to pay with his credit card until the attendant coughed to get his attention.

Adding a couple of Cherry Ripes to the tally, he tapped his card and smiled before heading back to the Troopy.

"I got you a present," he said, holding out the chocolate bar as he closed the door behind him.

"*Aww*," Eloise cooed. "Icy poles in the esky and overpriced chocolate at the servo. I'm spoilt today."

"I'm spoiling myself, too." Kyne held up his own Cherry Ripe, the wrapper crinkling. "We both need a pick me up."

Her smile barely touched her lips as she raised her hand towards the opal at her neck, though she stopped short of touching it.

Kyne blinked and looked away. "Right, let's get on the road." He turned the key in the ignition, the engine roared, and he pulled away from the petrol bowser, turning east onto Highway 1.

They were an hour out of town when she roused. "Before we get to Solace, there's something you need to understand."

Kyne knew this conversation was coming. He wanted to ask her about what'd happened at the billabong, about her full powers as a Celestial, and what ascension felt like. When she'd stood against Ilyana, she'd been so powerful and...*breathtaking*. Despite their connection bringing her back, he'd felt powerless next to her.

"Kyne?" she asked. "What is it?"

He worried his bottom lip. "You said we had to stand together, but I don't see how I can."

"What do you mean?"

"Well, I don't want to state the obvious, but..." He frowned, fixing his sights on the road ahead. Finally, he sighed. "I managed to find you with Coen's help, but it was nothing. Not like the power I felt in you at the billabong, or even now. You're just sitting there, and I can—" He closed his mouth, his lips thinning. He didn't want to sound jealous or resentful of what she'd been through, but what if, when they finally stood before the Old Ones, his lack of Celestial magic was the reason they failed?

"Kyne, I get it, but—"

"I don't resent you," he murmured. "It's not that."

"I know." Her hand slid onto his thigh. "You're not like that; you never have been."

"You say I need to stand with you at the end, but I don't... I don't feel worthy."

"Kyne, there's nothing special about me. I'm no better than you or any other elemental. We all have the same equal potential to unlock all the elements. It's just my journey brought me there sooner than yours." She took his hand while the other tightened around the steering wheel. "You're closer than you think. Don't give up."

"Maybe I should pull over," he muttered.

"Maybe you should keep driving," Eloise replied. "You're not going to crash."

He sighed and glanced at the side of the road, but there was nowhere to safely stop anyway.

"What I went through at the billabong changed more than just my appearance," she told him. "It opened up a whole new world, one I hadn't seen before but have always been part of because of what I was born as. You are the same. No ifs, ands, or buts."

If what she was saying was true, then her journey took a lifetime. If they drove all the way through to Solace without a break, he only had another thirty hours to reach the same conclusion.

"Maybe I should pull over," he said, slowing the Troopy.

The 4WD bumped over the flat ground at the side of the highway, the tyres kicking up red dust behind them. In the distance, a semi-trailer approached, the sun glinting off the windscreen.

Eloise turned in the passenger seat and took his hands, peeling them off the steering wheel. "First, know that our elemental power doesn't come from the Earth. It comes from above, from a place beyond reality." Her magic called to his, and he was powerless as her golden threads wrapped around his silver. "We are born of it, and it flows through us. The elements are manipulated by the threads that bind the universe together." Their magic flared softly in response. "Ilyana may have had the wrong intentions, but she helped me understand that I wouldn't realise my true potential until I opened up to it. It's our humanity that holds us back—fear, indecision, hope, longing, self-consciousness. Until we let it go and find peace, we can never ascend...or be strong enough to stand against the Old Ones."

As her magic entwined with his, Kyne felt the memory of her path opening before him. When her powers had awoken, the moment she altered her parents' perception, her period of homelessness, her travels, her arrival in Solace, and the realisation that she wasn't alone. Eloise's entire journey had led her to a place of understanding and forgiveness.

Kyne understood now. Elemental magic came from another plane of existence—a higher place amongst the universe—but it had to be *earned*. They didn't come as a full package from the day of their birth, not like a witch, fae, or even a created being like a vampire or werewolf. Elementals unlocked their truth over time... through the journey of life. With deep spiritual understanding came magic.

"We're not broken, we're something new," Eloise went on. "Something different and unique. We are true elementals—supernaturals born of two worlds and belonging to only one. We're not broken; we never were. All that we are, is just as we're meant to be."

"We were created to give this reality a chance," he whispered. "But..." His gaze met hers. "We have to want it." That's why Coen was so vague with him about levelling up his magic. He couldn't just show him how; he had to find it for himself, otherwise it'd remain hidden forever.

"You understood when you and Coen found me at the billabong," Eloise told him. "You know it's there."

She was desperate for him to follow her, to understand their true purpose, and his breath caught. "You think if you do this alone...it'll kill you."

Her fingers slipped out of his. "They sent twelve Celestials, Kyne. *Twelve*. We don't have time to find another ten elementals and help them on their spiritual journeys. If I'm not enough—"

"We'll be enough," he interrupted. "When the time comes, I'll find a way to stand beside you." He turned the key in the ignition, revving the engine with renewed purpose.

Eloise straightened up. "I can drive."

"I can do both," he told her, checking for oncoming traffic. "You need to rest, and I need to think. Driving helps me think."

There were plenty of things Kyne needed to mull over—from his mother's death to his travels across Australia's opal fields, to his first meeting with the Celestials, and even his relationship with the Exiles. Eloise said he was close, and he'd proven that by finding the Celestials the first time, but there was something stopping him from taking the final step.

"Kyne?"

"Check the phone," he said. "It should be charged by now, but I don't think we'll get a steady signal until Halls Creek."

"Kyne?"

He glanced away from the road and raised an eyebrow. "I'll be okay. I have to do this part on my own." No one could put a time limit on a spiritual awakening, but here he was, doing just that.

"Okay." Eloise nodded and picked up his mobile phone from the centre console, the USB cable trailing into her lap. "But I can drive for a while, if you need me to."

"What if the cops pull us over? You don't have license, remember?" He managed a smile and rubbed his palm over her knee. "What a story that'd be... 'Sorry, officer, I left my driver's licence in a gorge with a bunch of celestial beings who wanted me to ascend to a higher plane of existence...'"

Eloise laughed, the sound lightening the mood in the Troopy as if the sun had emerged from behind brewing storm clouds. "You never know, they might be impressed enough by my creativity to let me off with a warning."

He chuckled and tossed her his unopened Cherry Ripe. "Here. You better eat that before it melts."

"You sure? You might want the sugar hit."

"Yeah, nah. I got it for you, anyway."

As the wrapper crinkled, Kyne turned his sights back on the path ahead.

He had thirty hours minimum to find the missing link, resolve it, and level up. Sounded simple enough, but the mountain he had to climb was steep. Not Mt. Everest kind of steep, but straight up vertical with no handholds, kind of steep.

All Kyne could do was drive and hope he was on the right path.

CHAPTER 21

E loise shifted in her seat, trying to ease the ache in her backside.

They'd been on the road for almost twenty hours. She was impressed by Kyne's stamina, but she knew it was his Celestial powers—with some added human adrenaline—that helped keep him awake.

The soft green glow of the instrument panel ghosted over his face as the yellowish headlights lit up the lonely highway ahead. She felt the warmth of his magic simmer just out of his reach, the final barrier between him and his full potential still intact, even though it was wafer-thin.

I wonder if he realises, she thought, gazing at him in the dark.

"I can feel you staring at me," he said, glancing at her out of the corner of his eye.

"I can't help it."

He cocked his eyebrow.

"It's...complicated."

"Oh, I'm sure it is." He reached over and rubbed her shoulder. "Are you feeling any better?"

"My arse is numb."

Kyne chuckled and settled back into the driver's seat. "Do you want me to pull over so you can stretch your legs?"

She moaned and rubbed her backside. "Five minutes can't hurt, right?"

Ahead, Kyne guided the Troopy into a pull out and killed the engine. Eloise picked up the mobile phone and slid out into the night, her knees feeling like rubber as she put weight on them.

Above, the sky was ablaze with stars, the great arm of the Milky Way stretching from horizon to horizon.

"It's really bright tonight," Kyne murmured, following her gaze. "I wonder... Is it calling out to you?"

"No," she replied, catching onto his thought. "I don't think it works like that. It's a place that can't be seen, not by human eyes." Eloise remembered the partial ascension back at the billabong, even though she still wasn't certain *what* she was looking at, she at least knew *where* it was. "I saw what lives beyond. Past the purple limbo world, to where they wanted to go."

Kyne continued to stare at the sky and said nothing.

"You don't want to know what I saw?"

"I don't think it's for us to know," he replied, surprising her. "Not until we're ready to go there."

Eloise turned and smiled up at him. In that moment, she'd never loved him more.

"We'll save this universe," she told him. "We will save it on our own, and when the Old Ones are gone, I'll find the others."

"The other who?"

"Elementals. I'll find them all and help them understand they don't have to be alone anymore. We'll be the ones to protect this universe, not the Celestials. They failed us all." Her thoughts moved to Coen. "All but one."

"All but one," Kyne echoed.

Eloise sighed and lifted the mobile phone. When she saw there were three bars of 3G reception, she let out a yelp. "We've got a signal!"

Her fingers fumbled across the screen before opening the contact list. She called Vera first.

Kyne hovered by her side as the line clicked and the call attempted to connect. Five seconds later, three beeps sounded, and the call cut out.

Eloise looked at the phone, frowning. They had signal, but maybe Vera's phone was turned off? She knew the witch hated voicemail, so it was never turned on.

"Nothing?" Kyne asked.

"It didn't even connect." She tapped back to the contact list and scrolled to Hardy's number.

"She could've turned it off," the miner offered.

"I don't think she would," Eloise said as the call

tried to connect to the vampire's phone. "They'd be waiting to hear from us...unless the corruption has progressed more than we thought it would." The call dropped out again, and she shook her head. "Nothing."

It was the same with Wally and Drew. The calls wouldn't connect to anything, let alone ring. Not even the ancient landlines at the garage or pub worked. No messages had come through to their mobile, either.

"It has to be the corruption," Kyne said, "or maybe Finn's illusion is interfering with the signal. Try Clarke. He should be in the Ridge."

She found his number and tapped it. Thankfully, it rang.

The line clicked and a frantic voice answered, "Hello?"

"Clarke? It's Eloise and Kyne," she said, turning the call on speaker.

"Eloise? Bloody hell, am I glad to hear your voice."

"Me, too," she said with a relieved sigh.

"I hope you've got good news."

"We're on our way back," she told him. "We're just about to cross into the Territory."

"Damn, you're still too far..." The line crackled and his voice broke in and out.

"Clarke?" She took a step towards the highway. "Clarke, are you still there?"

"I'm still here, but Eloise... We've got a big problem."

Her gaze moved to Kyne, who swallowed hard.

"What's going on over there? I tried to call Vera and the others, but the calls won't connect. Have you heard from them?"

"When you left, Vera promised she'd call every day to check in, but I haven't heard from her in three days."

The blood drained from Eloise's face as Kyne placed a hand on her shoulder. "What?"

"Blue and I have been trying to get into Solace, but we can't get past Finn's illusion," Clarke went on. "I don't know if it's because we're human or what, but nothing's coming out and nothing's getting in." The line crackled again. "Eloise, I'm worried. I don't know what to do. I'm not supernatural, I..."

"Clarke? It's Kyne." The miner leaned close to the phone. "Listen, we're on our way. Hang tight, okay? We're driving straight through."

"Straight through?" the sergeant exclaimed. "*Mate...*"

"You'd do the same."

"Clarke?" Eloise said. "We've got what we need to stop this thing, okay? We'll call you when we're close to Solace."

"God, I hope so," came his terrified voice.

"I know Vera," she told him. "She's strong, capable, and can handle herself. And she's got Drew looking out for her. I have faith in them."

"They'd have to get through Hardy first," Kyne added.

"Stay strong," she added. "Call us if anything happens, okay?"

"Will do." There was a pause. "Travel safe."

The line cut out and Eloise stared at the phone for a long moment, her focus only breaking when the screen turned off.

Kyne ran his hands over his face. "Three days?"

Eloise slipped the phone into her pocket. "The day we reached the billabong."

"They have to be connected," he went on. "Like the Old One knew where we were. What if we triggered something?"

"It doesn't matter now," she told him. "We have to get back to Solace and end this."

Kyne took a step towards the Troopy and caught his boot on a tuft of grass. He stumbled and let out a curse, his short temper giving away how tired he really was.

"Kyne," Eloise said, laying a hand on his arm, "let me drive for a while."

"But your magic is still depleted and—"

"I'm fine. It's more of an emotional exhaustion than a physical one. Besides…" she gestured to the Troopy, "I've got hundreds of hours of van-life driving experience. There's no one else more qualified."

He hesitated, then slipped the keys out of his pocket. "Your license?"

"Now isn't the time to worry about the law."

Then, for the first time since they'd left Solace, Kyne allowed her to take some of the human responsibility. She'd already asked him to take some of the Celestial equivalent, so she figured it all balanced out in the end.

"It's heavy in the arse," he told her, "and the clutch—"

"Kyne," she interrupted with a soft laugh. "I've got it. Now get in the car."

Wasting no time, Eloise climbed into the driver's side and slid the key into the ignition. Kyne opened the opposite door as she was adjusting the seat. *Man, he has long legs.*

"Better fasten your seatbelt," she declared as the engine roared into life. "I've got a lead foot."

Kyne had never travelled so far, so fast, in his entire life. The vastness of Australia was an illusion in itself, so it was no surprise neither of them were up to making the marathon drive all in one go.

When they reached Mt. Isa, it was clear neither of them could continue without falling asleep at the wheel. Even with their magic—and an energy drink or two—boosting their alertness, it was too dangerous, so they stayed over at a caravan park on the outskirts of the city. But as soon as they both felt refreshed enough, they were back on the asphalt for the last leg towards Solace.

Kyne may have felt the benefits of a few hours'

sleep, but after hours and hours of lonely outback highways, he was still no closer to unblocking the path to his latent Celestial abilities. He just couldn't seem to find the thing that was holding him back, and by the time they were on the home stretch, it was clear he wasn't going to make any earth-shattering revelations. They just had to hope he came through when the time came.

"It's okay," Eloise said as they passed the large green sign that told them it was six kilometres to Solace. "You did what you could."

"You should call Clarke," he replied, not wanting to talk about it.

"I should, but there's nothing he or Blue can do. I don't think we should worry them until we know more."

Kyne nodded. He'd been thinking the same thing. They'd both want to come out here and help, but they'd only get hurt once the magic started flying—guns and tea towels would be useless against the Old One.

"There's still a chance you'll unlock your powers," she added. "I know we're up against it, but I have faith."

"Eloise, I—" The words died in his throat as they finally reached the end of the road.

Kyne eased his foot off the accelerator and let the Troopy roll the last hundred metres, where the highway was blocked with bright orange barriers. Beyond that, Solace was gone, the town replaced with an enormous sinkhole that had to be at least fifty metres wide.

"Finn really did a good job with the illusion," he managed to say, pulling on the handbrake.

They got out of the 4WD and walked towards the barrier. Kyne could sense where the edge of the magic was, but as he passed through it, nothing changed.

He looked down into the hole and frowned. "It's real... The whole illusion is real."

It was as if Solace had been torn from their reality, and their friends along with it. No wonder none of their calls would connect. Kyne was certain if he stepped off the edge, he'd fall down into the Earth itself—if Finn'd had the foresight to conjure what the bottom of the hole looked like.

"I don't understand," Eloise murmured, following his gaze. "Finn's illusions can't be manifested this way. That's not how his magic works."

There was only one thing that could've gone wrong, and neither of them had to say it out loud.

"We need help from someone who specialises in opening doors between realities," Kyne said.

Eloise looked to the east. "Andante."

"The one and only." Kyne took her hand. "Let's go. Time's a wastin'."

They both knew the way, so they started walking due east, following the path towards the karsts where the old druidess had made her home.

It wasn't long before the rock formations

shimmered through the blue sky and the banded domes towered over them. Maybe it was because he was with Eloise—her Celestial powers had given them the ultimate short cut through the currents and into the pocket of reality the druidess had carved out for herself—or maybe it was because the druidess was expecting them.

Andante was waiting on the path, sitting atop a rock overlooking the entrance to the caves when they arrived within her pocket of space.

"I saw you even before you decided to come," the druidess said to Eloise. "It seems *you* found what you were looking for." She glanced at Kyne and narrowed her eyes.

"Still pleased to see me," he declared, cocking an eyebrow. "I'm flattered."

"You shouldn't be," Andante grunted. "Are you a glorified chauffeur or an elemental? I still cannot decide."

"*Andante,*" Eloise said before he could reply. "Finn's illusion around Solace—"

"I sensed a shift in the threads three days ago." She stood and made her way down to them, moving lithely for an old woman. "Some latent power within the town has closed it off from reality. I suspect Finn's magic was simply conveniently placed."

"Has the Old One broken free?" Kyne asked.

Andante shook her head. "If it was truly free, then none of us would exist."

"Then we still have time," Eloise said. "We have to get through the illusion and stop it."

The druidess stood before the elementals and studied Eloise before turning to Kyne. "No."

"What do you mean, no?" Kyne demanded.

"You're not ready."

The miner's heart sank. He'd been hearing the same thing over and over. *You're not good enough. You're too broken. You're not ready.*

"After all you have seen, after all you have known..." Andante shook her head and rolled her eyes.

"I know you've never liked me," Kyne snapped. "Now's not the time for reminders."

"You are *still* blind." Andante flicked his forehead, the tip of her finger stinging against his skin. "What's the hold up?"

He flinched and scowled. "I've been trying!"

"Not hard enough, boy."

"Andante—" Eloise began, but the druidess held up her hand, silencing her.

"We are out of time. The path must end here." Threads of glowing blue magic grew in her palms, twisting into geometric shapes with sharp corners.

Always with the threads, he thought.

Andante held up her hands, angling the shining shapes at him. "It's time to wipe the shit out of your eyes and slap some sense into you, *boy*."

"Excuse me?" Kyne exclaimed. "Did you just say what I think you did?"

The old woman clucked her tongue. "He hears, but he does not *listen*. He watches, but he does not *see*." She lunged towards him, moving fast for such an ancient woman, and slapped her hand on his head. Her palm connected with is forehead and her magic shape blasted into his skull.

Kyne fell to his knees, his eyes widening as the druidess's power threaded into his mind.

"Andante!" Eloise cried. "What the hell?"

"*See*, Kyne Brady," she whispered. "Reach out and find your way."

The world tilted and went dark, then...

"Kyne." Fingers brushed his hair, the touch so gentle he almost didn't feel it. "Kyne, sweetheart..."

"Huh?" Stirring, he lifted his head, the rough blanket scratching against his cheek.

Through the blur, a white and turquoise room came into focus. Electronic beeps keeping time, murmurings from the hall, the faint sound of a name being paged over the intercom, the rattle of the dinner cart, a closing door. And that smell...antiseptic, medicine, and sickness.

He remembered this place.

Hospice.

"You fall asleep more than I do," a female voice murmured.

Kyne blinked and stared down at the woman lying beside him. "Mum?"

The chair was pulled up to her bedside as close as

he could manage it, the tubes and wires feeding into her twisted in an elaborate pattern around them. She lay in the centre of the bed, her cancer-ravaged body tiny and frail.

Her beautiful black locks had long fallen out from chemo and had barely had time to grow back, but he smoothed his hand over her cheek anyway, straightening the wisps of hair around her ear. Sunken blue eyes stared up at him and the ghost of a smile appeared on her lips.

This wasn't how he wanted to remember her, but he couldn't leave. She was all he had.

"You're eighteen now, Kyne," she whispered. "You're old enough to go out into the world."

"But it isn't fair," he said. "You should be with me."

"I know, sweetheart. Life can be cruel."

"I..." he trailed off, not wanting her to see him cry.

"I know you blame yourself," she told him, "but it wasn't your fault. There was nothing you could've done."

"Yeah, there was. There was plenty—"

"I never told you," she swallowed, the motion difficult, "but I named you after your father."

Kyne's eyes widened. "M-my father?"

"He was special." She sighed, the effort of the simple act of speech sapping her strength. "He chose me...to create you."

His Celestial father? How had he never remembered this conversation? Kyne tensed, his grip tightening around his mother's hand. It was another memory they took from him, it had to be.

"You're special, Kyne. So very special..." Her eyes drooped and he felt her grip on his hand slacken.

Tears filled his eyes. "Mum?"

"Don't... Don't be afraid..."

Kyne's heart sped up and he looked for the call button to summon the nurse.

His mother opened her eyes and reached towards him. "I knew. I knew this was the price, but I never forgot...even though...they tried..."

"Forgot what?"

"You have a destiny," she whispered, her eyes drooping again. "You only have to reach for it... Don't... *Don't let...*"

Her hand went limp, and Kyne leaned over her. "Mum?" When she didn't respond, he shook her shoulder. "*Mum?*"

She was gone.

"No," he whispered, tears streaming down his face. "*No.*"

The ground began to shake as he held onto his mother, then the equipment around the bed shook. Lost in his grief, he barely registered when the world began to jerk violently, the floor rippling outwards like waves in the ocean.

"Kyne!"

He looked up as the room faded around him, the white and turquoise walls shattering to reveal a dark purple-tinted landscape. The sky opened up, billions of silver stars igniting across the blackness, and he felt warm golden light wrap around his body. His Celestial side was waking up.

"Kyne!" the voice cried again.

"Eloise." He reached out into the darkness, his threads growing inside him.

"About time," Andante said, looking down at them.

Kyne blinked, the motion snapping him out of the vision.

Eloise was on her knees, her arms wrapped around his neck. "You made the whole place shake," she murmured.

"I saw..." He glanced up at Andante, but it was Eloise who replied.

"Your mother," she said, drawing back so she could look at him, and he knew her blue eyes mirrored his now.

That moment, when his mother had passed, was the thing holding him back. It'd been taken, twisted, and purposely blocked. Why would the Celestials do that to him?

Because they knew he'd never truly processed the trauma of that day. Because his mother was never meant to remember. Because he wasn't meant to *know* before his time. His path to the billabong hadn't *conformed*.

"I blamed myself," he said, staring into nothingness. "I blamed myself for her death. I-I should've seen that she was sick earlier. I should've..."

"It was never your fault," Andante told him. "It was the price they made her pay."

"Cancer?" Eloise asked. "The Celestials had children with human women, and they all...?"

"Unknown," the druidess told her, "but entirely possible."

"Life can be cruel," Kyne whispered, echoing his mother's words.

Andante looked towards the west, where Solace lay behind the solid illusion. "Whether they knew or not, or if all suffered the same fate, is irrelevant now. There will be no more Celestial-hybrids born after today."

Kyne grasped Eloise's thighs, lost in the turmoil of his awakening and the memories the vision had restored.

"I suppressed my grief," he murmured. "I'd never faced it. That's why they took it from me. I wasn't ready to realise my full powers...and they believed I never would be." The Celestials had blocked him from his birthright forever, until Andante had come along and shoved him through the proverbial brick wall. He never would have found it on his own. Was this irony? Sure felt like it.

"And now you have faced it," the druidess said. "And after all you have seen and felt since, you have survived."

Kyne lifted his hands, his breath catching as he saw

the shimmers of colour breaking through years of outback tanning. He looked at Eloise, his eyes meeting her iridescent blue, and he saw…

He saw *everything*.

"I see it now," Eloise said, tracing her fingers over Kyne's features. "Can you feel it?"

"Is that…?" he asked, reaching out to touch the threads of the universe. A river flowed around them, brushing against his skin like cool water seeping down from a mountaintop.

"The currents," she told him.

"I get it now." Kyne could hardly contain his elemental magic. He wanted to see it all, to hear, touch, taste, feel… "I get—"

Andante coughed, drawing them apart.

"I will help you break through the illusion," the druidess told them. "But we must go now. The wanderer has arrived."

Kyne frowned. "Wanderer?"

"Coen," Eloise said, her eyes lighting up. "Coen is back."

CHAPTER 22

Vera Walsh was in a goop-load of trouble—tied to a chair, sitting in a circle with her closest friends, imprisoned by a maniacal tentacle monster.

It'd been easy to hunt them all down. No one had suspected Siora except for Drew, and by the time Vera had realised the truth, she couldn't do anything about it.

Siora stood in the centre of the circle, her hands outstretched. Her eyes had turned completely black as the Old One manifested whatever crazy tentacle monster magic it needed to 'judge' them, which was as unpleasantly invasive as it sounded—all any of them experienced was a great deal of pain as she bore into their minds.

She'd also solidified Finn's illusion, trapping them inside an increasingly corrupted Solace.

Things had gone from bad to completely screwed in T-Minus a trillionth of a second. Their only hope was that Kyne and Eloise had found what they needed in the Pilbara and got back in time to stop Siora from hitting the delete key.

Why am I still calling her Siora? she thought. *Do Old Ones even have names?*

Vera tugged against the magic binding her wrists and ankles, but after an unknown number of days, it still held strong. It was no use fighting an Old One, at least not on a level playing field.

As a witch, she was brought up with the notion of working with the powers of the universe, that fate was fate and there was nothing anyone could do to change what the higher powers willed. Considering where she was now, it was a pretty useless teaching.

Drew moved in his chair and grimaced. "How long is she going to keep us here? I've got a numb arse."

"Hopefully, a long time," Vera replied.

"I feel like we're at one of those group therapy meeting," he went on. "Hi, my name is Drew, and I have anger issues."

"He finally admits it," Hardy muttered, who looked a little grey. Vera knew he hadn't had any blood in a while and was starting to desiccate.

"The lights are off, we're sitting in a circle in a pub..." The shifter narrowed his eyes and nodded towards the bar. "It's inappropriate to hold an AA meeting in a bar."

"My bones ache," Wally muttered.

"My veins feel like sandpaper," Hardy rasped.

"Since we're comparing ailments," Finn moaned, his head lolling, "I'm devolving into old boot leather."

"*Shh*," Vera hissed, glancing up at Siora. "Now's not the time to complain. We're representing an entire universe."

Drew snorted. "If we're the representatives, then we're fu—"

"*Drew*."

Siora's eyes snapped open, and she spun around.

"Uh-oh," the shifter muttered.

"I have seen," the Old One proclaimed, looking at each of them.

"*Finally*," Finn drawled. She hadn't said a word in hours, let alone moved.

Siora didn't seem to hear him. "I have watched your corruption grow, spreading across this planet and ruining everything you touch. Soon, your kind will find a way to reach the stars and spread your vile populace across the galaxy...and in time, it will devour *all*. Corruption must be cut out and destroyed."

"Funny, we think the same thing about you," Drew muttered.

"You." Siora pointed at Wally, who jerked back in his chair. "Your curse was made by corruptible supernatural humans."

"You." She turned to Hardy. "You are a product of corruption. You were made by the magic gifted to humans by the Celestials—a curse that spread from another reality. Perhaps one we should see for ourselves…"

Drew raised his eyebrows. "Celestials? What are—"

"*You.*" Her gaze fell onto the shifter. "Your spirit creature comes from something much older than the Celestials, but your humanity corrupts you."

Vera tensed, waiting for her assessment, even though she knew what it was going to be.

"You." Siora stared down at her. "You are born a witch, but you are still human. Therefore—"

"Yeah, yeah," Drew said, "we get it. *Corruptible.*"

"Technically, she said I wasn't corrupted," Wally said. "Just the people who made the werewolf curse."

"I don't think it matters," Hardy told him.

Vera sighed, her heart heavy. Hardy was right. Vampires, witches, werewolves, and anything with a human element had the potential to be corrupted, which meant they were all candidates for deletion. The Old One in the Black Mountain had known it all along, which is why it'd used them to help break the seals.

Honestly, she didn't think they had much of a chance at saving the universe. All of this was just buying time for Eloise to sweep in with her elemental magic and kick the Old Ones out for good.

Siora turned to Finn. "You are the closest thing to being pure in this world." She held out her hand to him and smiled. "We tried to corrupt you, but you resisted. If you choose, you may take our power."

The fae rolled his eyes. "I think I'll pass."

"So, you've deemed us all corruptible," Vera said. "Is that it? Is that your judgement?"

Siora looked down at her, her eyes eerily black. "You have more to say?"

"You've only looked at our potential," the witch went on, "but it says nothing for our actions. All living things are capable of evil, but it doesn't mean it's inevitable."

The Old One stood unblinking, her expression a wall of nothingness. Whatever effect this statement had on her thinking was unknown.

"Who will speak for you?"

"Eloise," Vera replied. It was worth a shot.

"Eloise is not here."

"Then I will."

"Very well." Siora reached out towards her. "Convince us."

"*Wait*," Drew hissed.

The Old One froze, her disembodied stare turning to the shifter.

"Remember what Andante said," Hardy murmured to Vera. "They don't care about us. They have no emotions. There's only one way this can end." *All-out war.*

"Then we have to hope Eloise and Kyne are on their way," Vera whispered. "And buy them some more time."

Drew jerked against the magic holding his wrists. "What are you saying?"

"I'm the least corruptible," she told them. "Without the Nightshade, there's only a slight chance the Old One can—"

"Vera," the shifter snapped.

"She's right," Hardy murmured. "She's the only one."

"*She can hear us*," Wally muttered.

"Mate," Drew said, "it doesn't matter. I reckon she knows what we ate for breakfast a week ago."

Hardy tried to raise his hand, but the magical binding stopped him. "Vera..."

"We made a vow a long time ago," she said, looking at each of the Exiles in turn. "We can't back down now."

Finn lifted his head. "It's been an honour, witch. *Rilae...*"

"I want to say something, but I was never good at this kind of thing," Wally told her.

"You don't have to say anything," she replied. "*I know.*"

Hardy nodded, but Drew... Vera was surprised to see tears in his eyes.

"May we meet again," she whispered, knowing nothing was on the other side of erasure.

Siora held out her hand and the magic binding Vera to the chair faded.

"Come," the Old One said. "Stand at the precipice and see truth manifest. It is time to speak for all."

When Eloise, Kyne, and Andante arrived at Solace, Coen was waiting for them.

"Hooray!" he cried as he laid eyes on the miner. "You can see!"

"And not a moment too soon," he said, glowering at Andante.

The druidess raised her eyebrows at the Celestial and clucked her tongue. "Your kind loves to meddle, but you are unlike any Celestial I've ever met."

Eloise hesitated and looked at Kyne, her eyes wide.

"I have a feeling druids are just as bad as Celestials," he whispered into her ear. "Best not to ask too many questions."

"Are you okay?" Eloise asked Coen. "What happened at the billabong?"

"The Celestials are contained within their sanctuary. Ilyana knows she can no longer reach you and has anticipated Kyne's awakening. They will not interrupt our work here—their fate is now bound to this reality."

"And *Marlu*?" The kangaroo had been a rare sight in the last month, and she'd been secretly hoping to see her one last time before the final battle.

"*Marlu* is with her joey," Coen replied. "I asked her to keep a safe distance. This is not a place for a kangaroo this evening."

Eloise nodded and turned to the illusion. When

they'd left for the Pilbara, she could feel the corruption touching everything. She couldn't see it then, but the sense of its poison was everywhere—in the earth, the water, the air, even the plants had begun to wither. Now, it was all contained behind the barrier.

"What do you think is happening in there?" she wondered.

"Judgement," Andante replied.

"*Judgement*," she whispered, her eyes widening. She couldn't even imagine what was happening to her friends or what 'judgement' from the Old Ones entailed. All she knew was that their task hadn't changed.

"Do you think you can break through?" Kyne asked.

"Let me see." Andante approached the illusion, her hands stretched out in front of her. Tiny sparks of her druid magic glowed on her fingertips as she sought out the edges of Finn's spell. When she found it, she tested the limits, her hands passing back and forth through the magical barrier. "It is complex and will take time, but I am confident I can create a path."

Eloise heaved a sigh of relief but was conflicted. "Are you sure you want to help us?" she asked. "I know you're risking a lot considering the covenant your people made with the Old Ones."

Her response was clipped. "It is the right thing to do."

"Please don't misunderstand," she said. "We're thankful for your help, it's just..."

"When it comes time for me to walk the Darklands in search of my homeland, the Old Ones will judge me. They'll likely find me unworthy, and I'll become a shadow, but that is a risk I'm prepared to take."

"A shadow like the ones I saw at the mountain?" Her thoughts drew her to the kadaitcha that'd plagued Solace and wondered if the vengeful spirits were the same thing—souls the Old One's had deemed 'unworthy'.

Andante lowered her hands and turned. "The shadows guard the Old Ones. Given enough time, they will do so here, so we must be vigilant."

Eloise nodded, wondering if the fae that'd turned into darkness at the mountain were deemed 'unworthy'. Only Siora had remained as she was.

"I still worry about you," she murmured. "I don't want to see you hurt."

"Eloise." The druidess had rarely said her name, so it sounded strange to hear it now. "I'm an old woman, not only to humans but to the druids. I have spent my life turning away from my responsibilities. All I can do now is try to find absolution in my final acts. My path led me here for a reason, and while fate can be cruel, it is what it is." Her gaze shifted to Kyne, who'd hung back as they'd begun to talk. "The animosity I felt towards you was misplaced," she told him. "It frustrated me that you could not see what was within your grasp. Now I understand that you were blinded against your will. I should have helped you see instead of turning you away."

The miner blinked in astonishment, his blue eyes shining. "Thank you."

"Now," the druidess turned to the barrier, "I have much to do. Please guard my back whilst I work." She raised her hands and pulled several threads out of thin air and began to weave. Each strand shimmered with purplish-blue light as they began to form simple shapes, then flared as they became more complicated.

"Her magic is rooted in the sacred geometry of nature," Coen told the elementals. "It is beautiful, don't you think?"

Eloise nodded. "I scarcely understand how it all works."

Coen chuckled. "Not everything is for understanding. There has to be some mystery or physical reality would be boring."

"The thrill of discovery is the spice of life," Kyne stated.

"Now is the time to rest and prepare," the Celestial said. "Watch the shadows, for they will lengthen before we cross into Solace."

As Coen wandered into the scrub at the side of the highway, Eloise and Kyne leaned against the bull bar on the front of the Troopy, watching Andante work. The road was silent and the outback was still, except for the soft hiss of the wind as it rushed over the plain.

"I reckon this might take a while," Kyne said. "We should crack out the camp chairs."

Eloise didn't care for sitting right then; she was too amped up. "What do you think we'll face in there?"

"Nothing good."

"The coral key kept the goop away," she mused. "But it's in my backpack...which I left at the billabong." Another casualty of the Celestials.

"No," Kyne told her. "It's in mine, in the back of the Troopy."

She pushed off the bull bar. "What?"

"I didn't trust Ilyana, so put it there when you were...*you know*."

Her heart leapt and she nudged him towards the Troopy. "Go get it then!"

Kyne chuckled and disappeared around the back of the 4WD. When he returned, he offered the flat circle to her.

Eloise grasped it and held the key to her chest, taking comfort that they at least had something she knew would definitely help them once they were inside Solace. Spiritual magic was so ambiguous, trying to wrap her head around the concept was giving her a migraine.

In that moment, she longed for Vera. The witch would know how to explain it.

"I'm afraid," she whispered as Kyne wrapped his arm around her. His warmth seeped into her body and their magic began to entwine. "What if they're already gone?"

"Don't dwell on the what if's," he murmured. "Have faith in the strength of our family."

Eloise sighed and leaned her head against his shoulder...and that was how they waited.

As the sun set and the shadows lengthened, Kyne got the lantern from the Troopy and set it on the road. The globe was one of those intense white LEDs that charged with a solar panel on the side. It cast a glow that spanned the width of the highway and misted the bordering scrub with a ghostly glow.

"It's so dark," Eloise murmured. She didn't mind the dark when she was in it; the creeps only came over her when she was within a ring of light that washed out the shadows outside it. The thought of not knowing what lurked beyond was the thing that got her, and now that she knew the kadaitcha could return, it creeped her out even more.

"It's a new moon tonight," Kyne said. "And clouds are gathering, blotting out the stars."

"No," Coen declared, "they are not clouds. The Old One casts a curtain...see?" He swept a hand out in front of him and the shadows wavered as if they'd turned into thick mist. If it weren't for the lamp, Eloise had the feeling they'd be swimming in it.

"The corruption is seeping through the illusion," she said.

"Soon the lantern will not be enough," Coen confirmed. "Andante will need our help then."

The mist was the prelude to the arrival of the shadows. When they were close to breaking through, the Old One would try to stop them from passing into Solace, using the 'unworthy' to do it.

"What's that?" Kyne asked suddenly.

Her heart twisted and she turned to the dark. "What's what?"

"There." Kyne pointed. "On the horizon."

Through the gloom, two points of light began to ebb somewhere off in the distance. They were blurry at first, mere smudges, then they started to grow.

"It's the Min Min," Coen said, grinning. "The spirits have come to help."

"The Min Min are spirits?" Eloise asked.

He nodded. "They are ancient voices of the land. Their song can be heard if you listen closely enough."

Kyne shifted, angling his body in front of Eloise. "Are they here to help?"

"Corruption cannot touch pure light," she told him, but how she knew was a mystery.

"We do not stand alone," Coen told them. "The few that can have come."

And it was definitely a few. Two awoken elementals, a descended Celestial, the Min Min, and a druidess were all that stood between the Old Ones and total destruction.

The shadows began to stir, and Eloise jerked

towards the north, the white strip in the centre of the highway fading into utter blackness...but she knew the night wasn't empty.

"They're coming," she whispered, grasping Kyne's hand. "*It's starting.*"

CHAPTER 23

Siora grabbed Vera's hand and pulled.

The witch's breath caught as the pub dissolved around her, the walls melting to reveal a nightmarish, blackened landscape beyond.

It was Solace—all the pieces were there, from Wally's garage across the highway, to Hardy's opal shop, and the *Outpost* beyond—but it'd been ripped from reality and placed inside a bubble of corruption.

The sky shone with silver stars and the great arm of the Milky Way arced from horizon to horizon, but the points hung on a sheet of total darkness. The ochre dirt was reduced to the colour of charcoal, and even the gum trees had turned into greyscale nightmares, their trunks growing strange, dark crystalline scales.

Vera ripped her hand out of Siora's and stepped out of the ruins of Blue's pub. It wasn't actually destroyed —what remained of the structure flickered like digital interference on a TV as she moved through the wall and into the yard. One step took her five paces, the next brought her back two, but she found her mark on the third.

"This is a place few creatures are permitted to see," the Old One said. "Behold." She swept her hand at the sky, which came alive with a swarm of blackened vines that oozed from the dark places between the stars.

Vera recoiled, her mouth falling open in horror as she realised what she was looking at. There were *millions* of them—countless entities that resided in a higher layer of reality, beyond anything she ever dreamed might exist.

"What is this place?" she managed to ask.

"Solace now sits in a place between," the Old One replied. "A single leaf of paper laid over countless universes, a page turn away from the higher place where we reside."

"Finn's illusion," she whispered. They'd been trapped in a twisted snow globe where they were the day's entertainment. Gladiators in a spiritual battle, where the victor would win the right to exist.

"It was an unexpected occurrence, but one we can use to our advantage, trapped as we are." The entity swept her hand through the air and the landscape began to waver. "This will serve as the place of judgement, as it has for countless others."

Solace faded behind the ripples and a new vision took shape, seamlessly merging with reality.

Vera blinked, her mind taking a moment to

perceive where they were...but it didn't take long. This place was intimately familiar to her.

They stood in her parents' living room back in Ireland, but it stood in disarray. The couches had been pushed back against the wall and the curtains drawn so the glow from dozens of candles could light the sacred space drawn within. A thick salt circle lay on the floorboards and a variety of crystals dotted through the complex sigil within...but it was what overlaid it all that still haunted Vera to this day.

Blood, chaos, and carnage.

Even though she'd let it go and made her peace with those who had inflicted it on her, there would always be a part of her legacy that would regret what'd happened to her family and coven that day.

A craglorn—a magic-starved fae—had killed them whilst they were in the circle, bleeding them dry of magic until it'd ripped them apart. They knew the risks of using their power, but they'd been attempting to suppress the Nightshade who'd taken up residence inside Vera. The evil entity driven by a curse that leapt from generation to generation in order to survive. It was the ultimate family curse.

Unable to dispel it entirely, the coven had opted to suppress it with magic.

That day, the spell was successful—the Nightshade had only resurfaced when the mountain corrupted her —but her family had paid the price. A whole coven for one witch. It hardly seemed like a fair trade.

In the end, all she had to do was let it go…but it'd taken half her magic with it. Her Nightshade legacy was no more, and because she was the last of the bloodline, the entity had nowhere to go. Thus, it was gone.

If her family still lived, then it would've simply jumped to one of them, and the mountain would've used them to break the seal. It couldn't have happened any other way…and knowing what she knew now, Vera would make it again without hesitation.

"How…" She turned away from the carnage and glared at the Old One. "Are you reading my memories?"

"No." Her smile widened, which was creepy considering they weren't supposed to have emotions. "We see all. We know all."

"I see," Vera muttered, her eyes narrowing. The Old Ones were more connected than they'd realised. They seemed to be separate entities but existed as a hive mind—every experience was experienced as one. Everything that'd happened with the mountain, Siora was aware of. That's how she knew all about the Nightshade.

"Is this how I will be judged?" she went on. "How I reacted to my family's murder? The circumstances of their death? The things I've done since?"

Siora grabbed her arm and wrenched her around, her fingernails biting into her flesh. "*Look.*"

Vera tried to wrench away from the Old One but

was held firm. She had no power in this place, only her words would help now.

"I don't want to look,'" she rasped.

"*You must.*"

Vera held her breath as she looked down at the remains of her family. There wasn't much left of the Brinewold coven, which included her mother and her Nightshade father.

"This was the fae," Siora said. "They sent their exiled here to devolve. Your world was their prison."

"And?" Vera blinked and shook her head. She was flagging but being magically lashed to a chair for an unknown amount of time would do that to a person.

"No one would blame you for hating them. Look what they did." She gestured to the carnage.

"I made my peace with what happened to them a long time ago," Vera hissed. "All you're doing is trying to trick me into saying something that will damn us all. I won't allow it."

"Did you know Finn had plotted with the druid to leave this world behind? If things became unsalvageable, he was going to take Siora and leave you all behind."

"He chose us," Vera spat. "He's sitting with us in the pub right now."

"Only because we took the choice away from him." Her smirk widened. "If he cannot return to his own world, he will not survive. And if we are freed, he will not survive."

"He *can* survive!"

"And what kind of life will it be for him? He will always be dependent on your magic. Finn has been reduced to nothing more than a parasite in this reality…and you have used him and his kind time and time again for your own gain. To save a world destined to destroy itself with its own corruption. In time, even your scraps of paltry magic will not be enough to sustain him, and he will devolve." Siora shook her head, her fingernails cutting into the witch's skin. "What happened to your coven will happen again. *Corruption.* This reality will never be free of it. It should never have been allowed to spread."

Vera squeezed her eyes shut, her heart thumping a painful rhythm in her chest as her energy faded. This was pointless. This whole vision, this whole argument was *pointless*.

"Do not turn away from the truth," the entity said. "Open your eyes and accept that your fate is out of your hands."

She only had one shot. One shot to keep them talking, to squeeze every second out of the vision she could, because once it was over…

"What are you trying to gain from all this?" Vera demanded. "Are you trying to conjure hatred inside me? Are you trying to trick me into a false confession?" She jabbed a finger at the remains of her family. "Life can be traumatic. The things other creatures do to one another can be cruel. But all you did was select the worst moment of my life to use against me. What about all the good ones? The love, the light, the laughter... You never once looked at them. I treated you with kindness, even after all the things Siora did to harm us. What about that?"

What was the Old One trying to gain from showing her this? It felt like pointless busy work designed to—

She jerked against the Old One's hold as exhaustion tugged at her legacy. Pointless busy work designed to use her magic to *help free it*. Siora was draining her magic and pouring it into the seal!

The ground jerked beneath Vera's feet, and she stumbled. A piercing crack echoed through the soupy air as the seal begin to shatter and a plume of blue bioluminescence billowed into the sky, coiling and clouding like ink in water.

"You're using me to break the seal!" Vera exclaimed. "You never wanted to hear anything!"

"It is not personal," the Old One said in an eerie monotone, "it is simply the natural order of things."

"*Bullshit.*" Vera knew she was going to lose—there were no two ways about it—but she wasn't going down without a fight. It was time to call on her legacy...every last scrap of it.

Eloise, if you're out there...hurry!

"To the Nightshades who bind the dark." Vera's magic began to gather, pushing back the darkness. "To the Crescents who lead us towards the light."

"Stop!" the Old One shouted.

"For the Earthstone who shelter us, and the Brinewold who carry us home." Her magic swelled, steely blue light gathering in her palms.

The Old One lunged towards her, desperate to reestablish its hold, but Vera stepped back.

"I am Vera Brinewold of the water on high, daughter of Claire Brinewold and Matthew Nightshade. I remember those I have lost." Her magic ignited, bursting from her heart, filling the void with the scent of salt and brine. "Their magic was taken from them, and if I am the last of my coven, I remain to guide them home. Though I am far away, *I will never forget.*"

The prayer held steady as she looked towards the sky. A cacophony of twisted shrieks echoed from above as the Old Ones bore down on Solace, desperate to extinguish her light. The split in the seal groaned as the meteorite fought to contain the entity, then cracked a little more.

Vera staggered as her magic bumped up against her tipping point.

"Eloise!" she shrieked, tears of blood streaming down her face. "*Eloise!*"

Eloise stood at the centre of the highway, staring out into the dark of night. Mist billowed around the edges of the light cast by the lamp, but it was already flickering, the battery draining as the oppressive power of the Old Ones closed in on them.

She could feel them out there. The shadows were legion, all descending on the last hope of the universe, arriving for the theatre of destruction that awaited all things.

Andante didn't turn; she continued to work on breaking through the illusion, her power weaving a tunnel of holographic light through the thick walls of corrupted fae magic.

"We must hold them back," Coen said as the Min Min raced through the mist and dove at the swarming shadows.

Eloise tried to swallow her fear, even as she took an uncertain step backwards. "What do I do? I-I don't..." She wasn't the type of person who got into fights. She'd never raised a fist to anyone before, so how was she going to fight shadows?

"Trust yourself," Kyne said. "I understand our path now. Our blood is memory and it'll show us the way."

She took a deep breath and remembered the kadaitcha. They'd swarmed Solace when the Nightshade and the witch Rosheen had been corrupted. They were not the same kind of shadows that bore down on them now, but the same principles applied.

"Light," she said. "Shadows are afraid of the light."

"Basic physics," Kyne murmured. "It's gotta apply, right?"

Coen joined them, standing on Eloise's other side. "The Min Min will help us." He lifted his hand and one of the spirits arced through the air, buzzing past the gathering shadows, landing in his palm.

The orb burned like a miniature golden sun, the surface undulating with scale-like waves. The second raced to join its twin, circling Kyne's head like a moth to a flame, before he, too, reached out and allowed it to land safely on his hand.

"I've seen you a lot over the years," the miner told it. "Glad to finally meet you up close."

The orb seemed to flare in response, but it was difficult to tell for sure.

Coen took Eloise's hand. "Come. Feel their energy."

As Kyne took her other hand, she felt the power of the Min Min flow through them, join with their own Celestial abilities, and into her.

She remembered the first rule of elemental magic that Kyne had shared with her—she could only manipulate what was there.

Grasping the light, she imagined it flying through the outback, illuminating the ochre earth, the bold greens of the trees and shrubs, the golden grass, and the midnight blue sky. Her will became reality as the ring of magic flared, pulling from the Min Min's essence and pulsed outwards.

Eloise faltered as she saw what awaited them in the darkness, and as she'd suspected, seeing was much worse than imagining.

Thousands of shadows writhed through the scrub and rolled towards them on the highway, their featureless faces a blank pit of nothingness. Their limbs were stretched at abnormal lengths, and they crawled like spiders, oozing over the spiky spinifex grass and around the gum trees. Nothing stopped their advance.

"Do not be afraid," Coen murmured. "We are stronger together."

Kyne's grip tightened on her hand. "Let's give 'em hell."

The light pulsed and she pushed it outwards again, the barrier holding against the shadows, but they continued to push against it, wearing down her strength.

"I can't destroy them," she gasped. "I can't—"

The Min Min lifted into the air and circled around the Celestials, moving faster until they blurred into a ring of gold.

Eloise staggered as she felt her magic respond, her mind unconsciously pulling from the building energy. The same force built up in Kyne and Coen until all three burned as bright as stars.

The Celestials may have been sent from the dark places between, but they were made of the fabric of the universe and the magic that bound it all together. They came from the place that lay beyond—another kind of reality that held infinite possibilities.

Their blood sang, calling out to the light…and Eloise pushed it all out into the darkness.

The pulse spread outwards, bowling over the shadows like skittles. The force buffeted them into the gloom beyond, their hollow shrieking fading as they tumbled away.

The Min Min slowed their buzzing and wavered lazily outwards, their path widening as they searched.

Eloise heaved a sigh of relief but tensed as she realised the shadows weren't gone. She felt their presence scattered across the outback, and they were already amassing for a second assault.

"They are tied to the Old One," Coen told her. "They will remain until it is banished. We can only hope to hold them back."

Kyne looked over his shoulder to where Andante worked. "Are you close?"

"I'm threading the last needle," the druidess replied. "The final stitch…" a whoosh of air blasted the Celestials' backs as the path broke through to the other side of the illusion, "is placed."

Eloise turned, and as she caught her first glimpse of what lay beyond the barrier, her hands slipped from Coen and Kyne's.

Darkness. Ruin. Blackened trees. A crystalline road. And thick, soupy corruption.

"I cannot keep the way open for long," Andante said, her voice strained. "The threads will break, and I don't have the strength to weave another."

Kyne turned to Eloise and softly kissed her lips. "You first. I'll be right behind."

Coen had already stepped into the opening, not wasting any time. The elementals followed, the web glowing around them, and stepped through to Solace.

Eloise looked back at Andante as the shadows appeared in the faltering lamplight. She gasped as they swarmed closer, her heart leaping into her throat.

"Go!" the druidess shouted. "My place is here."

She reached out a hand. "But—"

"*Go!*"

The tunnel spiralled closed, sending out a gust of hot air that buffeted the Celestials, and the druidess was gone.

"Andante knows what to do." Coen laid a hand on Eloise's shoulder. "We will see her again."

She opened her mouth to reply but was cut off as she heard her name being screamed from deeper within Solace.

"Eloise!" The pained cry shattered the darkness. "*Eloise!*"

And through the gloom, she saw a flare of steely blue light.

Vera.

CHAPTER 24

Eloise took a step towards the pub, her boot slipping on the crystalline road.

Kyne grasped her arm, steadying her.

"Kyne and I will repair the seal," Coen said. "It will buy you time. You must stand against the Old Ones."

Eloise hesitated, but Kyne pointed to the south. "There's no time to question. Vera needs you."

Without thinking, she shoved the coral key into his hands and turned, sprinting down the highway towards the steely blue glow outside the pub. The crystal asphalt cracked under her boots, the sound splintering through the air.

She passed the boab, the bulbous trunk had morphed into a shard of jagged obsidian. The *Outpost* was dark, the windows blackened and lifeless. Across the side road, the far side of Hardy's opal shop looked like it was melting, the brick wall dripping like candle wax, and beyond that, Blue's pub had been reduced to a smoking ruin. The half-dissolved walls glitched in and out of reality with sharp, pixilated crosshairs.

Blue light pulsed before it all, with Vera standing at the epicentre. An unknown woman with long, golden-brown hair loomed in front of her, silhouetted by the bright pulse of magic, trying to push through.

Eloise lengthened her stride as she felt the power within the woman and the flagging strength of her friend.

"Get away from her!" the elemental shrieked, running towards them.

Vera collapsed to her knees, her gaze falling on Eloise as her magic faltered. Blood streamed down the witch's face, falling from her nose and eyes as the Brinewold failed.

Eloise grasped Vera's outstretched hands, the yard fell into shadow, and she turned to face the unknown woman.

"You've come at last." The voice that came out of her was a lifeless monotone, devoid of inflection and emotion.

Eloise hesitated, her breath catching as she saw who it was. "S-Siora?"

"No!" Vera cried. "It's not her! It's—"

Siora let out a shriek, her mouth opening wide, and a plume of darkness grew in her throat. "*Katu, katu, makrz izish...*"

The same rasping words she'd heard on the mountain bore down on her—words that tasted like rotting flesh and tore at her willpower—and she knew...

"Stay down." She pushed Vera back and swung a clenched fist at Siora, but she wasn't aiming to strike her, not physically. It was time to take off her mask and see what lay beneath.

Eloise's magic ripped at the shell surrounding the Old One, and Siora's flesh fell away. The entity burst forth, a writhing mass of blackened tentacles and mist that grew until it towered over them.

"*Eloise...*" Vera rasped. "Please tell me you know what you're doing."

Eloise stood in front of her friend, guarding her from the hulking mass of darkness, and looked to the sky beyond, where more of the entities had gathered to watch the show of a lifetime.

She took it all in—the crystalline world that lay between Earth and the beyond, the poison twisting her home, the overwhelming power pressing down on her from above—and for the first time since she'd arrived in Solace, she wasn't afraid.

She knew exactly what she had to do.

Kyne flung open the hatch at the base of the boab, the handle hitting the crystal trunk with a thud that cracked off a slice of obsidian.

The black goop reached the top of the shaft and the surface rippled lazily as the outside air connected with it.

The only way was down, so he held out the coral key and hoped for the best. The tar began to bubble and dissolve, whatever magic the key held driving back the corruption.

The first rung of the ladder appeared, then the second.

"C'mon," he said, gesturing to Coen.

The Celestial darted down the ladder, the goop parting in front of him, then Kyne followed.

Inside the tunnel, the air was thick with the smell of rot and the oxygen thin. Kyne stumbled, his shoulder hitting the jagged wall, and gagged.

"What is this stuff?" he asked. "It smells like something decomposing."

"The physical manifestation of the Old One," Coen told him. "We are descending to the heart of the entity itself."

"This is the real deal, huh?" He swallowed the lump in his throat. The seal was where the Old One would fully appear in their reality, given half a chance.

When they emerged into the cave, Kyne wasn't prepared for the state of the meteorite the Celestials had placed eons ago. He knew it was failing fast, but he hadn't realised how close they were cutting it.

It lay in jagged pieces, like someone had come along with a sledgehammer and rammed it over and over onto the rock until all that was left was little more than pebbles. No wonder Solace had become a crystalline nightmare world. The thinnest of layers was all that remained between them and nothingness.

"Come." Coen grasped Kyne's hand and placed his other onto the destroyed surface.

The miner did the same, and the moment his palm connected with the shattered stone, he felt a sharp stab of pain tear through his arm. The Old One was thrashing against the last shred of power holding it back, desperately trying to free itself.

"Focus," Coen said. "Push back against the pain. Trust yourself, Kyne."

He felt his Celestial power build inside him, the echo of his elemental abilities calling to the earth around them.

The minerals in the seal began to vibrate, responding to his touch. Iron, nickel, aluminium, and sodium; silicon, potassium, and even molecules of oxygen. They all began to heat, and the cracks began to glow softly at first, then golden light pooled in the dark places, filling the holes with liquid gold.

A shriek ripped through the opening beneath their hands and the earth began to quake. Kyne stumbled and fell to his knees, his palm slipping across the shattered meteorite.

Coen tightened his grip on his hand. "Don't let go!"

A slab of rock fell from the cave ceiling, dropping with a boom that sent a splash of goop raining over them.

Kyne gagged as the putrid stench of rotting flesh filled his nose, and another rock fell until the entire cave roof seemed to be melting. Stones and shards collided with his back, pinging off him with silvery sparks as his Celestial magic tried to protect him from the corruption.

The sky opened as liquid gold continued to pour into the seal. He looked up, only to see the stars blotted out by millions of writhing, pitch-black tentacles.

"*Coen*," he said, his fear threatening to overwhelm him.

"I see them." The Celestial grimaced and his power ignited. "Do not let go!"

Eloise Hart was the only creature that stood between a mass of all-powerful celestial beings and nothingness.

The only thing that was stopping the Old One from ripping apart the universe was the last shred of the seal. If Coen and Kyne failed, then she wasn't sure she could hold back the onslaught. She was one Celestial-hybrid, as opposed to twelve full-blooded Celestials who'd been sent for the same mission forty thousand years prior.

"Only you?" the Old One rasped, its voice echoing painfully in her mind.

Eloise grimaced and stared defiantly at the writhing mass. "*Only me.*"

"Then it is time."

The Old One gathered itself and Eloise lunged, her body erupting into silvery-gold light as they collided. The force sent a shockwave through the air that shattered the crystallised trees, and blue magic flared as Vera threw up an arm to protect herself.

Threads gathered around Eloise, looping into the air and twisting with pitch-black tentacles, and she soared into the sky, taking the Old One with her.

They fought, tearing and ripping, twisting and turning, struggling for dominance. Solace fell away beneath them, fading into the inky mist that clung to the globe of reality.

The Old One shrieked, struggling to break free, but Eloise wouldn't let go. Her entire being was assaulted with pain, the corruption the entity had brought to Earth seeping into her blood, trying to take control of her mind. But she was not like the others.

She'd awoken.

They hit the topmost point of the illusion and their flight stalled. Eloise opened the last piece of her heart to her Celestial side and pushed, finally dragging the Old One through the layer covering the Earth. The fabric of reality opened like a leaf of delicate tissue paper, and they hurtled into open space.

The mass of Old Ones began to clamour around them, clicking and rasping in their strange language, calling to their brethren. She felt their overwhelming power, their desire to shape infinity, and the layer upon layer that soared above.

They were parasites, but they saw humanity the same way, so who was right and who was wrong? And did it even matter?

No, Eloise thought. This was the struggle of nature itself, of spirit, of the most ordinary and magical things that had ever existed. Only the strongest would survive.

As they soared through the swirling shadows, Eloise knew the only way she could close off their reality from this place forever was if she gave up her humanity...every last shred of it.

She had to become Celestial and ascend. She had to inhabit the same level of existence as the Old Ones, or she would fail. It was the only way.

"I love you, Kyne," she whispered as her human voice faded. "I love you, Vera. Drew. Hardy. Wally. Blue. Clarke. Coen. *Marlu. Finn.*" Even the vampire Joseph Cheapside and the witch Rosheen. She loved them all.

And so, she became pure light, her radiance shining down on everything she'd vowed to protect.

Vera huddled underneath the last spark of her Brinewold legacy as a blinding light erupted out of Eloise.

She was a star. A golden star woven with silver threads.

She stared open-mouthed as Eloise wrestled with the clump of black tentacles, and fell onto her back as they shot upwards, hurtling through the air faster than her eyes could follow.

Kneeling on the ruined earth, Vera glanced back at the pub, which had regained its walls and the Exiles within. But in front of her, a crater had opened up in the centre of the highway. The hole exposed the seal beneath and an impossibly bright glimmer of gold.

Vera dragged herself to the edge, her hands scraping over sharp crystal, and gasped as she laid eyes on what lay within.

Kyne and Coen knelt over the shattered seal, their hands pressed against the ruined meteorite. All she could make out was their outlines as the cracks glowed with metallic gold light. Her witch senses were going crazy; her third eye opening all the way, revealing a swarm of silver threads wrapped around their bodies. The amount of magic they were pouring into the breach was unfathomable.

There was nothing she could do to help. She was spent, and even at her strongest, she didn't have a hope of matching them.

Vera jerked as a hand slid under her arm.

"It's me," Hardy murmured, lifting her to her feet. "Are you all right?"

Vera nodded, her voice lost. A hot tornado of wind whipped around them, tossing strands of his curly hair loose from his man-bun.

Drew appeared at her other side, helping the vampire prop her up. "What's happening?"

"They're holding the seal closed," Finn said, kneeling at the edge of the crater.

"Where's Eloise?"

Vera looked to the sky, where the sight of the Old Ones had turned away from them and into a bright star within their midst.

"Bloody hell..." Wally whispered.

"What did they find out there?" Hardy murmured.

"The truth," Finn replied. "They found the truth."

Suddenly, the sky exploded, erupting with white light that blotted out everything.

At first, Vera wondered if she was dead...but as her vision returned, she saw Solace begin to emerge from the gloom.

First, the darkness above began to melt, the shadows dripping away to reveal the radiant sapphire sky she'd come to love. Then, the crystal cracked underneath their feet and shattered like ice as warm sunlight poured through the dissolving illusion.

"She did it..." Vera whispered. "Eloise did it."

"Yeah," Drew muttered, staring at the sky. "But where is she?"

Her hand fumbled for the shifter's, her heart twisting.

Kyne emerged from the crater, his face smeared with charcoal. "She's gone," he declared, falling to his knees with an exhausted sob. "*She's gone.*"

CHAPTER 25

Kyne sat on the ridge overlooking Solace and pulled down the brim of his hat. He didn't like to look at the sky anymore.

Below, the sounds of hammering and the thunk of a nail gun echoed through the still air. Someone let out a shout and laughter followed.

In the wake of the Old One's banishment, Solace had come alive. Not only had the plant life regained its former lustre—the boab had sprung back bigger and broader than ever before—but the animals had returned.

Colourful parrots and budgerigars soared overhead each morning, screeching and carrying on like pork chops during their morning hunt for water. Emus wandered in from the outback looking for food, as well as the mammoth goannas that Blue hated so much— they often tried to knock over the bins out the back of the pub—but it was *Marlu* who brought the kangaroos.

Her joey had grown a lot in the months following the restoration, and she'd collected a mob of greys and reds that liked to bask and graze through the grass on the side of the ridge as the sun rose. Seeing them idle peacefully made Coen happy, and he'd often linger in town, watching them on the hillside before he disappeared, travelling the rivers in search of who knows what.

Solace's businesses were faring even better than before, too. *The Outpost* was fully restocked, complete with a lick of paint. Wally's garage sparkled, the piles of scrap metal were gone, and the petrol and diesel tanks were full. Even Blue's pub was undergoing renovations, complete with a new kitchen and the long-awaited removal of the sticky linoleum flooring.

The highway was no longer a smoking ruin, thanks to Kyne's elemental affinity for rocks. Vera's dugout was free of goop and her furniture was returned to the pristinely clean home, and Wally even had a new secret bunker for his werewolf transformations.

In the absence of opal, Hardy had taken up silversmithing, creating outback and Celestial inspired jewellery. The latter, Kyne knew, was to honour what had happened here. It was the best the vampire could do in lieu of sharing the impossible with the world.

Hardy had also called in an Indigenous artist he knew through the community outreach program he donated opal potch to. The woman was nice enough, and she'd spent several weeks painting a mural on the water tank. It was another homage, this time to Solace's supernatural heroes. Under the great arm of the Milky Way, a dingo roamed with a kangaroo, a miner leaned against his pick, an Indigenous man cradled an orb of shining opal, and within the purple sky shone the brightest star of all.

Partnered with the repaired windmill, it'd already become a tourist stop, and cars and motorhomes pulled in to take photos while on day-trips out from Lightning Ridge. That's how Vera and Drew had come to the conclusion that Solace needed its very own caravan park, complete with boutique cabins situated in renovated dugouts up the side of the ridge.

They'd already began drawing up plans and researching permits, so Kyne had no choice but to invest in the project. He did own the land, after all. It was a good idea—Solace wouldn't be able to survive for long without a source of income. The miners were long gone, spooked off from the scent of opal by all the supernatural goings-on, and through traffic hadn't quite returned to its normal level yet.

All in all, things were going brilliantly...but none of it would be the same without Eloise.

Wherever she'd gone the day they'd fought the Old Ones, Kyne wasn't sure. All he knew was that she hadn't come back.

A shadow fell over Kyne, and he looked up to find Finn standing over him.

"Care for some company?" the fae asked.

"Sure." He shrugged and returned his gaze to Solace.

Finn sat, his fingers curling around the crystal talisman around his neck. In the absence of the Old One, he now relied on Vera's magical battery to keep him from devolving. It was working for now, but soon, he'd have to find a more permanent solution.

"You want to tell me what's on your mind?" Finn prodded.

He didn't really want to, but the fae would keep needling him until he gave in. It was best to not fight it. "It's been over three months."

"Our little desert pea did what she had to," the fae told him. "No one else had the power to seal this reality from the layers above."

"I don't think I can live without her."

"Of course, you can. Solace needs you now more than ever."

"More than..." Everything that'd happened barely seemed real to him. He was still an awakened Celestial-hybrid—though he preferred to call himself an elemental—with all the powers and good looks that came with it. The salt and pepper hair, the iridescent blue eyes, and the skin that shone like pearl when he used his powers. Thankfully, the latter was something he could keep on the down-low and the other bits were perfectly natural. Still, every time he looked in the mirror, he saw her.

"Yes, more than fighting tentacle monsters." Finn

shook his head and smirked. "Mate, you're bankrolling this entire operation. Solace needs a caravan park."

Kyne blinked. "Did you just call me mate?"

"Got your attention, didn't it?" Finn breathed deeply and a creepy smile appeared on his face. "I reckon it's hot chip o'clock."

Kyne made a face. "You can smell Blue cooking chips all the way up here?"

The fae clapped the miner on the shoulder as he stood. "Who said anything about smelling potatoes?"

<hr>

Purple. Purple stars, purple earth, purple plants. Her entire world was purple.

Eloise Hart sat within limbo, the place between one reality and the next, staring across the reflection of the outback.

It was so quiet, the lack of noise was deafening.

The last thing she remembered before she'd opened her eyes was pure, white light. Before that, she'd plunged into the higher place where the Old Ones resided—a nightmare realm, devoid of light, filled to the brim with writhing entities pulling infinite strings.

How many universes did they control? How many were erased and how many were created? It didn't matter; it was an endless cycle without a beginning or end.

Honestly, she'd expected to not open her eyes at all, and if by some miracle she did, it would be to literal hell. But neither of those things had happened.

She didn't know if it was her love for Kyne that pulled her back to the limbo world or if it was her longing for something familiar, but perhaps it was both. Solace was the first place where she'd felt like she'd truly belonged. The first place that felt like *home*.

"Ah, there you are!"

Coen's voice boomed in the silence and Eloise jerked her head up. She stared at him for so long, trying to figure out if he was real or not, that he began to chuckle.

"Yes, the thunder has come," he declared, plonking down in front of her. Crossing his legs, he held out his hand. "Would you like to pinch me?"

"No." She shook her head. "I trust you. No one else could find this place."

"No, they cannot. I am clever and they are not." He winked.

"How long have I been here?"

"It's difficult to say. Time moves at a different pace."

"Solace?"

Coen smiled. He'd been expecting her to ask. "They all survived. Life has returned. Finally, after so long asleep, the country comes alive."

"What about Andante?" The last time Eloise had seen her, a horde of corrupted shadows were hurling towards her.

"The covenant her people made spared her. She lingers in her hive, waiting for Finn."

Finn... She sighed, tears welling in her eyes. Without the magic of the Old One, he would wither away, but Vera's magic helped sustain him—the magic of the people the fae had caused so much suffering and heartache to. It was more than a simple symbolic gesture; it was the healing of a rift that was forged a thousand years ago. Maybe their story would spread and others would reach out the hand of friendship.

"Andante's waiting for Finn?" Eloise asked.

"Yes. She has promised to take him home."

After all he'd been through, he now had possibilities. She was glad, even after hearing all the Old Ones had accused him of. With her ascension had come understanding, not only of her place, but of what had been in order for her to reach it—and that included the choice presented to Finn through the reanimation of Siora.

Eloise grasped the opal hanging around her neck. "He would've done anything he could to save Siora, and I don't feel any hatred towards any choice he would've made," she said. "I hope he finds peace."

"As do we all."

Peace felt like a strange notion after so much turmoil. Had she ever felt it? There had been peaceful *moments*, but was that all it would ever be?

Yes, she thought. *There's no such thing as complete peace, for the path is never straight. It is the way it's always been.* Nothing existed in a straight line. It was up and down, side to side, back to front, all ways at the same time. It was now and then, the future and beyond. Night and day. It was one. It *was.*

"Coen?"

"Yes?"

"Why did I end up here? I ascended, but…" Eloise gestured to the purple-tinted limbo world. "Aren't I ready?"

Coen smiled. "If you weren't ready, you wouldn't have been able to do what you did."

"Then why am I here and not with the Celestials?"

"Love."

She thought of Kyne and tears spilled down her cheeks. *How she longed for him…*

"You can go back if you wish," Coen murmured. "Or you can travel beyond. The choice is yours."

"I can choose to descend?" Her eyes widened. "But what if…"

"You break as the twelve did?"

She nodded.

"Life, no matter its existence, is a risk."

Yes, it was a risk.

Even if Eloise chose to descend, she'd never be the same. She'd be a Celestial, not an elemental. How could she live amongst humanity, being and knowing what she was? Would she be satisfied with a simple life after all she'd seen?

She looked up at Coen. "Do I have any humanity left?"

"Humanity is a physicality," the Celestial told her. "Empathy, anger, loneliness, love...all the emotions you can think of. We feel them, too. They are not exclusively human sensations, Eloise."

"Oh..." She thought on it for a while, then asked, "What will you do?"

"I will return to the billabong," he replied. "It is where I belong. Without me to make up the original twelve, the remaining Celestials have lost their way. I will help them as best as I can. In time, I hope we can ascend again."

"I hope so, too."

"You are welcome to come with us any time," he added. "If your choice is to ascend, then the Celestials will welcome you. If not, you shall be received with open arms and the love of family."

"After everything Ilyana did?" Eloise asked. "No matter what?"

"You are one of us."

It was time to make her choice. She couldn't stay in limbo forever, even if she wanted to. Something was calling out to her already, opening a path that beckoned her to walk.

Eloise stood and wiped her palms on her shirt.

"You have made your choice?" Coen asked.

"Yes." She turned to face him one last time. "Will I ever see you again?"

"Perhaps." The Celestial smiled, his features igniting with his trademark cheeky grin. "That is the beauty of possibility."

"Thank you. For everything."

Reality peeled away at the lightest of touches as she stepped through the curtain into brilliant sunshine.

Her bare feet soaked up the warmth of the earth, and her skin glowed with a thousand and one threads of gold and silver, each lit by the radiance of the star shining down on her.

Kyne stood and whirled around. His expression fell into shock as he saw her standing on the ridge, naked as the day she was born, her translucent hair shining silver, her eyes glowing like pure sapphires plucked from the heart of the Earth itself.

He touched the opal at her neck and sobbed. "You came back to me."

"I came home," she said, wrapping her arms around him. "*I came home.*"

CHAPTER 26

Finn Oreah'anza sat on the newly installed bench seats outside Blue's pub, watching the sunset on his last night on Earth.

He felt Andante's approach as she let her magic unravel around the karsts east of Solace and saw the threads float through the sky like gossamer spiderwebs full of glimmering crystal.

Finn glanced to his side as Vera sat beside him, her gaze following the fluttering magic above.

"I wonder what the human world will make of the sudden appearance of a new natural wonder," she murmured.

He snorted. "There will be a dozen conspiracy theories relating to aliens and government coverups by dinner time."

"No doubt." She chuckled and leaned back, her elbows resting on the table behind.

Finn hated goodbyes, and he'd had to say a lot in the past year. Sometimes, he'd had to say them twice.

"It was the Nightshade that was corruptible, not you," he told her before she could get all soppy. "You do realise that, right?"

Finn knew she was probably one of the most powerful witches alive, only second to the Crescents who governed the Irish covens. Their magic came from something ancient tied to the heart of the universe itself. It was how she was able to stand against the Old One for so long. If it wasn't for the Nightshade, who knew where her path would have led?

"Yeah," Vera murmured. "I know...but not until I stood before the Old One and called on my ancestors."

Finn kicked the toe of his boot into the red earth. There was nothing more to say. They all understood who they were now and what they were capable of. If trouble dared to come knocking again, they'd be ready for it.

"You know I'll keep giving you magic for as long as you need," Vera told him. "I've got plenty to go around."

"Yes, but it's not your responsibility to keep me alive." He turned to look at her. "I can't keep living like this. It's not fair to you."

"What about Ireland?"

Finn smiled and shook his head. "Ireland is still Earth, and it's best I enter Lor'Iyslar in secret."

Her shoulders sank, but she let it go. "Will we ever see you again?"

"You're a powerful witch who just helped save this reality from total destruction. Once the Crescents find out about you, they'll bend down and kiss your feet. I doubt they'd deny a request to pass through their portal."

A smile spread across the witch's face and Finn knew she was thinking about what it'd be like to visit the fae world, but then she shook her head. "Maybe one day, but my place is here in Solace."

"And mine is in Lor'Iyslar."

It was time for him to return to his birthplace and find peace with the wrongs he'd done there. Helping save Earth was the right thing to do, but it didn't find him closure with the deeds that'd brought him here in the first place. Finn had found himself, and he'd become the fae he'd always wanted to be, but there was still more for him to do out there.

Vera worried her bottom lip. "You're going to miss the grand opening of the Solace Caravan Park and Resort."

"Resort?" Finn raised his eyebrows. "That's a bit of a stretch."

"Okay, the resort part isn't official...but it could happen."

He sighed and shook his head. People would flock to Solace with its quaint outback vibe and new natural wonder, and he'd stick out like a sore thumb. Magical creatures would live alongside humans, hiding their truth once more. It wasn't a world that was made for the fae. Witches, vampires, werewolves, shifters, and elementals...this place was for them.

"Others will come," Vera murmured. "This is a whole new world, full of possibilities. We won't be exiles anymore."

Finn patted her hand and smiled. "And I am happy for you." He lifted his hands to the talisman and went to take it off, but Vera grasped his wrist.

"Keep it. You never know when it might come in handy." She let him go and glanced over her shoulder.

"Eager to get back to your human?"

The witch held up her hand, showing off the glittering diamond on her finger. "Fiancé, thank you very much."

"I'm surprised Clarke didn't get you a slab of quartz. I know you witches love the stuff."

"Smart arse." She slapped his arm playfully. "I'm going to miss you."

"That's high praise coming from you."

Vera laughed, standing as Eloise appeared beside them.

The Celestial looked strange dressed in denim jeans, boots, a plain light grey T-shirt, and an Akubra hat. Her golden blonde hair was long gone, replaced with silver strands that shone with starlight, paired with shimmering skin, and iridescent blue eyes. What was the human word for that? Juxtaposition.

"I'll leave you to it," Vera said but then turned to Finn. "We'll be back for the big send off, so no scurrying away while we've got our backs turned."

The fae smirked and crossed his heart. "Promise."

Eloise sat gracefully beside him and sighed, closing her eyes as the setting sun caught her pearlescent skin.

"I'll never get used to seeing you like that."

Eloise laughed and picked up a strand of her hair. "Vera already tried to colour it. Didn't take. I might have to wear a wig."

"Embrace it," he told her. "It's beautiful."

They sat together and watched the sunset fade into the first glimpse of night. Andante's threads dissolved overhead, gleaming as they broke apart and returned to the fabric of the universe

Finn was glad Eloise wasn't trying to convince him to stay like Vera had. She understood why he had to return to Lor'Iyslar better than most.

"At the Black Mountain, Siora called me *Lor'astra*," she said after a while. "It means Celestial, doesn't it?"

Finn shrugged but couldn't hide his smile.

"You knew all along?"

"I suspected. There's a difference, *Shr'lei de Astrad*." Blade of the Stars.

Eloise laughed and threw her arms around his neck. "If they don't take you back, they're fools."

"Can you write me a reference?"

She pulled back and shook her head. "I'm going to miss your witty comebacks."

"You have plenty of your own, desert pea." His smile faded as he felt a pulse of magic appear in the last rays of sunset.

On cue, Andante appeared on the highway and walked towards them. She carried nothing but the clothes on her back and the courage in her heart.

Finn stood and greeted her. "I'm ready."

"Now hold on a second," Eloise said, putting her hands on her hips. "I just heard you make a promise to Vera not five minutes ago."

"I'm not big on teary goodbyes," the fae replied.

Andante raised her eyebrows. "Neither am I."

"One last meal," the Celestial said, threading her arm through Finn's. "For old time's sake." Andante hesitated, but Eloise smiled and nodded towards the warmth of the pub. "Blue made his famous vegetarian lasagne...*especially*."

Now Finn was the one hesitating. "Are there hot chips?"

"Of course!" Eloise laughed and pulled him towards the pub.

"Are you sure, because—"

"As sure as the sun will rise tomorrow."

Eloise Hart pressed her nose against the Troopy's side window as the dusty 4WD hurtled down the highway towards the city.

All things considering, she found herself enjoying long days on the road, watching the changing landscape hurtle by, and all the comings and goings in each town they passed through.

"You know, we could've just taken a short paddle down a certain stream," Kyne stated, glancing over at her from the driver's seat. "It'd be more cost effective."

"And appear out of thin air in the middle of Perth?" she asked. "I know we've both got all this fancy magic now, but it didn't come with an instruction manual."

The miner laughed and turned his gaze back to the highway.

Eloise hadn't been to her hometown in over ten years, not since she'd bought her van and hit the road. After her powers had manifested and she'd changed her parent's perception, she'd fled and never looked back, even though she'd been full of regret ever since. It wasn't until she'd repaired the seal inside the Black Mountain that she understood she could repair the damage she'd done to them, too.

This was the first step in the rest of their lives. She would make things right with her parents, then they would work to build Solace into something beautiful.

"Are you nervous?" Kyne asked.

Eloise watched the skyscrapers of Perth's CBD appear through the haze and her heart leapt. "I wasn't until now. I wonder what they'll think of me?"

"Whatever they see, it'll be of their own making," he told her. Which was the point. "And if it's only a drop of what I do, then they'll see how beautiful you are. Inside and out."

"Bloody hell, you know how to lay it on thick."

"Is this a bad time to ask you to marry me? I mean, I don't want to steal Vera's thunder, and I don't have a ring…"

Her already pale cheeks paled even more. *"What?"*

"Marry me?"

Eloise shrugged. "Sure, why not."

Kyne laughed and took the next exit off the highway, merging into Perth's outer suburbs. "Why not, she says…"

Why not, indeed.

She'd given this reality possibilities when she'd ascended and now, she had plenty of her own.

Marriage, love, family. *Hope.*

She thought about the lost elementals and knew she and Kyne would be there to show them they weren't alone anymore. They had a future, a purpose, and were perfect just the way they were.

Eloise and Kyne would guide them, and they would make new paths by walking together.

And all they had to do was take the first step.

The End…

Thank you for reading Australian Supernatural! I hope you enjoyed the adventure as much as I did writing it.

More Aussie themed stories are coming, beginning with a thrilling tale of revenge and magic set in the golden heart of the Victorian Goldfields...

Australian Supernatural: Goldfields is coming soon!

When Holly Bourke's eccentric aunt dies, she's drawn to the small country town of Dunloe.

Haunted by its Gold Rush past, the small community in the Australian bush hides more than the promise of gold beneath its rugged surface. Witches and vampires struggle for dominance, and a strange presence looms in the historic diggings, waiting for its chance to rise...

Trapped between two worlds, Holly must unravel the secrets hidden deep within the pages of history in order to save her future.

For without the power within, Dunloe doesn't stand a chance...

To be notified about the release of Australian Supernatural: Goldfields, follow along with Nicole's monthly newsletter at: nicolertaylorwrites.com/newsletter

Want more novels just like this one? Check out Nicole's other series:

THE ARONDIGHT CODEX - An ancient war with demons. A lost sword with the power to end it all. And a woman with purple hair is the world's only hope.

THE CAMELOT ARCHIVE - Set in the same alternate Arthurian world seen in **The Arondight Codex...** Deadly secrets. Murder and revenge. The end of the world is nye and Camelot is the last bastion of hope.

THE WITCH HUNTER SAGA - Vampires and witches collide in this thrilling Urban Fantasy adventure. You've never met vampires quite like these...

THE CRESCENT WITCH CHRONICLES - Witches, shapeshifters, and ancient myth collide in this colourful Irish flavoured series! Come on an adventure fraught with danger and forbidden romance... and the ultimate battle to save magic before it's gone forever.

THE DARKLAND DRUIDS - A woman with no living relatives travels from Australia to the other side of the world to find out the truth of who she is...only to land in the middle of a prophecy of destruction. Druids, witches, fae, and shapeshifters abound in this thrilling magical adventure!

FORTITUDE WOLVES - Werewolves and vampires are embroiled in a war for supremacy and a troubled woman is in the centre of it all...only she doesn't know it. Packed with suspense, action, and supernatural secrets, this series is sure to keep readers on the edge of their seats...

Find out more at: NicoleRTaylorWrites.com

See what titles are FREE at: Nicole's Free Reads

ABOUT NICOLE

Nicole R. Taylor is an Australian Urban Fantasy author.

She lives in the western suburbs of Melbourne dreaming up nail biting stories featuring sassy witches, duplicitous vampires, hunky shapeshifters, and devious monsters.

She likes chocolate, cat memes, and video games.

When she's not writing, she likes to think of what she's writing next.

Follow Nicole Online:

Website: www.nicolertaylorwrites.com
Facebook: facebook.com/nrtaylorwrites
Newsletter: www.nicolertaylorwrites.com/newsletter
Email: nicole.this.is@gmail.com